KU-637-536

The characters in this book are entirely imaginary and bear no relation to any living person.

I SHOULD HAVE KNOWN

When Shelley Bray was appointed governess to two young children in Monte Carlo, she thought that she would be in complete charge during their famous father's absence, until she met her employer's sister, a wheel-chair invalid. She had received no warning of her existence. Shelley quickly realized that she would be challenged and frustrated in her efforts to win her new pupils' love and trust, as she was forbidden to mention their beautiful mother. Worst of all, she was constantly made to feel small in front of her new employer, Esmond Torrington – and for some strange reason that mattered terribly to Shelley.

I SHOULD HAVE KNOWN

I Should Have Known

by

Denise Robins

Dales Large Print Books
Long Preston, North Yorkshire,
BD23 4ND, England.

British Library Cataloguing in Publication Data.

Robins, Denise
  I should have known.

  A catalogue record of this book is
  available from the British Library

  ISBN 978-1-84262-531-6 pbk

First published in Great Britain in 1961 by
Hodder & Stoughton Ltd.

Copyright © 1961 by Denise Robins

Cover illustration © Len Thurston by arrangement with
P.W.A. International Ltd.

The moral right of the author has been asserted

Published in Large Print 2007 by arrangement with
Patricia Clark for executors of Denise Robins' Estate

All Rights reserved. No part of this publication may be
reproduced, stored in a retrieval system, or transmitted in any
form or by any means, electronic, mechanical, photocopying,
recording or otherwise without the prior permission of the
Copyright owner.

678876

MORAY DISTRICT COUNCIL
DEPARTMENT OF
LEISURE AND LIBRARIES

Dales Large Print is an imprint of Library Magna Books Ltd.

Printed and bound in Great Britain by
T.J. (International) Ltd., Cornwall, PL28 8RW

1

On that hot sunny morning in June when I walked into the Monte Carlo tourists' agency to get my ticket for London, I think I was the unhappiest girl in the world. I hadn't slept all night. I left the Villa Arc-en-Ciel long before the rest of the family were up. It is never a hardship to get up early in the South of France when you can open the jalousies and let a stream of sunshine into your room, yet I had felt cold. I was trembling with nerves and agitation as I closed my two suitcases and crept down the long corridor, terrified that somebody would hear me. I did not want to see any of them. Certainly not *him*, the one whom I loved more than my life. Certainly not the woman who had been so cruel to me, so viciously opposed to my presence in the villa, and my happiness. And not even the children because I knew they would weep at my departure. Above all I did not want to hurt them.

But I had to go. The whole thing was too strong for me. I could no longer cope. My life had become insupportable. I stopped only once and that was in the hall. The villa was dim and shuttered, and I fancied I could just see the portrait which had once hung there – *her* portrait. That wonderful face, carved as though from ivory, with the huge dark eyes and the crisp upward sweep of flame red hair and just a hint of that same red in the fringed shawl that draped one bare shoulder.

Beautiful Veronica who had been dead all of three years, and whose loveliness was now ashes that had been scattered on the side of the mountains she had loved – way behind Monte Carlo. Veronica, who had died so tragically in a car accident on the Corniche road but whose personality had lived on and dominated this villa, just as she did the house in London where there hung yet another striking portrait of her.

There is a saying: '*The beauty that is the body perishes, but the beauty that is the soul endures.*'

Is this true? *Was it true of her?* Had Veronica ever possessed a beautiful mind or spirit, or had it been merely the memory of her grace and elegance and that fantastically glamorous colouring of hers that had settled like fine dust upon everything in the place, blurring it; just as it had destroyed the peace of mind of those who remembered her?

I do not know. I'm too confused now. Too heart-sick and worn out.

I had wondered when I looked at myself in the mirror this morning to brush my hair, why my tears had not worn away my very cheeks.

I left the Villa Arc-en-Ciel, I hope for ever. I dared not wait there until the ticket-office opened in case *they* tried to stop me from going.

So I sat for the next three hours in the gardens of the Casino, looking out upon the still blue waters of a sea that was as calm as a lake, mirroring a faultless sky.

How wonderful are these early mornings on the Côte d'Azur! Cool and delicious. How intriguing the Casino looked – not that I had often visited it. I am no gambler and nobody at the Villa Arc-en-Ciel ever gambled. But the exotic, sugar-coated building held a strange fascination for the onlooker, like all those expensive gleaming yachts in the harbour or the sleek cars, the air of general luxury that makes a little Monégasque town a veritable playground for the rich.

I sat motionless, trying not to think; looking at the dreaming beauty of the sea. The green palms and the lemon trees along the coastline. The gorgeous blossoms in the wide beds of the well-kept gardens.

I was leaving it all, and I didn't care. I did not even know what I was going to. I was just a young girl of twenty-three, hall-marked by the tragedy of a hopeless love and a sense of bitter loss and loneliness. I was quite alone, preparing to go back to London to face a new life. This time without glamour, without love, without hope.

At eight o'clock I had a cup of strong black coffee and a *croissant* in a little café which had just opened. At half past eight I was in the tourist office buying my ticket.

In twenty-two hours' time I would be back in London.

I scarcely knew how to pay for that ticket or how to face the journey, I felt so utterly desolate. *Oh, Esmond, Esmond, my love, my very life, how am I going to bear that life without you?*

All through the long train journey to Paris and then to Dieppe I remained miserable and afraid of the future. Sometimes I was filled not only with wild regret, but with the puzzlement of a bewildered child who has not yet grown up and is still unable to become mistress of a difficult situation. Yet the next moment I felt so old and wise, so experienced that I thought I saw things clearly, and could even blame myself for some of the awfulness that had happened.

Sometimes I stopped grieving and remembered only the loveliness of Monte Carlo and the glorious pride and joy of having loved and served Esmond Torrington.

It was only as we drew into Victoria Station that I made my decision to face up to facts more fully. To write them down without prejudice, so that the children, anyhow, might one day read my diary and understand why I had so suddenly left them.

Words come easily to me, and tears too, so it would seem, but I am glad I have kept a diary while I was in France and have written so much about my life there. Here in London I can just revise it and add the story of the terrible finale.

Now I want to begin at the very beginning. I *must* – in order to explain and rationalise my emotions, and re-shape my future.

Esmond, Esmond, will you ever see what I write, I wonder. Will you ever know what it all meant to me? But this I do know: I love you, and I shall love you until I die – and long after that.

2

The very first time I saw the Villa Arc-en-Ciel was on a morning such as the one I have just described. Golden-fine, exquisitely fresh. I had just got off the Calais–Méditerranée in which I had a second class couchette.

There had been three other women with me. Two young girls who left the train at Nice. French students who had just finished a year in London and were returning home. We three had gossiped most of the night, thankful that our number four was a very old lady – stone-deaf, so not bothered by our chattering. But as I, myself, had recently been a student, before I worked in a P.N.E.U. (Parents' National Educational Union) school, we girls had a lot to talk about. In fact we arranged to meet again, as they said they often drove over to Monte Carlo. One of them actually knew the villa to which I was going.

The Arc-en-Ciel was famous, she said. It had belonged to a well-known Italian Duc and had been sold a few years ago to the great English conductor, Esmond Torrington, who was at the moment giving a series of concerts in Southern France. She couldn't give me any more information about Mr Torrington although I eagerly asked for it. For he was my future employer. His secretary – an elderly and efficient lady, named Miss Collins – had interviewed me in London. All I knew was that Mr Torrington was a widower with two children – Conrad, a boy of seven and Kate, his sister, a year younger. Their mother was dead. I knew no further details except that so far they had had a nurse of the 'nannie' type, but their father considered they were too old for her now and wanted them to be trained under the P.N.E.U. system. That was why I had been chosen. I thought the P.N.E.U. curriculum a first-class training for small children.

When I first saw my future home, I felt enormously excited, and I am not by nature excitable. I am rather calm; shy until I get to know people, and although quick to feel appreciation, slow to show it. I've often been called too reserved. I wish I wasn't, because I've truly got very deep feelings. I just can't always produce them. I always hesitate to disclose my secret, inner heart. It is precious to me, like a jewel that I do not want anyone to steal.

But the sight of Monte Carlo on that glorious day roused even me, the calm Miss Bray, to enthusiasm.

It was simply lovely. From my taxi I caught a brief glimpse of the famous harbour; and the glittering Casino, the verdant shores, which at that time of the year were gay with azaleas, mimosa and carnations. The very air seemed fragrant with flowers.

And, of course, on the rock of Monaco, dominating the town, was the beautiful palace which I had seen in so many pictures at home. I thought rather tenderly of the ruler of this bijou monarchy; Prince Rainier and his lovely Princess Grace. I had watched their marriage on television, and thought at the time what a romantic, glamorous wedding it was! What girl wouldn't want to identify herself with such a Princess and find her Prince Charming and live happily ever after with her husband and children in that beautiful palace?

I am a lucky girl, I thought, it isn't everyone who can leave college on their twentieth birthday, have two years' experience teaching little girls in an English country school, then find a job in a place like this.

My sense of anticipation and pleasure increased as the taxi went through the open wrought-iron gateways over which hung the name Arc-en-Ciel (Rainbow – what a charming name!) I looked out on a perfect flower-filled garden. Quite different from anything in England. Much more artificial; but undeniably lovely. I couldn't put a name to many of the flowers. But I adored the pink and scarlet carnations which grew so profusely here. The oranges, the eucalyptus, and the rose-laurels. Now, suddenly, I saw the gleaming white of the villa, itself, half-hidden in purple bougainvillaea.

Green-shuttered, cool-looking, with a wide verandah, and an air of immense elegance and wealth, it seemed to be waiting for me; little Miss Bray! It was thrilling.

The taxi driver sprang out, opened my door and gave me a dazzling smile. A brown-faced, cheeky-eyed Provençal.

'*Voilà*, mademoiselle!'

A glass door, with a black lace grill of wrought-iron, opened. A bald-headed man wearing a baize apron came out. Obviously a man-servant, and obviously I was not expected because he stared at me, then spoke in rapid French to the driver who shrugged his shoulders, then they both turned and stared. I spoke to the man in the baize apron in my best French, which was adequate if not colloquial. He understood when I explained that I was Miss Bray and that Mr Torrington expected me.

His face cleared. He picked up my suit-cases and bade me follow him. I was about to settle with the driver when an English voice said:

'Let me do that.'

I turned and saw a tall thin man in grey flannels. He had grey thinning hair and wore horn-rimmed glasses. This was not the great Esmond Torrington, that most famous of English conductors. The grey-haired man smiled and said:

'Allow me to introduce myself. I am Sir Austen Warr. And you–?'

'I am Miss Bray. Shelley Bray.'

'Shelley!' he repeated. 'What a charming name!'

I blushed. I was not used to compliments, and I am quite sure I did not look 'charming' after an all-night session in the train. I felt hot and sticky. My cotton dress was crumpled, and although I had just powdered my nose and hastily brushed my hair, I was quite sure I was unprepossessing. Thank goodness, I thought, when the formidable Miss Collins had interviewed me in the Torringtons' London house I had looked more attractive.

'Now forgive me,' went on Sir Austen, 'if I do not yet know who you are, but please come in. Bertrand–' He turned to the man with the baize apron and told him to settle the taxi.

He then explained to me, as we went into the villa, that Bertrand was the 'treasure' of the family, and had been at Arc-en-Ciel with the Italian Duc who used to own it, and that he did five times as much work as any of the lazy girls. Then Sir Austen laughed, and giving me a kindly look, added: 'But I oughtn't to talk about lazy girls to you. I'm

18

quite sure *you're* not one of them.'

I then told him I had been engaged as a resident teacher (sort of governess to use an old-fashioned word) for Mr Torrington's children.

'Ah! now I understand,' exclaimed Sir Austen. 'Delighted to meet you, Miss Bray, and I'm sure we are all glad you've come. Those two poor children have been far too long with a doting nannie. They need a little discipline, although they're jolly kids. I'm devoted to them. I'm their uncle by marriage.' And he went on to say that he was married to Esmond Torrington's sister and that they, the Warrs, had joined forces with Esmond and made a home with him since his young wife died.

'Such a tragedy,' ended Sir Austen, and led me into the hall to look at the then unfamiliar portrait of Veronica Torrington in her Spanish shawl. In an undertone he explained that the late Mrs Torrington had been killed in a terrible accident, driving her own car to Villefranche.

'She must have been very beautiful,' I said.

'Very!' echoed Sir Austen. Then abruptly he turned and led me back into the big cool entrance which had a mosaic floor. After the strong sunlight it all looked rather dim, but splendid beyond anything I had ever seen out of pictures. Marble statuary, great bowls of flowers, handsome rugs, gorgeous striped yellow silk curtains. An air of brooding silence hung over everything which, I learned in time, seems always to hang over such villas in the hot languorous South.

'Is Mr Torrington at home?' I asked of Sir Austen.

I was, I must confess, a little surprised to hear that Mr Torrington's sister also lived here and wondered why *she* could not cope with her niece and nephew. She must be quite young. Esmond Torrington was only thirty-five. Incidentally, Miss Collins had not mentioned the Warrs when she engaged me. But now Sir Austen was enlightening me further as to the general set-up at Arc-en-Ciel. First of all, he said, Mr Torrington was away – he had been in Paris for a week but he was due back this morning. Secondly, Sir Austen's wife was a semi-invalid, and a good deal older than her brother. In fact, Sir Austen said with a little cough and a rueful expression, his poor wife was confined to a wheel-chair. Although barely forty-eight, she had for the last few years been martyrised by arthritis and could no longer walk. That was why Esmond had bought this villa, which was like an enormous bungalow – all on one floor. It made it easy for Lady Warr to wheel herself from one room to another, when she came to stay with her brother.

'And she has an active mind,' he finished. 'Wonderful little woman, my dear wife.

20

Controls everybody from that chair of hers.'

Just how wonderful Lady Warr – 'Aunt Monica' – was, and how active mentally, I had yet to learn. I had to learn, too, to my cost, the remorseless machinery of what her husband called 'her control', which, when it was set in motion, could be so dangerous that one had best beware of it and not step too near. But I knew nothing of that then, and when a smart-looking dark-haired girl in a white overall appeared, stared at me and said: 'Milady had heard that mademoiselle had arrived and wished to see her–' I followed the girl down a long corridor, full of eagerness to meet Lady Warr. I had no premonition that she would be a thorn in my flesh. I just wondered why Miss Collins hadn't warned me that Esmond Torrington did not live alone and that there was a mistress of the house. Later I learned that it was because Monica Warr liked to 'surprise' people – especially people whom she wished to intimidate. She believed that the element of shock often brought people to their knees the sooner. Well, I must say, now when I look back, that her ladyship needn't have worried about *me*. I suppose she thought that I might be one of those girls who hoped to take over not only the children but the father, in a job like this, in which case my lady meant to put a speedy end to my hopes.

Well, I was not prepared for what I found

when I first met Monica Warr.

She was already up and in her wheel-chair which was one of the very latest and most luxurious kind, padded with white leather, satin-cushioned, silver-wheeled. In that chair, with a light quilt of pale blue silk over her knees, sat a tiny little lady who at first sight might have stepped out of a Watteau Shepherdess painting.

Monica Warr was all pink and white ... pink cheeks (later I learned how long her maid took to tint those cheeks and darken those naturally fair brows and lashes), ash-fair hair dressed rather high; pearl earrings in small white ears. Diamond rings on small white hands that were as chubby as a baby's. Seated in that chair in her lace peignoir she was certainly plump, but still pretty. Quite youthful, too, for her forty-eight years. I, like so many when they first met Monica Warr, was deceived into imagining that anybody as petite and fair and crippled, must be a sweet sympathetic person whom one could easily love.

I had to get to know how pampered – and powerful – she was. Everybody in the villa was at her beck and call. Everybody adored her – except little Kate. *And she knew.* Some children are psychic, you can't deceive them.

However, I am letting my thoughts race too far ahead. Back to the moment when

Lady Warr first smiled at me, and held out one of her chubby hands, and said in that deceptively soft voice of hers:

'Welcome to Arc-en-Ciel, Miss Bray.'

I took the little hand and answered respectfully. I am not particularly ambitious by nature, except for the good of the children in my care. I had no desire to ingratiate myself with older people. Nor had I any airs or graces. I had come here as a paid teacher and was prepared to fill that place not humbly – because I hate humble people – but fully aware of my position. And I had absolutely no idea at this first encounter with Monica Warr of the dark and well-controlled furies that raged behind her pretty welcoming smile. No notion of her bitter jealousy because I was young and strong and could walk and do all the things that she wanted to do. And above all – because I was to take charge of young Conrad and little Kate whose upbringing she so badly wanted to dominate and organise herself.

But Esmond Torrington had no intention of letting an elderly woman, even his own sister, bring up his children. Conrad and Kate needed a young companion. Until they were old enough to go to boarding school he wanted them to live with someone like myself who could not only give them lessons, but take them for walks, swim with them, do all the active things that the old nannie and their aunt could not do – as well as give them elementary lessons.

'Sit down, Miss Bray,' said Lady Warr, 'and let us have a little chat.'

When the 'little chat' began Lady Warr could not have been more charming, although now and then she delivered small but definite 'digs' at me; one pencilled eyebrow raised.

I remember that interrogation so well, and her rather high-pitched metallic voice. Mine on the contrary is pitched rather low, with a slightly husky quality which I have always had.

'Miss Collins tells me you are twenty-two. A little young for the post. When is your birthday?'

'I shall be twenty-three on Christmas Eve.'

'That's quite a long way ahead. Christmas Eve. How charming! A nice present for your mother…' (That sounded acid.) 'May I ask some details of your education?'

'I was at Brighton High School until I was seventeen and then went to college to take a teacher's training.'

'Have you taught in school?'

'Yes, for two years.'

'You have parents living?'

'No. My mother died while I was still at school and my father a year later.'

'So you have no ties?'

24

'Only a brother.'

'Where is he?'

'Doing his National Service in the R.A.F. He hopes to get some sort of agricultural training as he wants to be a farmer.'

A delicate shudder from Lady Warr.

'I can't imagine why anybody wants to run a farm – all those odorous pigs and the manure etc., ugh!'

I smiled. I thought that sort of remark so artificial and stupid, but I was aware even at this early stage in my relationship with Monica Warr that she was far from stupid, but seemed somewhat anxious to make me feel that my family and myself were of small account.

'How old is your brother?'

'A year younger than myself.'

'Forgive my enquiring, but I presume you are not very well off.'

'Not at all well off, Lady Warr. Robin and I have had a struggle since my father, who was a small country practitioner, died. He left us only a life insurance but that is rapidly dwindling.'

'You are lucky to have been given the chance to come to Arc-en-Ciel in a private situation like this.'

Now I agreed with her ladyship whole-heartedly.

The questioning went on.

'You're not a bad-looking girl – quite

good-looking in fact. Did you never think of any other profession except teaching?'

'No, I love children and I want to work with them.'

Her allusion to my appearance embarrassed me. My brother (whom I adored) used to tell me not to develop an inferiority complex which I was in danger of doing. Actually he once said: 'You're a jolly pretty girl when you smile.'

Perhaps I don't smile often except when my sense of humour really comes to the fore. I am a little solemn and thoughtful, and even as a child used to hate strangers and bury my nose in a book.

I looked around Lady Warr's magnificent bedroom. Dove grey carpet, grey satin curtains lined with rose pink. A double bed with real lace spread, one headboard shaped like a shell, scalloped in grey satin. Everywhere, the hall-marks of luxury. It was quite obvious that the crippled Monica didn't intend to let her femininity, or whatever glamour she had had as a girl, die in the process of her increasing age and illness. Well, I admire courage and I admired hers. She seemed to have plenty of it in the physical sense.

Then I caught a glimpse of myself in the long mirror and didn't much like my own, ordinary appearance. Yet I knew I had a lovely skin, clear grey eyes and the sort of vital thick hair, brown as a horse-chestnut, that has a curl and lustre all its own.

I knew that I had a rather good figure – not tall but slim. But my chief 'beauty' my friends had told me from time to time are my white, quite perfect teeth, and I suppose I ought to smile more than I do just to show them. I have slender hands, too, which I am sensible of – and about. I look after them.

There was a boy who once fell in love with me – I didn't love him and sent him away, but I do remember one nice thing he said to me– 'You have gentle graceful hands, Shelley, and you are altogether a gentle graceful person. Your shyness is appealing.'

But I wished I could conquer it. I'm never shy with children, however, I can do quite a lot of laughing and talking naturally to them. Lady Warr's inquisition continued:

'Where is your home?'

'My brother and I share a flat – a garden flat actually – in south Norwood. It's shut up now that we're both away.'

'South Norwood?' repeated Lady Warr. I could swear I saw her shudder again. 'A long way from Monte Carlo.'

'A long way,' I agreed.

'Are you engaged?'

'No.'

'No – er – "boy-friend", as I believe it is called?'

'No,' I said and allowed myself to smile.

'Well, if you've come here with any hope

of finding one, I am afraid you will be dis-appointed, Miss Bray. We adults are older than you and we do not have many – if any – unattached young men coming to visit us.'

Now I felt a distinct resentment.

'I can assure you I didn't take this post with any thought of using it as a means to marriage, Lady Warr.'

'That's fine,' she said, and her voice was like cream. 'Just one more question. Are you musical?'

'Very. When you asked me just now, Lady Warr, if I ever thought of any other profes-sion, yes – I did – in my early teens I dreamed about playing the piano. But I soon realised that one has to be very much above average in order to make a profession of it. I only play a little. But I adore it.'

'I am afraid there will be no chance what-soever of your playing here. My brother's piano is in his studio,' said Lady Warr in a slightly sharper voice.

I looked at her, feeling slightly non-plussed. She was such a pretty little thing. It was so sad to think she was confined at her age to a wheel-chair. Yet somehow I felt she was not to be pitied. There was a sting behind her honey. I said:

'Miss Collins told me that although your nephew prefers sports, he takes after his father and is musical. I understood that I was to give him first lessons on the pianoforte.'

'Quite so. When Mr Torrington is out you will be able to give Conrad his lessons. I was merely referring to your playing for *pleasure*.'

'It would never enter my head to play here,' I said.

'Splendid,' said the little creature from the chair, with her dazzling smile. 'My brother, as you know, is a famous conductor. You will hear a great deal of music. He has a superb stereophonic radiogram and he uses it in connection with his orchestral work when he is studying for his concerts. That is the only sort of music that one *wishes* to hear at Arc-en-Ciel.'

'Yes, Lady Warr,' I said feeling that I had been suitably 'briefed'.

'And, of course,' she went on, 'you must understand that one of your duties will be to keep the children quiet and well away from the studio, when their father is here – busy, or entertaining. I presume you will have no objection to having a tray in your school-room when there are guests for meals?'

'None at all. It will suit me very well.'

I felt quite sure by then that Lady Warr wished she could organise things so that I ate all my meals in the schoolroom. But I was soon to learn that Conrad and little Kate were their father's dearest possessions. Because he was away so much (he conducted all over Europe), he insisted on having them at the table with him whenever

29

he was at home. (Which meant that I, of course, would then also be present.)

Lady Warr discussed my salary. It was to be ninety New francs a week while we were in France and adjusted accordingly when we returned to England. Esmond Torrington had a house in Eaton Square which was now closed. The family were likely to be in residence in Monte Carlo for some time.

Lady Warr then told me a bit about the establishment. The girl who had shown me in here was Yvonne, her special attendant. There was another resident maid, and a young daily girl named Thérèse, who was in charge of what her ladyship called 'the children's wing' (which included my bedroom). The cook, Louise, was an old retainer. Esmond Torrington had his valet, André. There were, of course, also the outdoor servants, gardeners, boys, etc., and Bertrand.

It all rather took my breath away. It seemed such a tremendous establishment. I was soon to learn that Sir Austen had always been a rich man, which was why Monica had married him in the first place, but that Esmond Torrington had had quite a struggle as a boy, and that it was only after he had reached fame as a conductor that he had inherited a small fortune from an uncle on the Torrington side.

It all seemed thrilling. Robin and I were used to pinching and scraping in our little garden flat. We had never known luxury. But here in Arc-en-Ciel, the ménage ran, as I was to discover, on oiled wheels; there was wonderful food, deferential service and even a visiting laundry-woman who in true French style washed and ironed everything in the house exquisitely.

An orchid atmosphere in fact. I wondered how the children fared in it – I was eager to make their acquaintance. After a few minutes Lady Warr seemed to be finished with me. It might be what Robin called the 'old complex', but I did feel, in spite of all her smiles and charm, that she was not really pleased with Miss Collins' choice, but decided to put up with me. She rang her bell for her attendant, and sent her to find Sir Austen. She then brought the subject round to the late Mrs Torrington.

'We do not mention her to the children. Her death was a tragedy, my brother does not like it mentioned.'

I felt suddenly shocked.

'Are the children not to be reminded of their own mother?'

Now Lady Warr, too, looked shocked – at my daring to express my own opinion, I suppose. She said, coldly:

'They do not know about their mother's accident. They just think she died naturally. I repeat, Miss Bray, the subject is *not* to be discussed.'

'Of course,' I said, stammering. She really did have the knack of making one feel small.

Sir Austen came into the room. He hurried across to the wheel-chair and put a hand on Lady Warr's shoulder.

'My darling is not tiring herself, I hope?'

'Certainly not. I've only just started the day. You ought to know that I do not tire easily and certainly never until I have done all the things I have to do managing a house like this.'

'Yes, yes, of course. You're always a wonder, my darling.'

'Miss Bray and I have had our little talk. I thought you might find Kate and Conrad and bring them here, please, Austen.'

'Yes, my darling, at once.'

I sat silent. Her ladyship spoke to her husband with a sharpness that seemed a poor reward for his exaggerated courtesy and attention to her. He was, I soon discovered, a weak, kindly, rather stupid man. And she was the uncrowned queen of Arc-en-Ciel. Everyone fawned upon her. I was never a very good 'fawner'. In my quiet way I've always been independent; candid to the point of bluntness at times. I did hope I wasn't going to tread on any of her ladyship's corns. I would certainly have to watch my step, I thought.

I was to grow used to hearing poor old Sir Austen utter those words: *Yes, my darling, at once!*' All the commands of the little lady in the wheel-chair had to be carried out '*at once*'.

I now felt hotter and stickier than when I arrived, and longed to get out of this perfumed and gilded bedroom. Sir Austen returned with the children.

'Why, hello,' I said to them. I could feel my own personality change. I became as I always was with children – friendly and unafraid. I held out a hand to each.

'This is your governess, Miss Bray,' said their aunt, and wheeled herself deftly around the big room and took up her position at one of the windows. She looked out at times, and at others, round at us. I was always aware of her scrutiny.

The children shook hands with me. Politely enough they greeted me with, '*How do you do, Miss Bray.*'

Their old nannie had certainly taught them manners. The boy at once reminded me of his famous father whom I had often seen at the Festival Hall in London. Tall for seven years old – thin, dark-haired, dark-eyed, he was brown as an Indian and wore those very short shorts that French boys wear, and a spotless sports-shirt. He had a rather defiant face ... as though he could easily be rebellious and difficult. He eyed me covertly. But the little girl, I found touching. She, too, had dark eyes but they were big and sad and not at all defiant. Her rich red hair resembled that of the woman in the portrait – her mother. The child was tall for her six years and much too thin. She seemed to be nervous and shy. She kept twisting her fingers and plucking at the little, short, dirndl skirt which she wore with a pale blue blouse.

The two were perfectly turned out. Too perfect, I thought. I would like to have seen them a little more untidy and childish and exuberant. Perhaps it was their aunt who overawed them. I swiftly drew my conclusions.

Conrad was not overawed by 'Aunt Monnie' as he called her, for he immediately went over to her chair, took one of her chubby little hands and kissed it.

'That's what all the Frenchmen do, isn't it, Aunt Monnie?'

'Why, you did it too, *most* gracefully, you darling boy,' said Lady Warr, looking delighted. 'Wasn't it sweet of him, Miss Bray?'

'Very,' I said politely, although the sight of the small boy kissing his aunt's hand rather irritated me. Surely, I thought, Mr Torrington would not want his son brought up like a foreigner, or was it just that Lady Warr liked to number even this child among her servitors?

'You'll find my nephew charming in every way,' added Lady Warr, proudly.

I saw Conrad eye me through his lashes. He grumbled:

'Why do we have to have a governess?'

'Now, Con, that's not very polite of you,' murmured Lady Warr. 'And it'll only be for a year and then Daddy's sending you to school, alas!'

Privately I thought it would be good when Master Conrad Torrington did go to school. It was evident he didn't fancy any control. I soon learned how completely he had been spoiled by both his aunt and the old nannie. But Kate was quite another cup of tea. She just looked at me with her huge eyes and remained sad and silent. Lady Warr said:

'Kate, you haven't kissed me.'

She hung her head.

'I don't want to,' she murmured.

'Now, Kate,' said Lady Warr in a warning voice, 'don't let's start today with another little scene like we had yesterday.'

The child turned scarlet. Knowing children so well, I could sense immediately that she was one of those who do not care for kissing or caressing, nor could she flatter people – as the boy had done. It was also obvious that her ladyship made a pet of Conrad, but did not get on with Kate. But I understood the little girl. She had my innate dislike of being asked to draw too near a stranger. She was antagonised by Lady Warr. *And she was bullied.* Of that I was sure.

Lady Warr spoke to her sharply:

'You're not at all affectionate, my dear, and you're not very obedient, either. I told you yesterday that unless you came and kissed me good morning like Con does that there'd be no swimming for you this morning. Miss Bray will give you some letters to copy out instead.'

On this glorious morning! And the child only six, I thought. So that was all that Lady Warr knew about children. And all because little Kate didn't wish to play up to her. Kate burst into tears. I took her hand, but before I could speak, Lady Warr said:

'No, Miss Bray, she is not to be coddled. She's a very naughty girl. I'm afraid her father spoils her when he is at home. He does not realise how difficult she is. You will find also, that you may have to watch what she says. We aren't always truthful, are we, Kate?'

That, I thought, was unspeakable. The child sobbed, her face hidden in her hands. I wondered just how much Esmond Torrington did know about what went on with his children. I had an uncanny insight into this matter. Lady Warr positively disliked her little niece. *Had she also disliked the mother whom Kate resembled? Was it the resemblance that annoyed the woman?*

I was to learn the answer to those questions in time – but not just now.

Lady Warr rang her bell again for Yvonne who was told to take me to my 'wing'.

'As soon as you are washed and changed you can take the children for a little walk, Miss Bray. And I repeat – no bathing for Kate, but Conrad can go down with you to the *plage* before lunch.'

I stood up. My passionate love for children gave me courage. Lady Warr had wheeled herself towards me while she was speaking. I looked straight down into eyes that were as cold and hard as blue stones. I said:

'Just to celebrate my arrival could Kate not be forgiven this time, Lady Warr. I am sure she'll come and give you a little kiss later on.'

Then the snake, coiled in the deceptive nest of flowers, struck. Lady Warr said:

'Please do not question my orders or try to alter them in any way, Miss Bray.'

I stared – dumbfounded. The little boy giggled. At once Lady Warr became sweet and correct again.

'There's nothing to laugh at, Con. It's *rather* impolite to Miss Bray. Now run along, all of you.' And to me, she added: 'We'll meet at lunch. I hope you'll be very happy with us at Arc-en-Ciel, Miss Bray.'

Very happy? I wondered. I could see that the little lady in the wheel-chair, and I, were going to clash considerably on the question of the children – if nothing else. But I knew that I must try to curb my own impulses. I must try to remember that *she* was 'the boss'. But I was fired by a sudden and quite ardent desire to champion poor Kate. So, as she continued to sob, I took her little hand and talked to her gaily while we followed Yvonne through the handsome villa.

'Don't mind too much about the bathing, dear. There'll be plenty of other times to swim. And it'll be quite fun copying letters. We'll make each one a different shape like a little animal, shall we? B for a bear, R for a rabbit, and T for a tiger, and so on.'

Her tears dried. Her fingers clung to mine. She began to giggle and talk. But Conrad lagged behind and I could almost feel his animosity in the air. I would have my work cut out to discipline young Conrad with that doting aunt behind him. I was sure he would always play up to her, cunningly enough.

Before I had time to reach my room I heard a deep man's voice calling:

'Conrad! Kate!'

They swung round. I, too, turned. With a little thrill of surprise and pleasure I saw the tall figure of Esmond Torrington. He had come early. He was in the entrance hall. Bertrand was behind him, carrying two suitcases. Mr Torrington moved towards us. Yes, those remarkable features of his were not strange to me. I had seen them in so many papers and journals. Conrad was certainly like him. But whereas the child had a furtive air, the great conductor looked frank, fearless, and quite wonderful, I thought. The most handsome man possible to imagine; mature for his thirty-five years, with a hint of silver in the dark hair brushed back above his ears. He was immaculately dressed in a light suit. I even recognised his fine long hands, with those flexible wrists. I had watched them many a time as he wielded his baton, leading his orchestra. During my adolescence, I used to feel quite a hero worship for Esmond Torrington.

I was speechless now that I saw him in the flesh. The children ran to him and he embraced them. Then he straightened and smiled at me. It was a smile that held infinite sweetness. He had the reputation for being a very sweet, human person for all his extraordinary success.

'You must be the new teacher,' he said. 'Miss Collins told me she had engaged you. Miss – er–'

'Bray,' I said.

'Ah, yes, Miss Bray. Have you been here long?'

'I've only just come off the train,' I heard myself stammering nervously.

'Indeed? I came over from Paris by plane. We seem to have synchronised. Well, I'm glad my two rascals are going to have some proper control and teaching now. They were getting a bit out of hand with poor old Nannie, I fear.'

'I'm not out of hand. I'm holding *Miss Bray's* hand,' said little Kate, her face all smiles now. 'Daddy, will you take me swimming?'

'Of course,' he said, 'I intend to have at least three hours' rest before I start my rehearsal this afternoon. I get far too little time with my children, Miss Bray,' he added to me.

Conrad put in:

'Aunt Monnie says Kate's not to swim because she's been naughty.'

I could have shaken him. Esmond Torrington was sorting through some mail that he had picked up in the hall. Of course he was a fabulously busy man and had little time to look into the details of his motherless children's upbringing. That was not his fault.

'Dear, dear, my naughty Kate! Well, you must always do what Aunt Monnie says.' And without noticing that little Kate's eyes filled with tears, he said to me: 'My sister's wonderful. As you will have seen – she's crippled by that terrible arthritis but we never hear a word of complaint and she runs the villa marvellously. A wonderful woman!'

Another sycophant, I thought.

It wasn't until later that I learned that Esmond did, in fact, owe a lot to his sister who was thirteen years his senior. After the death of their parents, she had brought him up – and, perhaps for the first and last time in her life, made sacrifices for another human being. She had allowed every possible penny to be spent on Esmond's musical education, for he had shown signs at an early age of the genius that had afterwards manifested itself in his conducting. She had seen to it that he studied not only at the Royal College in London, but afterwards in Paris and Vienna. Yes, he owed his sister quite a debt of gratitude.

I caught poor little Kate's hand and pressed it, trying silently to comfort her again. Then rather sharply I told Conrad to take her into the nursery and wait for me. Before I started my régime of control in this splendid villa, there were one or two things I wanted to know from the great man himself. I might never in a thousand years ask anything for myself, but I could dare most things in order to get what I wanted for the children.

'Come into my studio, do,' said Mr Torrington and opened the door close by which we were standing, to let me pass. I took a quick glance at a long room, with a dais at one end on which stood a black concert-grand. Everywhere there seemed to be sheet-music, scores, gramophone records and papers. Cool green walls covered with

41

signed photographs of famous artists. Overawed, I glimpsed such signatures as 'Flagstadt' ... 'Kathleen Ferrier' ... 'Yehudi Menuhin'. This man in whose employ I could now consider myself, had conducted many concerts at which *The Great* had sung or played. How tragic for him to have lost his wife at such an early age, I thought. No matter how fond he was of his sister and her husband, their presence could not compensate for the loss of all that a man of his deep nature must need.

Esmond seated himself on the edge of a large desk, and ruefully indicated a pile of correspondence.

'Thank goodness our Miss Collins will be down later on tonight to take over all this.'

'You must work very hard.'

'To achieve anything one must work very hard, Miss Bray. You, too, I am sure.'

I felt my cheeks grow hot.

'Oh, I ... I do nothing ... I am *nothing* compared with someone like you.'

'If you're good at your particular job, you're every bit as good as I am,' he laughed again.

I remained tongue-tied. He added:

'How young you look! Still in your teens?'

'No!' I exclaimed horrified. 'I'm twenty-two.'

'That seems young to me. I am rapidly approaching forty.'

42

I liked his humorous friendly manner. I felt so much at ease with him in spite of his being a distinguished musician, and so much happier than I had been in Lady Warr's presence, I blurted out:

'I'm just a little confused, Mr Torrington. I know you won't mind me asking … but I didn't quite understand when your sister … when Lady Warr…' I broke off, stuttering.

'Yes?' he asked gently, and his dark warm eyes encouraged me.

'I … it's about the children's mother.'

At once I saw his expression change. A mask fell across his face, shuttering it from me. He stood up and walked towards one of the three French windows. They all had wrought-iron balconies and striped awnings keeping out the hot Mediterranean sun.

'What about her?' he asked, without turning round.

'Just … that Lady Warr said I was not to discuss her at all with the children. I … please, don't they ever speak of their mother? Don't you wish them to remember her? I felt it a little difficult and I just want to know exactly what I ought to say … for instance, if they should mention her name.'

When Esmond Torrington answered, his voice was still friendly but I felt there was a cool almost warning note behind it now.

'My wife died in an accident two years ago. Kate hardly remembers her. But of

43

course Conrad does. And of course, if Conrad ever speaks of his mother, you must let him do so quite naturally. They both know and appreciate her portraits which hang both in London and down here. My sister...' Now it was Esmond Torrington's turn to break off. He tapped the end of a fountain pen on his blotter, frowning. 'My sister and I don't altogether see eye to eye on this subject, I admit. She thinks it would be best that Veronica, my late wife, should never be referred to at all. That, of course, is on her part, out of deference to *my* feelings.'

Or was it, I wondered, that Monica Warr hated the beautiful girl who had first taken her adored brother away from her. Was it because Lady Warr couldn't even bear her niece and nephew – the latter in particular – to give one shred of love to the memory of their dead mother?

I said nothing. Esmond Torrington went on:

'Just treat the thing naturally and with tact.'

'I will,' I said, relieved.

He changed the conversation. I was soon to learn that the subject of Veronica Torrington was not one that he ever wished to discuss. Somehow it filled me with curiosity.

Had he loved her very much? Had her savage death in that accident embittered him? Would he now remain a widower and devote the rest of his life entirely to his children and career? He cleared his throat. The mask fell away. He was all kindness and courtesy and charm again.

'One day, Miss Bray, you must come here with the children and I'll show you all my treasures,' he waved a hand around the photograph-covered walls, 'and my collection of famous batons...' He indicated a glass specimen case in which there lay many beautiful batons, some with carved ivory handles, some encased in silver and gilt; one with sparkling precious stones which had apparently been given to him by a Russian colleague. It had belonged to a famous conductor who once played at the court of the murdered Tsar.

'I hope you'll be very happy here, Miss Bray,' he said, 'and please use all your authority with my children and train them as you think right. Your time off also must be organised. You must have rest and recreation away from Conrad and Kate. Children can be very tiring.'

I thought him kind and considerate. I thanked him. He opened the door of the studio. I walked out; straight into Lady Warr who was wheeling herself towards us down the corridor. Her chair on its soft-tyred wheels was noiseless, one could not hear her coming. She propelled herself in it so dexterously that she could gather up quite a remarkable speed. One never knew where she came from or when she was coming. She would just appear.

She was fully dressed now, I could see, for the quilt had gone. Her legs – rather short and ugly – in nylon stockings; her shoes were pointed and fashionable. She wore a dark blue linen suit with a white chiffon pleated blouse. I could see better now how very plump she was. Her china blue eyes examined me closely. I felt the necessity to explain why I had been in Mr Torrington's studio, but could scarcely say what I had gone in to ask him without offending her.

She eyed me, I knew, with suspicion; with disapproval. She said in a high, silvery voice:

'You won't make a habit of worrying my brother with any of the silly little details about the children's lives, will you, Miss Bray? I can always solve your problems – we don't need to worry him.'

'Very well, Lady Warr,' I said, and bit my lips.

She wheeled herself into the studio. I heard her changed voice then, honey-sweet.

'Esmond, *darling* ... how marvellous to have you home again. How is my beloved Paris?...'

I shut the studio door. Full of conflicting feelings, I walked down the corridor to look for my own room, and the children.

3

I could not complain of my bedroom. It had none of the magnificence of the rooms in this villa that I had already seen, but a simplicity and charm of its own which I appreciated. It had obviously been occupied before by the old nannie who had been sent away. I was to hear more about Nannie and the part she played in the lives of these people.

My little room had a single tall window looking out upon an attractive stone-paved portion of the garden with a bed of English roses planted around a small fountain. The marble figure of a faun, with his lute to his thick stone lips, was bent on one dimpled knee, looking down into the basin of the water. It was delightful, I thought. The high wall beyond was crimson and purple with bougainvillaea. There were orange and lemon trees to give shade, and the little grotto had that touch of dank and gloom and antiquity which I learned was an essential feature of some French gardens. Somebody – I don't remember who – explained to me that Arc-en-Ciel was built after the First World War on the sight of an old *manoir*. So the little faun had played his lute here for at least three hundred years.

My room had long, light polished floor boards, two bright red rugs, striped blue curtains and, of course, the inevitable shutters religiously drawn by the servants to keep out the sun. I was to wage a regular fight to keep those windows open because I adored the sun and could not have enough of it. Both old Bertrand, who came around to clean shoes and move heavy furniture when the servants turned out a room, and Thérèse, the young daily maid, obstinately closed those jalousies as soon as I opened them. Old Bertrand would shake his head at me and mutter:

'*C'est mauvais, le soleil. Prenez-garde, mademoiselle.*'

Take care – of the sun? Not I! There were other much more pressing things to beware of at the Arc-en-Ciel!

Now when I examined for the first time my little room which was to become home to me far more than the rest of the villa, the children forgot their psychological disturbances and were natural and friendly, running around to show me everything. Even the boy eyed me with less disfavour.

Here was my wardrobe – pale yellow rather ornate affair, here, my dressing table, of the same French-looking wood. My wash basin was neatly enclosed in a built-in cupboard, and my divan-bed was covered with a woven spread of the same striped blue as the curtains. There was a pot of geraniums on the table in a wrought-iron *jardinière*. It had belonged to their Nannie, they said, who had carefully watered it each day. A modern-looking easy chair in which Nannie never sat, so they said, because she was always running around after them. I smiled and said:

'I shall not run around after you. You will learn to look after yourselves a little. You will see.'

'I can look after myself. I can jump,' announced Kate, scrambling on to my bed and jumping wildly on to the floor. The mat slipped from under her. She skated halfway across the room over the polished floor which brought a hoot of laughter from Conrad. Kate began to whimper. I picked her up.

'You are not hurt.'

'I am, I am!' she howled.

'You are not,' I repeated calmly, 'and when you jump in future it must be outside, and not *in* the house.'

'Nannie always kissed the place to make it well,' wailed Kate.

'Kate's a beastly little baby,' jeered Conrad.

I could see well what manner of upbringing these two had so far had. What could one expect with no mother, a doting Nannie, a father who was far too famous and busy to supervise, and an aunt who indulged in rank favouritism.

I soothed Kate's injured dignity by offering her a boiled sweet – I had a little bag of them which I had bought in England. Her tears dried like magic and she was then given the task of helping me unpack. Both she and her brother seemed interested in my luggage. Conrad was old enough to despise my very modest wardrobe.

'You've only got four dresses!' he exclaimed as I hung them up.

'I have also two skirts and a blouse or two,' I smiled.

'Aunt Monnie has *hundreds* of dresses.'

'I am sure she has, Conrad. Your aunt and I are not quite in the same position.'

'What does *posishion* mean?' asked Kate.

'The way of life in which we move,' I explained. 'Your aunt is Lady Warr. I am Miss Bray, your teacher.'

'Why can't a teacher have hundreds of clothes?' demanded Conrad.

'Because she has to earn her own living and use her money sparingly and wisely.'

I saw a look of undisguised scorn in the boy's dark brilliant eyes.

'Are you poor then?' he asked.

'Very poor,' I smiled.

He stared.

'Like Thérèse? She is poor. She scrubs the floor here and she told us that they only have meat once a week in her family.'

'I'm not quite as poor as that,' I told him.

'Nannie was rich. She was always giving us francs out of her nest egg. Do you know what a nest egg is?' demanded Conrad.

'Yes, it is one's savings. Nannie was lucky to be able to save. I haven't been able to do so, so far.'

'Won't you give us francs then?'

I looked him straight in the eyes.

'No, my dear. No doubt your father gives you pocket money. I don't think you should have taken Nannie's francs.'

'Why not?'

'Because she was old and trying to save her money in order to live when she could no longer work. You should never take money from such people.'

'Aunt Monnie says that money is more important than anything else,' said Conrad lifting his chin in a way to which I was to become accustomed, with that slightly sneering stubborn *'I defy you'* tilt.

He was a little boy with great potentialities. A quick brain, which if not properly guided, could be cunning. A facility to absorb all that he learnt too easily. But, unfortunately, he did not always absorb the right things. Nor was he fond of hard work. What he had just said made it clear to me that Lady Warr had not instilled the best ideals or principles into the boy, but rather

51

those that appealed to his sensuous and lazy side. So long as he buttered her up the right way, she would not allow that there were defects in his character. Whereas Kate was still a baby and not nearly as bright; but much more generous and loving by nature. Suddenly, still sucking her sweet, she put her sticky lips against my cheeks and whispered:

'I like you, and I hate Aunt Monnie.'

'I shall tell her you said that,' declared Conrad, and made for the door. I immediately barred his exit.

'Conrad,' I said, 'it is a pity you and I should come to grips the very first moment we meet, but I'm going to be quite frank with you. I do *not* like little boys who tell tales. You told your father one just now about Kate. Do you *like* seeing her get into trouble?'

His long black lashes flickered down. I thought how magnificent they were against the golden tan of his cheeks. *What* a good-looker he was! Then he flicked the lashes up and gave an insolent laugh.

'Aunt Monnie told me always to tell her what Kate says and does.'

Heavens, I thought, how difficult my position is going to be in this house if every standard I set and everything I believe in is going to be 'downed' by Lady Warr. But if the thought depressed me I was not going to show it. There is something in my nature which does not allow me to be easily beaten. I tried to reason with Conrad.

'You must not always be guided by what you hear grown-ups say. That applies to what I say, too. You must learn to make your own judgments and form your own opinions. People who have no opinions of their own and just allow themselves to be blown to and fro like a straw in the wind, are weak and useless. You must learn to become strong and individual. To do good because you *want* to do good and not because you *have to*. To speak the truth because you believe in truth and are ashamed to be a liar. To be frank because it would seem low down and unsporting to gain what you want by deceit. I do not believe, Conrad, that you would really like to see Kate punished while you go free, and that you will enjoy your swim this morning knowing that your little sister is sitting in the schoolroom copying letters on this hot day. Tell me, truly, am I right or wrong?'

For an instant, he hesitated. I could see him struggling with his thoughts and against his worst instincts which had undeniably been fostered by that foolish and, if I judged rightly, rather wicked aunt of his. I wondered what weakness of character he had inherited from his beautiful mother or if there was anything in him of that fine man, his father? Then to my relief the good won. Blushing, he kicked his toe against the floor and muttered:

'I want Kate to swim with me and I don't want to get her into trouble.'

'Good! I'm delighted,' I said. 'Now take me and show me the schoolroom.'

It was, of course, only a temporary triumph. I was to have many battles with Master Conrad in the future, and one couldn't in a few hours eliminate the wrongful impressions that had so far been absorbed.

Conrad was an excitable child, up one moment, down the next, and one never quite knew what mood he would be in. But just now he seemed to wish to be friends with me, for he showed as much pleasure as Kate in dragging me from one object to another in their schoolroom, and chattering.

Until a week ago this had been the nursery. They both seemed rather proud of its new importance. They described how the painters and decorators had come and the old nursery paper had been pasted over with a more suitable one of plain soft green. The woodwork was all polished and of some foreign tree that I could not put a name to – like the golden floor.

It was a cool, big airy room with two windows leading out on to a verandah which had a scarlet and white awning. I could see at once that one could put some tables out there and enjoy some very pleasant open-air studies.

There were plenty of cane chairs with scarlet cushions, a long wooden table and two little painted desks which, Kate proudly informed me, Daddy had bought for them because they were to 'go to school' in here. There was even a blackboard. On a high shelf running all round the room, there was an amusing assortment of carved animals and French dolls and a built-in bookcase full of children's books.

'Are you going to teach us out of our old books?' Conrad demanded.

I said 'no' and immediately fetched some of my Parents' National Educational Union manuals – illustrated history, geography and botany books and the little supply I had brought with me of exercise and notebooks which the children use at home in the system in which I had been trained.

Both the children were intrigued, and Conrad, with his alert mind, at once grasped the things that I told him he would do. I could see that he would be an adept pupil *if* he worked. But I discovered that his powers of concentration would have to be increased before he turned into a serious student.

Nevertheless I was not discouraged with the first hour or two that I spent with my small pupils, and only too grieved that I had to put poor chubby little Kate to her pun-ishment task, instead of taking her down to the *plage* with her brother. But as I changed into my one and only pair of shorts and a shirt and, with towel and swim suit rolled under my arm, walked along the corridor with Conrad, the door of Mr Torrington's studio opened. He thrust out his head.

'Ah! I thought I heard your voice, Con. What about this dip? I'm all ready for it.'

'Then perhaps I need not go,' I began, 'I can stay with Kate?'

'Nonsense,' Esmond said, 'we'll all go.' And gave me his swift sweet smile. 'Just give me a moment to change. Where's Kate?'

I reminded him that Lady Warr had said she was to be punished for rudeness.

His brow puckered. He put a finger to his lips.

'H'm. Well, well, perhaps I'll square my sis-ter, Miss Bray. It's a bit tough on such a small mite being kept in on my first day home.'

I said nothing. It was not my place to agree with him, but I foresaw trouble. It came when the four of us (Kate now in ecstasy clinging to her father) were seen by her ladyship who was seated in her wheel-chair out on the terrace facing the main drive.

'I thought I said that Kate was to forego her swim,' she said sharply, addressing me.

I remained silent. Mr Torrington spoke for me.

'Let her off this time, Monnie. I don't suppose her crime was very sinister, was it?'

I saw Lady Warr's delicate face grow hot and pink with annoyance.

'Now, Esmond, you shouldn't interfere. I've repeatedly asked Kate to say good morning to me and she never will.'

Kate shrank back against her father. She looked so small and adorable, I thought, in the diminutive pale blue bikini and pants which she had proudly given me to put on her, and her little white towelling robe. I could see she was going to burst into tears. I prayed fervently that Esmond Torrington would stand his ground. He did. He gave a laugh, pulled Kate's curls, and said:

'She didn't mean any harm, Monnie, I'm sure. She's a bit shy like her papa.' And he actually *winked at me,* showing for the first time that boyish humour that was natural to the man when he was not harassed by over-work or sunk in the gloom which had, it seemed, encircled him ever since the tragedy of his young wife's fatal accident.

Lady Warr obviously had to sit on her own feelings in order not to annoy her brother. She gave a high-pitched laugh and shrugged her shoulders.

'Oh, very well, but you do spoil the children disgracefully.'

'Well, I've got a restraining hand about the place now,' he laughed. 'No doubt Miss

Bray will be very stern and I shall not be allowed to break the rules in future.'

'I doubt if the rules that *Miss Bray* makes need be observed by *you,* dear,' said Lady Warr acidly. 'That is going *too* far.'

Now she turned her china blue eyes upon me.

'I don't think there's any need for you to go down to the *plage* if Mr Torrington is going to take the children, Miss Bray.'

Once again before I could answer, Esmond spoke.

'Do you want to do something else then, Miss Bray?'

'No,' I stammered, 'I'd adore to bathe...'

'Good, then we'll all go down,' he broke in.

If looks could have killed, Lady Warr would have killed me then, I am sure, but I could not resist a human feeling of pleasure as I followed Mr Torrington and his children through the beautiful gardens to the gate outside which one of the loveliest cars I had ever seen waited for us. An open Rolls-Bentley – white and coffee-coloured which Esmond liked to drive himself. Conrad sat beside his father. Kate cuddled up to me. As we drove off I looked at the back of Esmond's proud dark head and could scarcely believe my good luck. To be in *his* car, driven by him through Monte Carlo on this sparkling day! He was one of Europe's greatest conductors and, so I quickly felt, one of the most charming and endearing men alive – absolutely without conceit and of incorruptible integrity. A man to inspire hero-worship, not only in an insignificant person like myself but many who were almost his equals. How lucky indeed, I was.

I saw how he cast off the mantle of care and responsibility and greatness, and became a youthful, laughing companion for his children. He chatted to Conrad as to an equal and friend. I thought how sad it was that the boy could not see more of such a father and be left less to petticoat government. I resolved there and then to do my utmost to train Conrad's young mind and character to the very best of my ability ... no matter what opposition I met with from Lady Warr.

Typical of the great man's kindliness and thought for the least of his acquaintances, Esmond went out of his way to make a detour and show the new English teacher a little of this delightful Monégasque capital. We passed the Exotic Garden full of strange and exquisite flowers which, Esmond told me, had been originally planted by Prince Albert the First. One day, he said, he would take me with the children to see the Grotto of the Observatory which should interest my student's mind, for it belonged to the Neolithic period and was full of marvellous shapes moulded by thousands of centuries one hundred and sixty-four feet below ground.

We turned, too, into some of the quaint old streets of sixteenth-century design. Then I was shown one of the more modern boulevards, full of expensive glittering shops.

I stared, wide-eyed at the Opera House in which Esmond Torrington had so often conducted, and so we moved along the esplanade, and stopped at the bathing beach where the pine groves looked cool and dark and welcoming in the heat of the midday sun.

Even I was beginning to realise how hot that Mediterranean sun could be. I felt my whole body bathed in perspiration.

Of course the Torringtons had a private bathing hut and their own table and chairs under a scarlet white-fringed umbrella. Before us stretched the radiant deep blue sea, glassy in the heat but tempting enough. We were soon all out in it, and I, who had so little opportunity in my restricted London life of swimming but loved it, struck out with vigour. I had to be called back by my employer.

'Hi there, Miss Br-r-ay! *Hi there* – don't go out too far.'

At once I turned and swam back, remorseful because I had for a dizzy moment forgotten my duties and left Kate on the beach.

Breathless, glowing, I pushed the thick hair back from my face and apologised to Esmond. He had just been out for a swim himself and was rubbing his hair. He looked tall and brown and rather splendid, with his wide shoulders; but on the whole too slender – almost thin, I thought.

'I don't want to have to show off my abilities as a lifesaver,' he grinned at me. He was polishing his dark glasses. 'But you seem to be quite a strong swimmer.'

'I'm all right, but I'm afraid I quite lost myself – it was such a treat!' I said breathlessly.

I saw his handsome eyes – like his son's – looking at me with frank curiosity.

'You are not used to this sun – cover up or you will burn,' he said.

Embarrassed, I grabbed my towel and wrapped myself in it.

'I'll get dressed,' I said.

'You looked like a child, coming out of that water,' he said, as though my appearance surprised him. 'What a little slip of a thing you are to be a trained teacher.'

'She's very poor, Daddy, and can't save,' Conrad suddenly volunteered to my complete confusion. I noted Esmond's expression of surprise, but immediately he corrected the boy.

'We don't make personal remarks of that kind, old boy,' he said gently, and added to me: 'You will forgive him, won't you, Miss Bray?'

'Of course – of course,' I stuttered, and quickly, to hide my embarrassment, picked up little Kate, set her on her feet and walked with her down to the sea – there to supervise while she paddled and pretended to swim in an inch or two of water.

She looked enchanting when her red curly hair was wet, and curlier than ever, and all her nervousness and that anxious air that had sat on her when she was with her aunt vanished. She kept close to my side. Nothing was more revealing than when she kept saying:

'I love *you*. Aunt Monnie says I ought to be punished because I won't swim like Con, but he's 'older an me' isn't he?'

'Yes, yes, but you must love Aunt Monica, too. You'll learn to swim in time. I'll teach you,' I promised her.

At once her face screwed up.

'I don't want to.'

'Then you shan't – until you do want to,' I soothed her.

'Goody goody!' she exclaimed and was happy again, but that promise from me was to have unfortunate results when it was repeated to her ladyship.

Back to that dazzling glorious hour on the beach with Esmond and his children. I felt that if I were told to pack up and go home that very afternoon it would have been worth while to have spent even those moments watching, listening to *him*. Not the conductor standing like a god on his rostrum – awe-inspiring, inaccessible – but an ordinary charming man in swim suit and bath robe smoking a cigarette, arms hunched around his bent knees, talking to me as well as to his children. When for a moment they were engrossed in watching a speedboat cut through the radiant water, he turned his attention fully upon me.

'I still find it difficult to believe that you are nearly twenty-three.'

'Oh, I am. I am!' I said. 'Sometimes I wish I were huge and fat with spectacles, then people wouldn't treat me like a child.'

He laughed.

'I'm quite glad you're not huge and fat, I assure you. But I've always relied on Miss Collins' taste.'

A light compliment, but enough to bring the colour back to my cheeks. I took refuge in combing back my hair. It was nearly dry. It was so baking hot on the *plage*. We sheltered now under the striped umbrella. Esmond added:

'I'm interested in this P.N.E.U. system. Tell me a little about it.'

Eagerly, because here at least I was on firm ground and knew my subject, I explained a little of the system that that great woman,

Charlotte Mason, had devised. Of how much she believed in nature and in probing the heart of a child, as well as his brain; helping him to grow and develop according to his own character. How she made that great difference between autocracy and the sort of intolerant discipline that can hurt sensitive minds. How we teachers were taught to study the children as well as educate them.

'I agree with every bit of it so far,' nodded Esmond. Then quickly handed me his cigarette case. 'Do you smoke?'

'No, thank you.'

'Sensible. Wish I didn't. I'm trying to cut down. Go on – tell me more about your P.N.E.U.'

There was so much to say I could only give him a mere idea of it all.

We have so much to watch out for, I said, such as want of concentration or lack of vitality – coaxing the backward and not allowing the brilliant child to rush ahead at too great a pace. How all lessons should be made happy and imaginative and enjoyed rather than enforced. How good will and thoughtfulness were encouraged in the schoolroom. These and many other things I told him, and gave him an impression of the kind of lessons Conrad and Kate would have – according to their age.

'It sounds just the very thing,' said Esmond. 'And it should be interesting for

64

you because my two are so different. Kate is of course still a baby.'

'But anxious to learn, and affectionate,' I said.

'More so than my son,' said Esmond with a slight smile. 'He is rather too self-assertive, and spoiled hopelessly, I fear, by both my sister and his old nurse. He has tremendous charm, but that is one of the most dangerous assets that any human being can have if there is no real goodness, no honest depths behind it.'

I nodded. I could see how understanding the great man was of human nature, which further confirmed my opinion that he *was* a great man. He gave me that warm smile that encouraged and delighted me, and went on:

'Well, I'm sure even if you have your work cut out to make anything of my two rascals, you'll do it. I know I've been pulling your leg about your youthful appearance, but I can see there is a determination in the curve of that chin.' He laughed heartily now, and I laughed with him, thinking: *It can't be true. I can't be sitting here like this with him as though we were old friends. He seems so simple ... so ordinary, and yet when Esmond Torrington enters an auditorium, people stand up and cheer...*

Suddenly, rather shyly, I volunteered some of my knowledge.

'It may interest you to hear that our motto

in the P.N.E.U. is: *"I am, I can, I ought, I will."'*

He blinked.

'H'm! There's a whole history of human endeavour in those few words. How many of us ever live up to them?'

'I know.'

'Tell me more about the type of lessons you give.'

'Oh, there's much too much – it would bore you. But please, one day, come in when we are having school and listen.'

'I will. I shall listen and learn.'

'I couldn't teach you anything,' I said with hot cheeks and fluttering pulses.

'My dear little Miss Bray, we all go on learning until we die,' he said. 'Personally I often think I ought to go back to school. My parents died when I was quite young and my sister Monica, to whom I owe so much, made a home for me because she was so much older so that I had somewhere to go back to when I was on holiday. I started with an English prep. school, and then, because I had asthma as a child, ended up at one of the big Swiss public schools which was good for me because of my health and a help in my musical and artistic education. After that I was lucky enough to get scholarships and go right ahead with my training as a conductor. But after a Continental schooling, I sometimes feel I've missed English education and shall certainly send Conrad to Eton.'

I listened intently, hardly daring to speak in case he would put an end to these reminiscences which I felt honoured to hear. He was in a dreamy expansive mood, and as he went on, I could understand very well why he felt a particularly affection for and gratitude towards his sister. Whatever Monica Warr had become since, she seemed to have been at one time devoted to him. It was only after he left home that she had married. And then at an unusually early age she had been struck down by this incurable arthritis. Then he diverted the conversation from himself, and turned back to the subject of his children's education.

He was interested when I gave him some idea of the curriculum, and pleased by the thought of the painting and drawing, the reading of poetry, study of nature and good books to which I was to introduce them. Then we came to Conrad's music, and in this the great conductor was naturally more than ordinarily interested. When I said that I had brought such books as *Modern Course for Piano* by John Thompson and *Teaching Little Fingers to Play,* and that in our system we also like to play gramophone records to the children and instil musical appreciation into them, he was delighted.

'Sensible and up-to-date,' he said. 'And

you shall bring the children into my studio and I shall choose the records – at least when I am home.'

That will be something to look forward to, I thought happily.

'Miss Bray,' he began, but broke off, then he added: 'What incidentally is our Miss Bray's Christian name?'

When I told him, he took the cigarette from his mouth, with a look of surprise.

'Shelley! How very unusual.'

'Yes, everybody says so.'

'How did it come about?'

'My mother,' I said, 'always had a passion for Shelley's poems. Incidentally she was a teacher in a country school and my father a young doctor in the same village, Dymcross in Sussex.'

'Dymcross, I know it well,' exclaimed Esmond. 'How *very* strange. My wife and I–'

He paused. Now that mask fell across his face that I was always to see when Veronica Torrington's name was mentioned. And what he had been going to tell me I never knew. I could only suppose that at some time he and the girl who had died must have visited Dymcross. It was one of the most beautiful old places in the south of England, and famous for its wide street and Georgian houses.

'Go on with your story,' he said abruptly.

I felt sure that anything I could tell him

about myself would bore him, but one of Esmond Torrington's most charming characteristics was the way in which he interested himself in the least of his friends or associates. He made you feel when you talked to him that you were the only person in the world. *He* most certainly had what he called that 'dangerous asset – charm'!

Out came the story of the romance that had blossomed between my parents, and of how Mummy had left the school and devoted herself entirely to Daddy, then to me when I was born, still in Dymcross, and twelve months later, my brother.

'But unfortunately,' I sighed, 'the war ruined everything. Daddy went off to the Middle East in the R.A.M.C. and Mummy was left to look after us, and when Daddy came home it was because he was invalided out with some sort of bug they couldn't cure. It greatly hampered the rest of his life. He had hoped to become a successful doctor, but had to be content with a very minor National Health practice near Brighton where my mother died. Then Daddy just faded away, and my brother and I joined an aunt in south Norwood, but she didn't live very long. We still occupy her flat.'

'How sad for you,' said Esmond sympathetically, as though my insignificant little history really distressed him. 'From a young age you have had to work. What happened to your brother?'

I explained about Robin doing his National Service and warming to that subject (because I was devoted to Robin), said what a darling he was and how fond we were of each other.

'Well, I'm glad you've got someone,' said Esmond gently, 'and you must ask this brother to come down to Arc-en-Ciel for a day or two and spend it with you when he gets leave.'

That was too much. Even though I had only been down here a few hours, I was positive that such an intrusion would not please Lady Warr. I stammered:

'Oh, I couldn't ... I wouldn't dream of it ... how terribly kind of you ... but you hardly know me or anything about me. You may send me packing next week.'

'I really can't see why,' he laughed, re-gained his feet and called to the children. 'Come along, poppets, we must get back to lunch. My sister is a punctual person,' he added.

She was, indeed. Waiting for us in that wheel-chair on the terrace with Sir Austen on guard behind her, I could almost feel that she had kept on asking him what time it was. My heart sank as I saw that expens-ively dressed little figure (as it was to sink so many times in the future when I looked at Monica Warr). I felt absurdly depressed because that heavenly hour down on the beach talking with Esmond Torrington had finished. I wondered how long it would be before I would get such a chance again.

4

Lunch was an informal affair in a singularly beautiful *salle à manger* as they called it there. A long low room with four windows that folded back and so opened the whole room out to a terrace on which the family could eat under an awning, and look upon the cool of the romantic gardens – so green and beautiful with their tall cypresses pointing to the sky, and a glimpse here and there of a white statue on a pedestal – in Italian fashion. I felt transported into another world, and had to pinch myself in order to believe that I was actually here and not in the dingy kitchen of our suburban maisonette.

The dining-room was panelled in silver grey wood with an acid lemon carpet. There were high-backed painted wood Italian chairs with brocade seats of the same sharp beautiful colour around a long green and black marble table on gilded wrought-iron legs. I'd never before seen anything like that table as laid for the Torrington family lunch; with hand-painted mats, tall crystal wine glasses, a huge cut glass bowl full of the most exquisite fruit as a centre piece, encircled by low curved narrow vases full of freshly cut roses, and marvellous table silver.

Mr Torrington sat at the head of the table. There was no one at the foot, in fact no chair was put there. Obviously nobody was allowed to sit in that place. Lady Warr sat on his right and Sir Austen on his left. The children and I were further down.

I had hurriedly changed into a cotton frock and combed back my unruly hair. I could feel my face burning from the unaccustomed sun, even though Esmond Torrington had made me take care. I was sure my nose was going to peel and that I must look like an awkward schoolgirl to these smart sophisticated people to whom such a meal was just a 'picnic'. But in the grand manner – a manner to which *they* were accustomed.

I tried to make myself small and remain unnoticed and addressed myself entirely to Conrad and Kate. I busied myself cutting up Kate's cold chicken for her. But now and again Esmond spoke to me in his easy kindly way. Sir Austen asked me what I had thought of the *plage*. Lady Monica Warr did not open her mouth to me, but I could feel her cold blue eyes continually slanting in my direction as though waiting to pounce should I say or do something she did not like.

The meal ended – such a delicious assortment of cold food faultlessly served by yet another domestic in smart uniform. (She, I learned, was called Lili and lived out.) Coffee was served, but I did not wait for it. I thought it more tactful to take the children out and leave the grown-ups alone.

I saw Kate trying to get out of the room before her aunt spoke to her, but the woman turned the wheels of her chair and propelled herself up to the little girl who then stood still as though mesmerised, thumb in mouth.

'Now, Kate, take that thumb out – you are no longer a baby,' admonished Lady Warr.

The child remained sullenly silent.

'Kate, do you hear me? You're much too old to suck a thumb.'

The child continued to nibble at it nervously and then turned her large eyes on me as though for defence. I could say nothing. But I remembered in my teaching how it was always thought that to stop a child from sucking its thumb, even so old a child as Kate, might have a psychologically poor effect and often start up worse habits.

Monica Warr, I could see, entertained every old-fashioned hide-bound idea about children that could be dragged out of a now obsolete method of training. For the third time she said:

'Take that thumb out of your mouth and obey me at once, please Kate.'

Esmond Torrington was not in on this. He was engaged in a political discussion with

74

his brother-in-law and the two men got up, and lighting cigars, seated themselves on the balustrade. The field was clear for Lady Warr. Her tight little mouth became tighter. She said:

'This disobedience has got to stop, Kate. You're getting absolutely out of hand. I insist you do as I say or you go to bed and stay there the rest of the day.'

Down on the beach I had promised the children that I would read to them while they had their after-lunch siesta then they would show me, they said, the Zoological Centre which had been founded by Prince Rainier, six years ago. I personally adore animals, and Conrad had informed me with some excitement that two new rare specimens had just arrived and he wanted to see them.

I knew how bitter Kate's disappointment would be if she was sent to bed instead, and I was furious with the woman for being so harsh over so petty a matter. Of course it wasn't just the fact that the child was sucking her thumb as that Monica Warr was being opposed. She couldn't tolerate opposition.

I bent over the little girl.

'Take your thumb out, darling. Be sensible,' I began.

Lady Warr snapped at me.

'I did not ask you to interfere, Miss Bray.'

I drew back, stunned, and felt my heartbeats quicken. Resentment made me unusually bold.

'I apologise, Lady Warr. I thought I was here in the capacity of governess to these two children.'

Her eyes shut between pouchy lids.

'Quite so. But *this* trouble is between Kate and myself. As you saw this morning, when I asked her to kiss me, she showed hostility and impudence. If she does not take her thumb out for *me*, why should she do it for *you?*'

Oh, I thought, the *stupid* woman; and of course trouble came!

Kate immediately drew the thumb out of her mouth, tossed back her red pony tail, rushed to me and clasped me with her arms.

'I *will* take it out for Miss Bray. I *love* her. I don't love you, Aunt Monnie.'

There was a deathly silence. Conrad giggled. Lady Warr even turned on him, her favourite.

'Be quiet at once.'

Then Lady Warr addressed me.

'Kindly take Kate to her bedroom and undress her. She will remain in bed for the rest of the day.'

I was so upset I didn't know what to do. I couldn't bear the thought of this harsh and unjust punishment for so paltry an offence. The woman didn't begin to understand small children but only wanted to appease

76

her own vanity – her desire to dominate. Kate, of course, let me go and set up a howl.

'I don't want to go to bed. I want to go to the Zoo with Con and Miss Bray.'

I saw Lady Warr grip the side of her wheel-chair. I saw her face grow hot and pink as though she were in a flaming rage and trying to control it.

'Take her to bed, Miss Bray, and no cake or biscuits for her tea. Only bread and butter.'

'Lady Warr–' I began.

'I will not have my authority undermined, Miss Bray,' she broke in furiously, 'and I consider this a very bad beginning for us – a very bad beginning indeed. What right have you to come here and start exerting your authority over mine. Of course if you've been *bribing* Kate with sweets or toys–'

'Lady Warr!' I interrupted hotly, 'nothing is further from the truth. My teaching does not allow me to *bribe* children. I like to win their affection and trust and I believe that affection and tolerance help to gain their confidence but–'

'I do not need a lecture from you,' she broke in, 'and you, Kate, stop screaming or you shall have further punishment.'

In despair I looked out on the terrace praying that Mr Torrington would hear his small daughter whose screams had now reached a shrill crescendo. I burned with indignation. I said:

'I'm afraid I shan't be able to work under these conditions, Lady Warr. Either I do have control of the children, or you have, but it will be impossible for us to work together. I cannot maintain any kind of level discipline if I am forced to go against all my own teaching.'

Her mouth fell open. Her round blue eyes stared as though at a phenomenon. I could see that she had not expected the 'shy little nonentity' to speak her mind. Well I am timid and, in a way, a pacifist, but injustice I will never tolerate, and I was not going to be spoken to in that manner by Lady Warr or anybody else without making a protest. As I had hoped, Mr Torrington now came into the room, holding his cigar between his fingers and wondering what the row was about.

'Kate – Katie, *please!*' he exclaimed, putting both hands to his ears, 'Daddy loves music but your voice is so *very* unmusical, lovey, when you raise it like that.'

She calmed down and sniffed and snivelled, instead. Before any explanations could be given to Mr Torrington by either Lady Warr or myself, Conrad volunteered:

'Aunt Monnie told Kate to stop sucking her thumb but she wouldn't so Aunty said she was to go bed and then Miss Bray told her to take her thumb out and she did, and

Aunt Monnie said Miss Bray had been bribing Kate with sweets. What's bribing mean, Daddy?'

There was another deathly hush. I'd never felt so tongue-tied as I did then. The fat was really in the fire. I saw the tolerant smile leave Esmond's fine-cut face and a more serious look cross it. Then he spoke quite sharply to his son.

'Take Kate and go into the nursery – or rather the schoolroom – right away, Con, no arguing.'

Conrad pouted but did as his father told him. Esmond closed the dining-room door. Then he came and stood by his sister's chair.

'What in the name of fortune is all this about, Monnie?'

I thought the little lady in the chair was going to throw a fit, her face was so congested, her breathing so rapid. I could see that she was longing to make fresh accusations against me and blame me for the whole silly episode but couldn't, so she amazed me by resorting to the most feminine and what I call 'below-belt methods'. She pulled a handkerchief from her bag and began to weep in it.

'Oh, oh, Esmond, I'm so *hurt!* I love those darling children as though they were my own, and they only *hurt* me – or at least Kate does. She does not love me at all. Miss

Bray has only just arrived. She may think Kate very easy but she'll soon find how difficult she *is*. I try my best but *everybody is ungrateful*...'

'Now Monnie, dear, what nonsense!' exclaimed Esmond and put down his cigar and rested a hand on his sister's shoulder. 'We are all most grateful for the wonderful work you do here for us and for the love you give Conrad and Kate...' He turned to me... 'My sister is a most wonderful woman, Miss Bray. 'We are *all* indebted to her for the way she has managed both the staff and the children since ... since...' He broke off.

Hurriedly I put in:

'Oh, yes, I am sure ... I am *sure* of that, Mr Torrington.'

Lady Warr continued to weep. In came Sir Austen.

'*My darling!* What has upset you? Oh, my *dearest*...'

And now she had just what she wants, I thought. One man on each side of her, trying to comfort her and extol her virtues.

I stood silent, inwardly despising her. I saw her eyes regarding me rather malevolently over the crumpled ball of her handkerchief. The truth was not told. It never would be told regarding either the children or myself, as I was to discover in the future. And Esmond Torrington was far too occupied with his work and his personal life to probe too deeply into the details of what went on in Arc-en-Ciel. Like many men he was only aware of what he saw on the surface. Lady Warr now affirmed that Kate was disobedient and didn't show the love she should show to her adoring aunt. I could have told Esmond Torrington just how wrong his sister was in her attitude towards little Kate. I was also burning to ask him to give me complete authority over the children, but that was out of the question. The incident ended, however, with him once again appealing for Kate to be pardoned and Monica Warr then produced an angelic smile and a sweet reply, that *of course* she would overlook it all. But I felt apprehensive. I knew that if and when Kate's father went away again and such incidents recurred, there would be little mercy shown to the small girl.

I felt irritable. It was so easy to gain a child's love and confidence if one went about it in the right way. This selfish woman was nothing less than a megalomaniac.

It was only when she stopped crying and consented to smile again and let Sir Austen hold her hand and give her a sip of Cognac – 'my brave darling' he called her – I felt sick, that Esmond remembered what his son had said.

'What was all this about bribery and corruption?' he asked me, smiling and on a more cheerful note.

I saw Lady Warr looking intently at me. I had no wish at all to cause trouble. I said:

'Oh, it was just some nonsense ... nothing at all... I assure you I don't bribe children.'

'I don't know where he got hold of that word,' said Lady Warr.

Esmond said:

'Well, Monnie, you must pay more attention to your health and your own life now and let Miss Bray manage my tiresome pair. I'm very glad for your sake that she has come. I thought she managed the children excellently down on the *plage*. A very different cup of tea from Nannie. Miss Bray understands control. I think you can safely leave the children in her care.'

I could have embraced him. Lady Warr did not dare argue. But what followed was not apt to increase her liking for me, for Esmond picked up his cigar again and said:

'Did you know, Monnie, that our little teacher's Christian name is *Shelley?* Now isn't that charming. We will hail her as the new "blithe spirit" of Arc-en-Ciel.'

'Don't think I've ever heard the name Shelley for a gal before,' put in his brother-in-law. Sir Austen had forgotten Shelley's Christian name – he was so forgetful.

Lady Warr maintained a freezing silence. With burning cheeks I hastily made my exit but I heard her sharp voice as I closed the beautiful panelled doors:

'Really, Esmond, don't let us get on to Christian name terms. It is best for the governess to remain Miss Bray.'

I heard Esmond's light tolerant laugh and not what he said as I fled down the corridor, only too thankful to tell Kate that she could go with us to the Zoo.

5

One evening about six weeks later I finished the meal which had been brought to me on a tray – Lady Warr was giving a dinner party – and went for a walk in the garden.

I always enjoyed this cool hour out of doors, when the sky looked like blue velvet sown with magnificent stars and the air blew fresh and crisp after the heat of the day.

Around a corner of the orangery I suddenly collided with a man – a stranger to me – who drew back and apologised, in French.

For a moment I stared at him.

He was smoking a cigarette in a long holder, which I was afterwards to associate with him for he was seldom without it, and always in rather a quick way either putting in or taking a cigarette out of that holder. I knew he was not English because of his Continental-style white dinner jacket and black satin cummerbund. He was not at all what I would call 'my type'; of medium height with very fair smooth hair and sharp features and eyes that seemed to be closed they were so like slits. Yet they obviously took in all he saw. They were very shrewd. He was quite young and good-looking, I suppose, yet to me his appearance was curiously foxy and unattractive.

I had to say something so answered him in English.

Then he said:

'Ah! You must be the English girl who has come over to teach *les enfants.*'

He spoke in my language now – with barely a trace of accent.

I nodded. I was always so tongue-tied at first with total strangers. I saw his half-shut eyes raking me, possibly thinking as everybody else did, of how young I looked. I am afraid that the light Mediterranean breeze which was cooling the heat of the day, had blown my hair into disorder.

He voiced my thoughts.

'You only look a child yourself, if I may say so, mademoiselle.'

'Oh dear!' I said, wishing devoutly that I did not always strike people this way.

'But *charming,*' he said with a bow, released the spring in his cigarette holder and sent the end spinning into the bushes.

I bit my lip wondering what to say next. He then supplied his name.

'May I introduce myself – Dr Valguay–'

I was surprised. He was a bit of a dandy – and so very smooth. Not my idea of a doctor; although of course I couldn't set my standards by my darling dead father who had been such a simple blunt lovable fellow – typically English – caring rather more about the health of his patients than what he looked like; never able to afford an expensive wardrobe anyhow. But Lucien (that I learned in time was his Christian name) Valguay was a smart medical man who made a fortune on the Côte d'Azur out of rich women's ailments. He now told me that he was Lady Warr's physician. And certainly one of her most attentive followers.

I wouldn't like to think what she paid out to him for all the little boxes of tablets he gave her during the year – plus charm and sympathy. It appeared that she adored him, and sent for him on every possible occasion. He was also called in for the children's ailments. (That he was far less tactful with them than with her ladyship, I was to discover.)

'I live just through the trees there,' Dr Valguay murmured, waving an elegant hand on the little finger of which he wore a large black onyx ring. 'You can cut through those trees right into the grounds of my own place – Villa La Gioconda.'

'Oh, yes,' I said vaguely nodding.

'You've only just come here?' he asked.

'I've been here six weeks,' I said.

He now shot personal questions at me. He was smiling all the time, examining me through those slitty eyes which I found embarrassing and disturbing. I didn't like being cross-questioned by Dr Valguay. Neither did I care for his fulsome compliments. He said that in spite of being so young, I was *ravissante*. (An absurdly exaggerated thing to say to Shelley Bray with her solemn young face and wind-blown hair and cheap cotton frock.) I saw him glance at my ankles and my hands and *could feel* at once somehow that he was picking out all my good points and that he was as quick, if not quicker, than the average Frenchman, to try and establish contact; that kind which, no matter what one said, always had 'sex' at the back of it.

He was a great success with his women patients, so I heard, and whenever anybody was really ill, cleverly passed them on to somebody more knowledgeable than himself. He ended by saying that it was going to be very pleasant to have such a person as myself living at Arc-en-Ciel.

'We have a need of the *"Jeunesse dorée"*,' he ended bowing.

I almost laughed. I could hardly connect myself with the words 'golden youth'. Then he said:

'I came over a little too early. Lady Warr does not expect me until half past eight. They never dine till after nine, and I see you are not yet dressed.'

'I've already had my meal, doctor.'

He assumed an expression of disappointment.

'Then you won't be at dinner, mademoiselle?'

'No.'

'Sad,' he sighed, 'I would like to talk to you.'

'Another time perhaps,' I said.

I expect he thought me unfriendly, but nothing ever deterred Lucien Valguay.

'Let us take a turn together. Perhaps you have not seen the lily pond and rockery – over there. It looks exquisite in the moonlight.'

'I – I was just going in.'

'Take pity on me. I have had a long boring day and some very trying patients who think themselves ill but are not.'

'Then why do you waste your time with them?' I asked, always too blunt I suppose. He did not take offence. He laughed.

'*D'accord*, but one has a living to earn, *chère enfant.*'

I objected to being called 'dear child' in that intimate way, and wished that I could make my escape, but could see no way of doing so without being really rude which I must avoid since he was the family doctor. I must grow used to the fact, but I could not help wondering whether Mr Torrington liked this man – and called him in as his physician. I found out, in time, that Esmond had as little use for the smooth-tongued debonair *médecin* as I had, and only suffered him at Arc-en-Ciel because he seemed to bring a certain amount of relief to Monica. She was so devoted to him. But Esmond, himself, when he was not well (which appeared to be rarely), consulted an older man. Dr Valguay was only about thirty-two or three. He had only been established in Monte Carlo as a doctor for the last five or six years. A Parisien, and unmarried, and with a reputation which I was to hear about – for indulging in love affairs which never seemed to end in matrimony.

I found myself walking with Lucien Valguay – unwillingly, but he talked to me without drawing breath. Oh, he was a great talker! I heard that the reason why I had not seen him at the Arc-en-Ciel before was that he had just come back from a trip to South Africa.

'Thank heavens,' he added, 'milady did not have one of her "turns" while I was away. You see I had the opportunity of accompanying the Vicomtesse de' – he mentioned the name of a well-known Frenchwoman who was a millionairess and reputed to be in her eighties – 'to Durban. She wished to visit a grandson, but would not go without her medical adviser and of course it was a wonderful chance for me.'

I remained silent. Of course it was wonderful. A free holiday in luxury! I felt that I despised any medical man who could have used his skill and knowledge in the service of humanity but dissipated it in such a way. Now Dr Valguay began to discuss the family which, even though I thought it tactless, held more interest for me.

'Milady is a darling but not really as much of an invalid as she likes to pretend. One has to play up to such people. I am sure you understand, mademoiselle. Milady is largely what one calls a *malade imaginaire*. The arthritis is not as serious as she thinks. She *could* get about with crutches, but does not care to make the effort.'

'But she should be encouraged to do so,' I said indignantly.

'Ah!' said Dr Valguay shrugging, 'she is so much happier in her chair. It excites sympathy and attention. All women like those things, do they not, mademoiselle, am I not right?'

I suddenly hated him. I had to speak my mind.

'If that his true, Dr Valguay, then it is a question of mind over matter. She should be encouraged to walk. It struck me when I first came that she was very young to be so crippled.'

'*Chère enfant*,' said Dr Valguay in that affected way of his, waving his cigarette holder in the air, 'take away her ills, you would take from her her greatest joy and refuge. She *enjoys* poor health – and her chair. Have you not seen how her husband and even some-times the great Mr Torrington himself, croon over her – filled with sympathy and admir-ation for her courage? Remove that and you steal her *raison d'être*. It would be cruel. I, myself, suggested the pretty silver electric chair,' he ended, with his glittering smile.

I hated him even more, and felt hot and cold. Yet I knew that much of what he said was true, and that Monica Warr without the citadel of pathos that she had built around herself might easily crumble. She *did* enjoy her *'ill-health'*. Now Dr Valguay touched upon Esmond. A wonderful conductor and a fine man, he said.

'But never quite with us,' he went on with a rippling laugh, 'not in our world. Always in the rarefied atmosphere of a great artiste. He sees nothing of what really goes on in Arc-en-Ciel.'

In a way I had to agree with that but I asked the doctor rather irritably:

'What more is there for him to see, *monsieur le docteur?*'

Lucien Valguay stopped in order to fit a cigarette into his holder. His thin lips lifted in an enigmatic smile. He cocked an eye-brow at me.

'Ah – mademoiselle, I assure you that many things go on that he *ought* to see – or ought to *have* seen.'

The cryptic words intrigued me against

my will.

'Such as what?' I muttered. I did not like this sort of gossip behind the backs of my employers and yet confessed myself fascinated by what this so-called family doctor said. Then out came the name that was never mentioned here.

'You should have known Madame Torrington.'

'Well, I didn't,' I said stupidly.

He sighed and looked up at the sky.

'Ah! There was an interesting character. B-eautiful! *Comme un ange!* Sometimes *comme un diable*. But b-eautiful.' He kissed his finger tips, 'Monsieur adored her. We all did.'

'So I understand,' I said coldly.

'Have they told you about her?'

'No, Dr Valguay, she is never spoken about.'

Now Lucien Valguay's artificial gaiety vanished. His face grew a little sad and cynical.

'It was a gr-reat tragedy.'

'It must have been.'

'She was in her new Citroen – she had only had it a month – she was driving to Cannes. Like a demon, they say. You know these hairpin bends on the Corniche Road, they cannot be taken too fast. When they picked her up she was dead. The car was a total wreck.'

I shivered. I thought of the lovely red-haired girl in the portrait which I passed so often in the villa. The woman *he*, Esmond Torrington, had loved. The mother of my two pupils. Lying dead in her wrecked car. It was a sombre thought.

'Don't let's speak of it,' I said.

'Are you going to join the others in this conspiracy of silence?' he asked me.

'I don't know what you mean,' I stammered.

He shrugged.

'Her name must not be mentioned – you, I am sure, have been told not to speak of her to the children, have you not?'

'Yes, but–'

'The girl is too young to remember, the boy, I suppose, does not speak of her,' he added thoughtfully.

'No. But if there is all this mystery why do they keep her portrait upon view?' I blurted out, my curiosity getting the better of me.

'Lady Warr wished it to be taken down but monsieur would not have it touched. He at least did not want altogether to exclude her memory.'

'But why should it be excluded at all? I do not understand,' I broke out again. 'Dreadful though the tragedy was – surely the memory of a loved wife and mother should be cherished?'

Dr Valguay stopped now and smiled down into my eyes in rather too intimate a fashion to my liking.

'I see mademoiselle is romantic at heart. But it was not all romance here, you see. Those two were an odd pair. I saw things … as the family physician often does, for I used to attend the lovely Veronica. She suffered from migraine – genuinely. I often helped her. She relied on me – as Milady does. Her husband was too occupied to be of help.'

I felt a sudden desire to uphold Esmond.

'Mrs Torrington may have suffered physically, but she was an adored wife. They say Mr Torrington has never been the same since the accident.'

'That is true, but he was also very jealous. Sometimes insanely so. A beautiful woman can suffer through a husband's jealousy, *chère petite mademoiselle*. Although, of course, you are so typically the English girl who knows more about sport – healthy outdoor sport – than the passions that can tear the hearts and minds of men and women to pieces.'

I did not know what he was talking about. I said so frankly. He shook his head at me.

'Ah, my dear, you will understand in time. But I repeat – jealousy is a terrible thing, and it must be even more terrible to be forced to look upon the broken body of the beautiful wife you have loved so madly, and to wonder how she came to die.'

Now I felt a positive loathing of this indiscreet Frenchman, who was putting all kinds of ideas into my mind which had not been there before and opening it up to the most unattractive possibilities. To situations appertaining to the life of my great hero of music, and his wife. Surely, I thought, the past should be allowed to fade into the limbo of forgotten things and not be raked over, even if there was truth in what Dr Valguay was hinting.

'Mr Torrington has never struck me as being either a violent or jealous man–' I began hotly.

'Ah! You have only just met him. Remember that I knew this family when they first came to Monte Carlo five years ago. And I have been a frequent guest at Arc-en-Ciel as well as a visitor in professional capacity.'

I must admit that I was longing to ask a dozen questions now – my mind seething with strange impressions and ideas. Yet I hated to connect Esmond Torrington with any emotions that were as exaggerated or savage as Dr Valguay would have me believe. *Was the doctor not,* I thought, *trying to suggest to me that it was her husband's jealousy that drove Veronica Torrington to her death?*

My next remark was meant to be innocuous but flung me into deeper waters.

'Nobody has ever given me details of Mrs Torrington's accident, but it *was* an accident.'

'*Or suicide?*' said Lucien Valguay softly.

I felt shocked and revolted.

'Oh! Really – please.'

'It might well have been. She was in a very emotional state before she went out. I know because I attended her.'

I did not answer. I was aghast by the suggestion. Then, seeing my expression, Valguay laughed and spoke on a lighter note. 'Ah well. Never mind. It's old history. I could a tale unfold, but everybody here clamps down on the whole affair and at the inquest the verdict was of course, "Accidental Death".'

'I must go in,' I said in the iciest voice I could muster.

'Of course you will keep what I have told you in confidence, *chère mademoiselle,*' he reminded me.

'Very much so,' I said, my cheeks burning.

'We will have another talk some day. The story of Madame Torrington is very intriguing. It is the one thing that even milady will not discuss with me. But I know the part *she* played in it. She was as jealous of Veronica as of her brother, only in another way. She was jealous of Esmond's love for his wife.'

I really felt that I could not stay one moment longer to hear more of this shameful gossip. It did Dr Valguay no credit, and in some vague way I resented any aspersions that it cast upon Esmond Torrington. During the month and a half that I had been at Arc-en-Ciel my youthful admiration for the great conductor had increased. He was so kind and considerate to me, so appreciative of the fact that I was doing my utmost for his children. I did not want to hear one disparaging word about him. I was utterly thankful that I need not appear in public again that night and that I could escape to my own little room, there to read and try to forget all that the doctor had said.

But I did not find it easy. The seed that Lucien Valguay had planted in my mind on the subject of Veronica Torrington's death was poisonous, and it was to bring forth poisonous fruit – as time would tell.

6

There followed two – nearly three – eventful weeks, during which I settled down to my work at Arc-en-Ciel. Nice Miss Collins, Esmond's secretary, who had engaged me and might have been a friend to me, unfortunately fell ill. She had to have an operation, after which she was not able to return to her strenuous job with the famous conductor. She was replaced by a young Frenchman, Monsieur De Vitte. He was, however, rarely at Arc-en-Ciel. He took letters only for an hour in the mornings when Mr Torrington was at home – then departed. In order not to make a busy office of the quiet villa – for Lady Warr's sake – the greater part of Esmond's business was conducted in London by his agent.

During all the weeks I had spent at the villa, I don't think I set eyes on Monsieur De Vitte more than once or twice. He never seemed to cross my path.

During that time, of course, Lady Warr and I were often at loggerheads – try though I had done to toe the line with her and not let her think that I was trying to usurp her position. But Esmond Torrington had entrusted his children to me, and I was not going to be diverted by anybody on earth from giving them the sort of discipline and instruction I thought proper and to which I had given my life. Otherwise I got on very well and seemed to fit in with the staff – all of whom were nice to me except Lady Warr's attendant, Yvonne. Yvonne was a sharp-featured, rather sly Parisienne. I thought she might very easily be a spy for her mistress too, for whenever she visited the schoolroom she seemed to come with a smirk and an unpleasant message from her ladyship.

But Thérèse, the little peasant daily, who came from some farm in the hills beyond Monte Carlo, adored me and could not do enough for *'Mees'* as she called me.

Kate was now my shadow – I found her easy to train and, when she was with me, sweet and compliant. Conrad had his bad moods and could be insolent and difficult, but generally after he had been alone with his aunt.

The clash between her and myself nearly always came on the subject of character forming rather than lessons in which she had no interest. But when now and again their father came into the schoolroom to find out what progress was being made, he seemed delighted, and examined the children's exercise books, their drawings, their nature studies and so on, with interest. On one occasion he laughed and said to me:

'I think I'll have to get you to improve my handwriting. Nobody seems able to read it.'

Nice to me … oh yes … always kindly and charming. Only I saw so little of him. I did not dine with the family at night and often during the day he was out. But I grew to look forward to his visits – to the sound of that clear modulated voice, the sight of that tall graceful figure, the moments when he would whisk the children and myself into the Rolls and drive us either down to the sea or along the coast toward Cannes.

Such excursions were few and far between, but I treasured each one and wrote about them to Robin. The great conductor, I told him, never 'threw temperaments' or created scenes but was easy and delightful, when he was in his home. Yet it was said that in his rehearsals he was a tiger ready to pounce on the slightest fault, and he worked his orchestra sometimes to exhaustion pitch because as a conductor he would accept nothing less than perfection.

From time to time I met quite a number of visitors to Arc-en-Ciel, despite Lady Warr's efforts to keep me out of the family circle as much as possible. Esmond seemed to sense this, and firmly – if tactfully – manoeuvred me into the gatherings from time to time. For instance, a memorable occasion, when Madame Ala Gunther came to a Sunday lunch party with Jean-Max Callot who was Esmond's first violin in his own orchestra.

Madam Ala was one of the world's great sopranos. A tall radiant woman rather like a golden-haired valkyrie with her tall, large figure and superb bearing. I could not count the number of times in the past I had switched on my little radio in south Norwood, when I knew she was to sing either at Covent Garden or a concert. I had always admired her voice. I suppose at some time (when I had dared to talk music with Esmond), I must have let drop this fact, so in his kindly way he gave orders that the children were to be at lunch that day and Miss Bray with them. It would be an education for the children and a treat for me. Such consideration on the part of a famous and busy man, touched me deeply. I could *never* connect him in my mind with the violent man whose frenzied jealousy had driven his wife to take her own life. That horrible story told to me by Dr Valguay haunted me, but I refused ever to believe in it.

Madam Ala spoke a few gracious words to me which I shall never forget. And there were others who came to the villa – Monte Carlo socialites, personal friends of Sir Austen and Lady Warr, etc., and such grand people as the Duchesse Secundo di Freitas

– a famous Spanish lady who was a patron of the arts and no mean pianist herself.

That afternoon I took the children into the studio to hear her play. Even they, who were usually fidgety and often naughty – apt to show off in front of strangers – sat on their little stools in respectful silence while the Duchesse gave us a Chopin recital in Esmond's room, where the acoustics were wonderful.

As for me – I sat spell-bound and wondered why I had been given such unforgettable moments.

Afterwards, the Duchesse spoke to Conrad whose handsome face and that rather bold insolent manner that he could adopt seemed to fascinate women. She stroked his head and said in her pretty broken English:

'From your gr-r-reat father I have hear zat you play the piano – no?'

'Yes, I play jolly well,' said Conrad promptly.

Esmond who was standing by – his usual cigar in one hand – gave a tolerant laugh.

'You give yourself a very fine write-up, my boy. *I* wouldn't say you played jolly well.'

The Duchesse laughed.

'He is char-rming. He shall play for me. Come!' And she led Conrad to the big open Steinway grand at which she, a few moments ago, had performed like a professional.

After eight weeks of struggling to make

Conrad play even his scales with any kind of intelligence, I felt my cheeks grow hot. I hissed in his ear:

'Make an excuse. Say you can't, please...'

But the terrible boy seated himself on the stool and began to show off. His father raised his eyes heavenwards. The Duchesse laughed and kissed him and said:

'*Olé*,' in true flattering Spanish fashion, 'we have with us a budding genius, I am sure.'

I dared not look at Lady Warr. She was sitting in her chair by one of the open windows with Sir Austen as usual in attendance. But as I hastened to take the children out of the studio she propelled herself towards me and took this opportunity of spoiling my glorious treat.

'I should have thought by now Conrad should have learnt to play a piece. You must work a bit harder, Miss Bray.'

I felt indignant. I seemed always to be on the verge of having to justify myself to Monica Warr. She made such catty remarks. But I buttoned up my lips. I could easily have told her that Conrad had none of the musical talent that his father imagined and that it was actually the little six-year-old Kate who could sing enchantingly, memorise quite difficult songs and was a good deal more like Esmond Torrington than was his son.

Once back in the schoolroom, I tried to

instil some sense into Conrad.

'It's better, dear, when you're invited to show what you can do in public, and you know you're no good, to refuse to do it. You made rather a little jackanapes of yourself.'

'Jackanapes! *Jackanapes!*' repeated Kate, finding the word funny, and screamed with mirth. My lecture fell flat, and in the end we were all laughing. Well, there were many kinds of episodes like that when I tasted all the excitement of sharing in the entertainments that so often took place at Arc-en-Ciel. But only when Esmond was at home. When he flew to Paris or to London to fulfil one of his engagements, everything changed then for me, the real heart of the place went out of it. Gloom descended.

I had become fond of the children. I took an enormous interest in training their minds. I enjoyed our games and walks. I began to know Monte Carlo as well as I knew my London. My own French was improving by leaps and bounds, and I lived in luxury. But when Esmond was away, his sister for some reason inexplicable to me (except that I suppose she just didn't like me), deliberately opposed me and made my life difficult.

Nothing I ever did was right in her eyes. When she could, she undermined my influence over Conrad, and because, I think, that she knew it upset me, she continued to be unkind and intolerant in all kinds of petty little ways to poor wee Kate. *And* I was forced to see far too much of Lucien Valguay.

The doctor called three or four times a week upon his wealthy doting patient with whom he had so cunningly ingratiated himself. On each occasion he turned up, uninvited, in my schoolroom and tried to start one of his frothy gossipy conversations which I detested. He always kissed my hand when he left me, looking at me through his slit eyes in a way which made me feel most uncomfortable. Once he told me, openly, that he found me attractive. I found him the reverse, and was very unresponsive. He must have said something to Lady Warr, because she pulled me up about it.

'I would like to know why you make yourself so disagreeable to my capable and charming doctor,' she upbraided me on one occasion. 'It is very impolite. Besides which I notice that you have an uncomfortable habit, Miss Bray, of being uncommunicative and awkward with certain people but *quite* the reverse with others.'

'I don't understand what you mean, Lady Warr,' I said, colouring.

'Do you deny that you were very abrupt with Dr Valguay when he visited the children, after seeing me this morning?'

'I was in the middle of a lesson, Lady Warr.'

'Lesson! Anybody would think you were

running a proper school here.'

'I like to take my work as seriously as though the children *were* in school, Lady Warr.'

'There is no reason why you should not have broken off and let the children have a game with my nice doctor. He was used to Nannie receiving him like the family friend he is, and giving him a cup of coffee. But you practically turned your back on him and went on with your so-called *lesson*. He was very hurt.'

I kept silent. I found it imperative to do so or fly out at her. I did not intend to give her cause to complain of my being rude and disrespectful to *her* so that she might have an opportunity to dismiss me. I was far too happy here. (Much *too* happy when Esmond was at home!)

Then suddenly I remembered something she had said which I could not let pass. I looked up at her, well aware that my face was flushed and defiant.

'Lady Warr, you said just now that I am awkward with certain people but quite the reverse with others. I would be glad if you would explain that to me.'

Lady Warr withdrew her stony blue gaze from me. She looked so very pretty and dimpled; pink and white and ash-gold in an incredibly lovely dress and jacket of pastel blue broderie anglaise. She wore magnificent aquamarine earrings which were only a little paler than her eyes. To look at her you would have thought she was a delicate angel. But I could think of another name for her which no lady would mention. Then, drumming her rose-varnished nails on one of the wheels of her chair, she turned to me with a glittering smile and said:

'Well, I have noticed that you do not continue with your lessons and turn your back on my *brother*, for instance, when he visits the schoolroom. He was having morning coffee with you a few days ago, and I heard you laughing as I came down the corridor. You will remember that I joined you.'

I did remember. And 'Aunt Monnie' had been furious because she had found Esmond sitting on the schoolroom table relaxed and happy, pretending to be a pupil, and raising his hand to answer the simple questions in arithmetic that I asked him in turn with his children. I was no fool. I knew that Monica Warr could not bear Esmond to like me or play any part in my personal life. But now I said:

'I cannot ask the father of my pupils to leave the room, Lady Warr, since it is his house. More especially so because such a busy man has only too few opportunities of seeing his children.'

'Isn't that an excuse?' sneered Lady Warr.

I swallowed, my breathing quicker.

'An excuse for what?'

Again her gaze avoided mine.

'To appropriate my brother's time.'

'Appropriate his time–' I echoed, gasping.

Now her jealousy and hatred of me found words – hot and hasty.

'You never lose a chance when he is at home to follow Mr Torrington around, or use the children as a means of getting yourself noticed by him. You are young and inexperienced and no doubt you have formed one of these 'schoolgirl crushes' for a very distinguished and handsome man, but I think you make it rather too obvious, and it would be more in keeping with your position here to make yourself scarce when Mr Torrington is at home, and to be friendly and polite to a man like Dr Valguay. He was very distressed by your attitude, and asked me why you disliked him.'

I felt too aghast to speak. I trembled. I could not bear to have this horrid little creature drag my feelings out into the open like this with such malice and cruelty. Even if she genuinely believed that I had a 'schoolgirl crush' on Esmond, it was unspeakable of her to say so. But good heavens, I thought, I hadn't even admitted so much to myself. *Was it true?* Yes. I did adore him. I worshipped his shadow. I would do anything in the world for him or his family. But as for Lucien Valguay ... what, I wondered, would her ladyship say if I repeated to her some of the disgraceful suggestions *he* had made to me relating to Veronica Torrington's accident.

I suppose I could have told Lady Warr that – and other things such as that Dr Valguay came to the schoolroom to torment *me*, not to play with the children in whom he had no interest. I might have made a lot of mischief. But I wasn't going to do so even in order to put myself in the right. It would only come back on Esmond. He was satisfied with me. He had said so many times, and with my upbringing of Conrad and Kate. Besides, I felt thoroughly obstinate and proud and I just *wasn't going to* let Lady Warr drive me from Arc-en-Ceil. But I was so upset about what she had said about my attitude towards Esmond that I could not trust myself to accept her bullying with my usual meekness. I rushed out of her sight.

A little while later her maid, Yvonne, brought me a note. By the time I received it I had recovered myself. I felt only a cold scorn of Monica Warr as I read what she had written.

Perhaps I was mistaken in what I inferred just now. Anyhow we will say no more about it. I have special permission to take the children up to the Palace to see some of the historic treasures this afternoon. Sir Austen will accompany me, and I shall be happy for you also to come with us.

This note written in a large ornate loopy kind of hand, was signed *M. W.*

At first I thought of refusing to join the party. It was the first time Lady Warr had ever invited me, personally, to join her in any kind of outing. It was quite obvious that she thought she had said too much and gone too far and that this was her way of making amends. Whatever she felt about anybody else, she adored her brother. She knew that he approved of me as the children's governess, and that he would be furious if she drove me away. I supposed I must meet her halfway, although I felt rather bitter and quite alarmed by my own reactions to her accusations. I still did not dare to allow what I really felt for Esmond Torrington to come to the surface.

But I sent a message back by Yvonne to say that I would have the children dressed and ready to accompany Sir Austen and Lady Warr to the palace after tea. I had not yet seen the interior of the palace of Monaco – and the ancient residence of the Grimaldi would of course be tremendously interesting.

But I didn't want to go, and although Lady Warr was unusually pleasant to me, so far as I was concerned the outing had been spoiled before it ever began.

One night Esmond insisted on giving me a

seat for one of his concerts in Cannes. I went with Sir Austen. A dear, polite, weak old man well under his wife's thumb, but kind to me. How I enjoyed that night! Watching Esmond's wonderful figure and the power that he seemed to have over all those men and women in his orchestra. Never have I heard the Prelude from *Tristan and Isolde* conducted with such brilliance, and when he turned and bowed, receiving tumultuous applause, I clapped my hands as frenziedly as the rest and felt the tears rain down my cheeks. I hurriedly wiped them away. I did not want Sir Austen to go back and tell his wife that 'Miss Bray' was too emotional. A teacher must not show her feelings.

But that night was not to be forgotten, for it ended in the most extraordinary way for me. Lady Warr of course was in bed and asleep by the time we got back. The concerts in this part of the world did not start until late. Sir Austen vanished and I was about to follow suit when Esmond called me back.

'Do you know, I'm hungry. Yes, I know they wanted me to have supper at the Hôtel de Paris, but I didn't feel like a party and now I'm hungry. Aren't you?'

'A little,' I said shyly.

'Let's rifle the kitchen,' he said.

My heart leaped. Oh, what fun, I thought, and followed eagerly, the tall beautiful figure still in white tie and tails, red carnation in his buttonhole; and with that air of elegance and dignity which was part and parcel of Esmond Torrington's make-up.

In the big well-planned kitchen, spotlessly left by Louise, I found myself at midnight sitting on the edge of a table munching chicken sandwiches which I had cut and sipping some white wine that Esmond uncorked. And the great conductor became suddenly a tired homely man; coat off, shirt-sleeves rolled up, talking to me in uninhibited fashion.

'What did you like best in tonight's programme?' he asked.

'*Tristan*,' I said promptly.

'Yes, they played it well.'

'It was the way you conducted it,' I said.

He eyed me over the rim of his glass. At once I became conscious of how I looked. I hoped not too shabby and insignificant tonight, because in his honour I had put on my very best dress – my *only* party dress – grey silk with little yellow flowers on it; a low neck, a tight bodice, a wide skirt. After I had got the children to bed I had spent an hour madly pressing it; rolling up my hair, creaming my face. I rarely used make-up except a little pale pink lipstick, but tonight I had dared to darken my lashes, too, and I had seen for myself that it made my eyes look big, and that I *was* what dear brother Robin called 'quite a pretty girl'.

Mr Torrington's next words confirmed it.

'You're looking rather sweet tonight, our Miss Bray.'

I gulped.

'Thank you.'

'I fully see now why Miss Collins sent you to us. You've been a great success with Con and Katie, and are most tactful.'

I want to be a success with you, I thought, but kept that very much to myself.

'Quite happy here?' next he asked.

'Oh, *terribly!*' I broke out.

'Well, I don't know why you should be. You don't seem to do anything but hide yourself with those children and work. You never seem to have any fun.'

'But I do. It's all such fun to me. Like tonight – it's *wonderful.*'

I saw his eyes rove restlessly round the kitchen.

'Yes, *this* is fun ... a midnight feast when everybody's asleep ... when life seems simple ... uncomplicated ... even childish. Yes, I find this fun. I am taken out of myself. I detest formalities. My sort of life and career insist that I adhere to a formal existence, and when you are always in the public eye you have to be very correct. But do you know, Shelley, when I was a young man and first married, I often used to go like this into our kitchen – and Veronica would cut sandwiches for me and we would laugh and chat together and I could relax and throw off all my cares. It was splendid…'

He broke off and tossed down some wine. I held my breath. I could scarcely believe my ears. First that he had called me *Shelley*, and secondly he had spoken about *her;* uttered that name that was so rarely mentioned at Arc-en-Ciel.

I was hoping that he was going to tell me more about himself and his marriage – and about the mysterious Veronica – but he seemed to be annoyed with himself that he had brought her into the conversation. He changed the subject abruptly.

'You ought to turn in. You look tired.'

'But I'm not!' I exclaimed indignantly.

He finished a sandwich, gained his feet, and put his plate on the draining board of the sink.

'Well, I must say I am.'

'I'm sure you are. You work so terribly hard. A conductor's life must be so exacting,' I said.

'Rewarding, too,' he said. 'You know, there was a time when we were supposed to be an unmusical nation, and when I was a boy, the standard of orchestral playing was by no means as high as the level of our choral singing. But now that is all changed. We can hold our own with any country in the world. I love the young enthusiasts who come to my concerts, or queue all night for an uncomfortable seat in the 'gods' for the opera. I appreciated my reception tonight – very humbly.'

I listened with absorption. Every word that Esmond Torrington said was as glorious to my ears as the music which he discussed.

When he stopped, I timidly remarked that it was his conducting that had brought the tumult of applause. It was the conductor whom one must praise when an orchestra was a success, and I told him how everybody around me had said how marvellously he had led his orchestra.

He gave me a smile followed by a sigh.

'Thank you, Shelley...' (Again my name!) 'I must make you my press agent. You have too good an opinion of my talent.'

'But not only I. The whole of Europe agrees with me.'

Now he laughed outright.

'You are a sweet kind child. Thank you again and good night. And by the way, one of these days I'll let you come down to a rehearsal, then you'll see that I'm not at all kind or nice but a fierce bully who reduces the members of his orchestra to nervous wrecks...' He laughed again.

I laughed too, but as I walked to the kitchen door I thought uncomfortably of that word *fierce*. *Could* he be fierce? *Was* he capable of the bitter passions that Lucien Valguay had attributed to him? I came to the conclusion that I didn't even care if he was. I adored him. With everything that was in me I adored him. But I was so scared of the very emotions that he roused in me that I dared not allow myself even to dwell upon them.

In the corridor outside the kitchen, I saw a light flick on and off and heard footsteps. Surprised, I walked more quickly, wondering who could be up so late at night.

I reached the staff staircase just in time to see the figure of Lady Warr's attendant, Yvonne, wearing a Japanese type kimono and with her black greasy hair in a long plait, disappearing up those stairs. I knew without doubt that she had seen me in the kitchen with Esmond and that I would hear more of it.

I did. That next morning just as I was settling down to lessons, I received a summons to her ladyship's bedroom. Yvonne brought it with that smirk on her face which always betokened trouble for me.

Rather apprehensively I knocked on Lady Warr's door. I found her sitting in her sumptuous bed wearing a white chiffon frilly jacket. The plump pink and white face held no smile of greeting. Lady Warr eyed me with a dislike which I could no longer ignore. But although I knew it was there, I was not going to let it frighten me away from Arc-en-Ciel.

I bade her good morning brightly. My very

brightness seemed to annoy her. She launched directly into a tirade.

'I happen to know that after Sir Austen brought you back from the concert last night you did not go to bed but followed Mr Torrington into the kitchen where you had some kind of midnight supper-party with him. I would like some explanation of this, Miss Bray?'

Biting my lips, I looked her straight in the eyes.

'I was not on duty with the children. It was my evening off and surely I do not have to account for my actions in such circumstances, Lady Warr.'

'Don't be impertinent.'

'I don't mean to be, but I really cannot see why you should be angry because I ate a sandwich with Mr Torrington after the concert.'

She tossed her head.

'I know my brother sometimes likes to have a little impromptu meal when everybody else is in bed and asleep, but why should *you* join him? The last time we spoke, I told you you made yourself extremely amiable to *him* rather than to *others*. And as you are a young English girl over here in France under my care, I feel responsible for you, and I do not like the way you conduct yourself.'

Now with burning cheeks, I interrupted.

'Forgive me, Lady Warr, I am not a teen-ager. I am over twenty-one and quite used to taking care of myself. Besides, are you hinting that I was in any *danger* through joining your brother in the kitchen last night?'

She went scarlet with anger. I knew she did not like my sarcasm. She literally hissed at me.

'How dare you speak to me in such a tone.'

'I apologise if I offend you, but I consider *your* suggestions most offensive.'

She gasped and struggled for words. None came. Her chubby horrid little hands tore at the French newspaper which she had been reading. I could see that she scarcely knew how to control herself. I added:

'I presume Yvonne spied on me. She is always following me about. I must also presume that she reports regularly to you about my movements.'

The little creature in the bed now fixed me with a baleful look which was totally out of keeping with her ash-blonde curls and skilfully-tinted face. She said through her teeth:

'Miss Bray, you will leave this villa today. I will not have you here one hour longer. You are a trouble-maker. No matter how good you are at teaching children, or how much they like you, you make trouble for the adults, yes. I refuse to put up with it any longer.'

118

Goodness, I thought, now the fat is in the fire. She really *does* hate me. All jealousy, I suppose.

The September morning was humid and clammy. I felt terribly hot and nervous and a little scared, now. Scared because I did not want to leave Kate and Con and my job here, and oh! above all I did not want to be banished from *his* house; never to see him again.

'You'd better go and pack,' said Lady Warr.

Then my courage returned. I said:

'I don't think you have any right to dismiss me at a moment's notice. I've done absolutely nothing wrong. I know that you do not like me, Lady Warr, but I have never wilfully tried to cross your wishes or offend you. Honestly, it is I who should take offence at what you inferred. And you *do* get Yvonne to spy on me and I don't know what she told you about last night, but I am completely innocent. I don't think you only cast a slur on my character but on Mr Torrington's by suggesting that he shouldn't have invited me to have some supper with him. As for your allegations that I am continually pursuing him – they are totally unfounded and undeserved. I never see Mr Torrington unless he comes into my schoolroom or issues an invitation to me like he did last night.'

Silence. I could see her mind working. I

knew that she was making some effort to calm down. She said:

'*So you were invited* to eat sandwiches in the kitchen with my brother.'

'Yes, Lady Warr, I was. If you wish I will go and fetch Mr Torrington and ask him to tell you that it was so.'

'Ah! Didn't I say that you were a trouble-maker!'

I shook my head.

'No, Lady Warr, I am not, but I like justice and you are being extremely unjust to me. The last thing I wish to do is to drag Mr Torrington into this. It would distress him, and I don't think he would understand any more than I do why you are dismissing me. But of course if your dislike of me is so acute, perhaps I *had* better go and pack.'

Another silence. Monica Warr tore a strip right off the paper and scrunched it into a ball which she hurled on to the floor like a petulant child.

What a distorted mind she had! I began to feel that Dr Valguay had had some justi-fication in saying that my lady was a *malade imaginaire*. Mind and body both crippled, for some dark secret psychological reason. Possibly, I thought, there had never been anybody in her life that she cared for as she did for the brother whom she had brought up and cherished, and of whom she was so justifiably proud. It was obvious that her marriage to Austen Warr gave her no real happiness. She despised the poor weak old man. She lived in a world of her own … a world in which Monica Warr was the central figure who must be spoiled, worshipped and obeyed. She had hated me from the start because, like little Kate, I was not to be drawn into the spider's web and devoured.

Oh, I thought, how I wished that I knew more about her association with the dead Veronica. Had she been as fiendishly jealous of Esmond's love for his wife as she seemed to be of everybody else who came in contact with him? I knew from little things I'd heard from one person and another since I came to Arc-en-Ciel, that before Veronica had died, Sir Austen and Lady Warr used often to stay here or at the house in London. Yet how *could* she be jealous of me? Poor little me! The penniless employee, who was of no consequence whatsoever in Esmond Torrington's life, but just the one who looked after his children and to whom he was unfailingly kind?

Suddenly I broke out:

'Lady Warr, this is ridiculous. Do let us try to understand each other a little better. I don't want to leave. Believe me, for the children's sake, if for none other, I don't want to, because they are just beginning to understand what I am teaching them, and getting on so well. It would be bad for them to have another change.'

Still no answer. I could only gather that Lady Warr longed to tell me, again, to go and pack but that something held her back. I understood why when at last she brought herself to speak to me.

'Well, I must admit that I don't want my brother worried, so I will overlook your behaviour this time,' she said sullenly, forcing the words.

But now my own pride stepped in. I spoke more sharply than I intended.

'Lady Warr, I do not consider I have behaved badly so if you still feel that I have, I would prefer to leave.'

She pressed her lips together.

'No. It would upset my brother. He is satisfied with the way you are handling the children. We will say no more about it.'

But my blood was up and I held my ground.

'Lady Warr, I cannot stay if you still infer that I behaved badly by accepting the invitation to eat a sandwich alone with Mr Torrington last night, or shall I call him in now to settle this dispute?'

That defeated her. I could see that she dared not let me call him in. It would make her look so stupid. More than that, it would precipitate a row with him which she definitely did not want. For she knew that she had absolutely no justifiable cause for dismissing me. She had lost her temper – that was all.

I was a little baffled when suddenly she changed her whole tone. She allowed her cold blue eyes to fill with tears, and held out a hand to me.

'I'm sorry, my dear. I'm a silly creature. Of course, you did no harm. But you must just try to understand me. I am always so anxious about my brother. He has had so much trouble in his life. And, once we had a young nurse here when old Nannie was on holiday – who set her cap at him and worried him out of his wits. Of course I have no real reason to believe that *you...*'

'None whatsoever, Lady Warr,' I broke in stonily.

'No, no, of course not, I have been very hasty,' she said. 'Let us, as you say, try to understand each other better. I have had a bad night. Sometimes I suffer such pain that I lie in torture, but I refuse to take Dr Valguay's sleeping pills. I try to do without them,' she said in martyr's voice.

I remained silent. I could not bring myself to take her hand or commiserate with her. Somehow I knew that she was a hypocrite. And I cherished no fond illusion that she was being suddenly nice to me for any good or generous reason. However, the dangerous moment passed. With a sigh of relief, I left her room and returned to my pupils.

But even while I was reading a chapter from *Our Island Story* to the children, I kept thinking of all the nasty malicious things their aunt had said to me. That story about that nurse who had set her cap at Esmond. It possibly wasn't even true. Lady Warr was just trying to excuse herself for her unpardonable attack on me. But the joy and happiness I had been feeling through my association with Esmond Torrington – my delight in his warm friendliness – were destroyed. Every time I saw him now, I would have the uncomfortable feeling that Lady Warr was watching, waiting to pounce and to make false accusations.

One afternoon the children and I were in their father's studio and I was putting on the records for their 'appreciation lesson'. He, himself, had chosen the programme. Some extracts from *Figaro* – (he told me that he wanted them to get to know and like Mozart's gay delightful music). Some brilliant Chopin piano recordings actually played by the Duchesse Secundo di Freitas herself. And two exquisite simple little songs by Vittoria los Angeles. Conrad fidgeted a little and bit his nails – a habit which I was trying to break. Kate, my dear little chubby Kate, sat listening quite soulfully, now and again reverting to a childish giggle and throwing roguish sidelong glances at her brother. But on the whole they seemed to enjoy the music which I explained as it went on. In the middle of this lesson, Esmond came in. He had been at a rehearsal. It was a sultry afternoon. He looked hot and tired but he smiled at us all.

'Better get this session over or you'll be adding thunder to your music,' he said, 'the sea looks like ink.'

'Oh, goody!' exclaimed Kate. 'The angels are going to bang the clouds together and make a noise.'

Esmond threw himself on to a sofa on which he sometimes rested in the middle of work, and grimaced at me.

'Is that our little Miss Bray's delineation of thunder?'

'No,' I said promptly, 'it's not. I try to give them a proper scientific explanation. I think *that* is one of Nannie's left-over stories.'

Promptly Conrad said:

'Why doesn't Nannie come to see us?'

I saw that strange shuttered look cross Esmond's face which was so fine drawn and, I imagined, pale under the coating of Mediterranean tan. He lit a cigarette and leaned his head back on the cushion.

'Maybe she will one day.'

'I want her to come tomorrow,' said Kate, who had no use for anything but the present and to whom 'one day' meant a long, long time.

'One day, one day, darling,' repeated

Esmond (rather curtly, I thought).

'I'm going to change the record,' announced Conrad and went over to the magnificent record-player that stood on a dais at the far end of the long handsome room.

Esmond beckoned to me to come to his couch and said in a low voice:

'I haven't ever said much to you about poor old Nannie but she turned into rather a trouble-maker toward the end of her days here. I'm not anxious for her to come back. She would talk too much and too foolishly about things which did not concern her.'

I nodded. I had already gathered this fact from the rest of the staff. I believe there had been several blistering rows between the old woman and her ladyship. Esmond said:

'When my ... Veronica, my wife, was alive – Nannie was in my wife's confidence. She often "maided" her – looked after her clothes and so on. I never felt that she was as much to be trusted as my wife thought. Later she proved that was so.'

I hadn't the slightest idea of what this was all about, and then Esmond met my questing gaze and he gave a short laugh and took a breath of his cigarette. 'But of course, that's all in the past. I won't say any more.'

No, I thought, *nobody ever says any more. They all begin about Veronica and then break off. It's so maddening.*

I could see that Esmond wished he had not

even mentioned his dead wife. But suddenly for some perverse reason, Conrad walked across to his father's side and spoke of his mother, which he had not done as far as I could remember during all the time I had been at Arc-en-Ciel – except in a desultory fashion. Such as to say: *'Mummy took us to the Zoo'* or *'Mummy used to brush my hair...'* childish talk and nothing informative. But now, suddenly, in a child's unpredictable fashion, he persisted:

'Why don't we ever play Mummy's record? We always used to.'

I was watching Esmond. I saw his mouth tighten and a strange deep look come into his eyes. One might almost call it a wounded look; indescribably painful. I could see that he had even to force himself to make a casual reply.

'I think it's broken, old chap,' he said.

'No, it isn't,' argued Conrad, 'I saw it just now, lying behind a lot of others, with a white label. I showed it to Kate. Let's put it on, Daddy.'

Esmond got up.

'No,' he said in a voice that I did not recognise because it was rough.

I would like to have warned Conrad to keep quiet, but he still persisted.

'I want to, *I want to,* Daddy...' and he turned to me petulantly... 'It was a record Daddy and Mummy made when I was little, but I remember it. We all sang songs into a thing that made the record and then Daddy had it made into a proper one.'

Kate now ran across the room with the record in her hand.

'Play it, Daddy, play it, I want to hear Mummy.'

'She doesn't remember hearing Mummy speak. She says so, but I do. I do!' shouted Conrad.

'Now, Con,' I began, 'if Daddy doesn't want–'

But this was where Esmond interrupted.

'Put that record back where you found it, please Kate...' he spoke in a very cold voice. I thought:

I understand. It would be very painful for him to have to hear her voice. He must have loved her very much.

But this sort of thing was hard on the children who were both too young to appreciate adult emotion.

Then the accident happened. Conrad tried to snatch the record from little Kate and pinched her finger. She dropped the disc. It fell on the parquet floor and smashed into pieces. It was one of the old, breakable, kind.

I felt most distressed. Conrad stood still, losing some of his healthy colour. Kate burst into tears. I dared not look at Esmond, but I hurried forward and started to pick up the pieces.

Then Conrad, who had a hot ungovernable side to him, turned on his father.

'It's all *your* fault, Daddy. You *made* us break it. I heard Nannie tell Thérèse you broke Mummy's harp!'

Dead silence. My heart seemed to stop beating. Her *harp* ... what did he mean? Did he mean her *heart?* I knew that he did. He hadn't understood what the gossiping old nurse had said. But he recalled a word that sounded like *'harp'*. Then when I glanced, feeling absolutely scared, at Con's father, I saw that he knew, too. He stood there like a figure of stone. His face was ghastly. He stammered:

'Mummy didn't ... you didn't ... there was no harp ... you mean her *heart,* I suppose?'

'Yes,' said Conrad sullenly.

I made a desperate effort to put an end to this.

'Con – Kate – come with me...'

'No,' said Esmond. 'Stay here, please, Miss Bray. You two children – go back to the schoolroom.'

Conrad began to snivel, knuckles to his eyes.

'I didn't want the record to be broken.'

'I'm sorry. Forget it,' said Esmond harshly.

The brother and sister trooped out. Alone with Esmond, I felt hot and then cold, and thoroughly uncomfortable. I had now picked up all the pieces of the record and flung them into the waste paper holder under Esmond's desk.

He walked to one of the windows and leaned his head out. A low growl of thunder broke the silence. He turned back to me, wiping his face and neck with a white silk handkerchief. He was wearing a light grey suit, I remember, and a buttonhole that had withered. It didn't look gay but sad. And he looked so sad that I could have wept. He said:

'I apologise for all that. It must have seemed quite ridiculous and incomprehensible to you.'

'Incomprehensible, yes,' I said. 'But it doesn't really matter. I'm just disturbed for you and ... and for the accident. But I'm sure Kate and Con didn't mean to break the record.'

'I'm sure they didn't,' he said. 'Anyhow I have wanted many times to break the thing and never brought myself to do so. It's better broken. It's too ... painful to me to hear it ... all our voices ... hers ... when we were so happy.' He swallowed convulsively.

'Yes, yes, of course,' I muttered.

'You understand things,' he went on. 'You're a strange, quiet, retiring little person and you never intrude ... yet I feel the strength of your presence Shelley. You're ... a comfort to me. I like to know you are with my children.'

My whole body flooded with a deep pleasure, an utter joy, as I heard those words. I felt incapable of answering them, but thought that if I brought any comfort to *him* I had not lived in vain. He continued to talk to me in that tired, unhappy voice ... his manner absolutely changed from his usual buoyant self ... the famous musical conductor who held thousands in his sway.

'Poor old Con. I was too harsh with him. Of course he doesn't understand ... at seven, how can he? And what he heard ... oh, well – now you realise why Nannie had to go ... she lived on stupid dangerous tittle-tattle...'

Like Lucien Valguay, I thought.

'The word Con meant was not *harp*, of course,' said Esmond. 'My ... late wife was not a musician. She played no instrument. Con meant that Nannie said that I broke her *heart*.'

I nodded miserably.

'It isn't true,' he broke out with sudden passion, and the muscles of his face worked. 'It was a dastardly thing to say. I adored Veronica. But I have no intention of dragging the past into the open or involving *you* in it. One has no right to bring outsiders into these family affairs. But you are in charge of my children and have become almost one of us ... you are bound to hear things ... and it must be difficult for you at times. Now

131

perhaps you realise why I do not encourage conversation about … my late wife.'

I did not understand now any more than before but I let him speak.

'If anyone's heart was broken, it was *mine*,' he added tersely. Then he completely changed his tone and in a high clear voice apologised again for the whole episode, and told me to try and wipe the memory of it from the children's minds. I was also to take the note he handed me and buy Conrad something that he wanted when we were next at the shops. He wanted to make up for the lost record.

'Thank you for being so understanding, and thank you for all you do for me,' he ended.

'I do nothing for you at all,' I stuttered.

'Yes, you do by your very presence here – your care of Con and Kate. They are so greatly improved as to be unrecognisable, both in their manners and what they are learning.'

'I'm terribly glad you're pleased, Mr Torrington,' I said breathlessly.

He lit another cigarette. *He smokes far too much,* I thought. *He is nervy and on edge.*

I felt an unutterable and inexplicable tenderness for him. I wished I knew more about Veronica, and yet glad that I didn't and glad that I hadn't known her, if she had hurt him. How terrible to think that a woman could be capable of breaking *his* heart!

He walked across the studio to open the door for me in his graceful courteous fashion. He even managed a smile.

'All forgotten?' he asked.

'Of course,' I assured him.

'Thank you, my dear, and don't think that all your little services pass unnoticed. You're very tactful and things can't always be easy for you.'

I knew that he alluded to his sister's many spiteful actions. I fancied that once or twice lately he had been astonished to find out how malicious Monica really was and that it hadn't enhanced her in his eyes. But that didn't please me. I didn't want to be the cause of trouble in this house that had already known such great tragedy. But as I walked out of the studio, leaving him in there alone, I made a passionate vow to go on serving him in any way that I could. Nothing would induce me now to let sister Monica drive me away.

I actually felt for the first time that *he* needed me at Arc-en-Ciel as well as the children.

It was a tremendous, blessèd, ecstatic thought for me.

7

I was almost glad at the end of that week when Esmond left Arc-en-Ciel for Milan where he was to be guest conductor for a new Benjamin Britten opera which was being performed over there for the first time.

Yet I hated it when he had left. I did not see him after that, for quite a month. As soon as he left, Lady Warr sent for me and told me to pack the children's things and my own. The heat right down on the Côte d'Azur could be stifling, and was particularly so at the moment. Dr Valguay had suggested that it would do her Ladyship good if we all went up to a hotel in the mountains for some fresh cool air, otherwise both she and the children would begin to flag.

'And Dr Valguay is coming with us,' announced Lady Warr brightly, 'isn't that nice of him? To get away and join us just to look after me.'

My heart sank. I wasn't at all keen on the thought of being shut up in a hotel in the mountains in the company of Lucien Valguay. It was hard enough to get away from him down here. But of course I had no choice. I just thought: *What a doctor! ... if he can leave his patients 'just like that' to a locum whenever he chooses. I wonder what he is being paid for his holiday at her ladyship's side?*

My thoughts turned wistfully to Milan … and the great man who was conducting there.

I did not think it a good thing for the children to break their schoolroom routine so soon, but of course their health came first, and they were wild with delight at the idea of the three weeks in the mountains. The hotel was up above Mont Viso, in a glorious position commanding a view of the valley which stretched for miles. And it just suited Lady Warr because it was built all on one floor like a colossal bungalow, in colonial style, with wide verandahs and big airy rooms with long pullman windows.

There was a swimming pool and tennis courts and it was all very expensive and luxurious. I was beginning to grow quite used to this life in which money was of no consequence. And I had been able to save, too, and send Robin a nice cheque for his birthday which pleased me. I had also bought some material from one of the shops in Cannes when I took the children over there to lunch, and was making myself a new flowered cotton skirt to wear in the evenings. I hoped that I would have plenty of time to sew, up there in the Hôtel de Montagne as the place was called.

I tanned a shade browner in that mountain air – constantly swimming, or out in the gardens with the children. I think I might have enjoyed it because it was certainly easier to breathe up there than down in Monte Carlo, but there were two snags. First and foremost, the constant presence of the detestable Lucien, and secondly, because I found that I missed Esmond so badly – much more than I had any right to do. I dared not ask for news of him. I never dared mention his name to Lady Warr. However, he sent postcards from Italy to the children and so I always knew from these how he was faring. And once ... (oh, ecstasy!) he mentioned *me*. Unfortunately for me, by my Christian name.

Remember me to Shelley...

I hoped Lady Warr would not see that card, but Conrad showed it to her at lunch the day on which it came.

'Daddy's sent his love to Shelley.'

'Well, well, how nice,' said Sir Austen, looking at me over his glasses.

But the lady in the wheel-chair narrowed her eyes to slits.

'To *Shelley?* You mean Miss Bray, dear.'

'No, he said *Shelley*,' said Conrad.

'That char-rming name,' put in Lucien Valguay giving me one of his languishing glances.

I felt myself grow hot.

Lady Warr took the card, glanced at it and returned it to her nephew.

She said not a word. But one could have cut the atmosphere with a knife.

Poor Esmond, I thought, you little know what a hornet's nest you've roused by your kindly remembrance of me and that casual use of my name. She misinterprets and misunderstands *everything*. Sometimes it is hard to believe she is your own sister – your natures are so different.

For reasons which still mystified me, Lady Warr had continued to be pleasant to me since the day when she had so completely lost her temper. We had not had one wry word since coming up to the mountains. Now she drew a letter from her bag and addressed the doctor.

'I must let you into a little secret, Lucien. Austen was so thrilled when I told him. You remember that charming woman – the Comtesse de la Notte.'

'Ah, yes, indeed,' said Lucien. 'The so-beautiful Sophie.'

'Well, you know she was separated from her husband.'

'I do, and she has a little girl, Renate, hasn't she? I attended her for tonsillitis last winter when they were in Monaco.'

'Exactly. Well, the husband has died and Sophie is free again. Such a delightful girl – so much too young to be widowed – barely thirty you know, and Renate's the same age as Kate.'

'The Comtesse's father is a millionaire, I believe.'

'Oh, yes, she will be one of the richest women in France. I remember meeting her mother who told me what a tragedy it was that she married de la Notte when she was barely of age. A playboy – no good to her.'

'She should find no difficulty in getting another husband,' remarked Dr Valguay lighting the cigar which Sir Austen offered him. 'Rich and beautiful – *tiens!*'

'Exactly,' said Lady Warr, 'and this is where Esmond's letter comes in. He seems to be seeing quite a lot of Sophie in Milan. She went over there especially to hear the opera and stayed on. She's very musical. I said to Austen, didn't I, Austen dear, that it would be wonderful if–' now her eyes turned to me– 'if dear Esmond were to find married happiness again with a woman like Sophie.'

Sir Austen gave his tolerant laugh.

'Are you matchmaking, my darling?'

'I couldn't bear the thought of Esmond marrying again, unless it was to somebody I really liked,' she sighed. 'But Sophie has always been sweet to me ... and is such a *sweet* person.'

I don't know why, but I felt sick. I certainly knew that this conversation between Lady

Warr and the others was meant especially to impress *me*. But I hope I showed no sign that I felt in the least interested in Mr Torrington's personal affairs. I rose and bade the children to come along with me and have their rest.

As we walked out, I felt Lady Warr's gaze burning my back. I heard her voice:

'Of course one mustn't jump to conclusions or say a *thing* outside the family circle, but I just *hope* something may come of this. Esmond said how adorable Sophie looked in a wonderful Dior gown on the first night. They had supper afterwards with–'

I heard no more. But my heart was beating quickly as I reached the children's bedroom. Mechanically I listened to their chatter. They wanted to go for a picnic this afternoon beside a certain mountain stream we had just discovered. Conrad said:

'Please while I am on my bed can I write to Daddy?'

'Yes,' I said.

'My writing's better, isn't it, Miss Bray?' he asked.

'Much better.'

'I'll show it to you when I've finished,' he said.

'Can I write too?' said Kate.

'She can't write,' jeered Conrad.

'I can so!'

A fight began. I ended it by giving them

both pencil and paper and promising to help Kate with hers.

I thought:

I would like to write to him too, but I daren't.

I thought of the beautiful wealthy Comtesse de la Notte who was being his constant companion in Milan. A woman who had everything to offer him – looks, experience, money, musical appreciation as well.

I thought with sudden hot uncontrollable emotion: 'Oh, I wish I were Sophie. *I wish I were Sophie!*

I knew then that I was in love with him. That my original hero-worship for a great conductor and my admiration since I entered his service, had culminated into a deep and absolute love. The revelation shook me to the foundations. I stared facts in the face and was dismayed – even terrified. I knew that I had no right to think of Esmond in such a way and that I must take this love and pluck it right out of my heart – quickly before it grew one whit stronger.

Heavens! Was I going to give Lady Warr cause for all her insinuations of the past? No, *no.* Once I returned to Arc-en-Ciel I must keep out of Esmond's way, or, indeed, leave his service and say goodbye to Arc-en-Ciel.

The children brought me their little letters to post on our way to the river picnic. Kate had faithfully copied out a few large loving words which I had written for her. Conrad's note was childish and misspelt but quite revealing to me.

I hop you are well. I liked your p.c. of the Kathidrl in Milen. We are going to fish in the river with Miss Bray. I like the mowntins bettrn home. But I don't like Dr Val. He's a sneek.
Love from Con.

I had to swallow twice as I read this, knowing that Con's bright penetrating gaze was upon me. Then I said:

'Why do you say that Dr Valguay is a sneak? And by the way it's spelt SNEAK.'

'Because he is,' said Conrad.

'Would you like to tell me why you think so?' I asked.

The boy's marvellous lashes flicked and he grinned.

'I bet you know.'

I did know. I felt most uncomfortable about this and I didn't see how I could let such a letter go through to Conrad's father. It would only worry him. But it just happened that a week ago I had had one of my awkward moments with Lady Warr. She had been annoyed, as usual, because Kate didn't want to sit with her while she read a book to Conrad (much too old to amuse little Kate, and it is so difficult for a six-year-old to sit still and twiddle her thumbs). So the usual mean paltry punishment had been administered, that Kate was forbidden to paddle in the stream and look for tiny fish with Conrad.

It was a warm afternoon. The ice-cold mountain water was tempting. Perhaps I was wrong, but in the end I let her take off her socks and dip in her hot little toes. Lucien Valguay turned up. I anticipated trouble because Conrad, with childish tactlessness, at once told him that Aunt Monnie had forbidden Kate to paddle but that I had allowed it.

'Isn't Miss Bray a sport?' he had exclaimed. Bit by bit Conrad was melting towards me and we had established by now a fairly firm friendship which only fell apart after Lady Warr had breathed some of her hopelessly wrong philosophies into his receptive ear.

Lucien Valguay had smiled and looked at me.

'Indeed she is a sport. But I personally would like her to be a leetle more "sporting" shall we say.'

That meant nothing to the children who went on with their paddling; but I understood and I suppose I looked cross because he put an arm in a light but too familiar way round my shoulders.

'You are never spor-r-rting with me, are you, Shelley? Always so r-r-remote,' he rolled his r's richly. 'Like the snow on the

142

Alps. Yet I do not think you are snow. I think there is a leetle fire burning somewhere deep down, *hein?*'

I wriggled away from that arm feeling crosser than ever.

'You talk a lot of nonsense, Dr Valguay.'

'S-strange,' he said, putting a cigarette in his long holder and regarding it thoughtfully, 'but you do not like me, do you?'

'Is that so strange?' I asked rather rudely.

He gave me a sidelong smile.

'Most women do.'

'Then I'm not "most women".'

'No, I confess, you are unique. I have been watching you since we have been up at Mont Viso. You have the external appearance of a so-slender schoolgirl. Just now in your blue linen jeans and T-shirt, with your untidy curls, you might be a charming boy. Yet there is a clever brain behind it all. You are no fool. I have admired the way you came to Arc-en-Ciel, and tackled those difficult children.'

'I do not find them difficult,' I broke in.

He ignored this and went on.

'And I've admired the way you stand up to her ladyship. But I know Milady better than you do. Whether you like me or not, I shall give you a leetle warning. Be a *leetle* more careful of the way you handle dear Monica. The leetle lady can be very powerful and rather malicious behind her mask of Pathos-tied-to-a-wheel-chair. The gr-reat conductor admires you. She knows it. And–'

'Dr Valguay,' I broke in. I was furiously angry, although not unaware of the fact that it made my heart leap to be told so openly that Esmond admired me, and I could not even believe it. 'Dr Valguay, will you please not say these sort of things to me. I am not afraid of Lady Warr or of you, or anybody, and I am just going on doing my duty as a teacher as well as I am able. But please leave me alone.'

His charm, his smile, his wheedling manner suddenly vanished. I could see that he had lost patience. He sneered:

'I find your unassailable virtue almost alar-r-rming. But I still warn you not to upset Lady Warr. The beautiful Veronica found that it didn't pay, *tu sais?*'

He said those last words very softly. The significance of them could not fail to strike me and rouse the usual violent curiosity which I confess I felt whenever that name was spoken. Lucien Valguay never came into the open but perpetually insinuated things. Anybody with an imagination like mine could build up a very unattractive story ... a picture of Esmond's lovely lively wife at the mercy not only of a jealous husband but of a cruel and jealous sister-in-law. The very idea cast a sinister shadow even here in this sylvan glen, where the stream gushed from

144

the rocks and down the mountain side between verges starred with flowers; where the air was full of the scent of wild thyme and heather and sun-baked grass. Below us stretched the glorious valley, above us the heavenly blue sky. The atmosphere was translucent. In the silence could be heard the pleasant tinkle of cow-bells, for there was a mountain farm not far away. To me it was a place of peace where I could come with the children and where I could be sure Lady Warr could not get up to join us in her chair. Now that peace was broken by this detestable man who had not stopped trying to get on to more than friendly terms with me since we arrived at the hotel.

Lady Warr actually seemed to encourage it – she was always suggesting that he should come with me and the children for a walk, or that I should go for a drive with him alone. And whereas at first I had thought nothing of it, I had ended by being forced to believe that she approved of the persecution.

Perhaps she believed that I might fall for the suave handsome French doctor, and so divert my attentions from Esmond. The very thought of this was ridiculous to me. And always he said something about Veronica Torrington ... threw some new slant upon her life ... and death. Anyhow he was so fed up with my lack of response that afternoon, he left us abruptly and I presume that he went back to her ladyship and told her about Kate. Not only was Kate punished in some other way but I was 'given a rocket' in front of the children which I always found most humiliating. Conrad actually disliked seeing his aunt's displeasure with me and that was why he had called Dr Valguay a sneak.

But I *could* not let Conrad's letter stay as it was.

'We have agreed that we don't tell tales, Con,' I said calmly, 'and you are not to tell tales about the doctor. Please give me the scissors and I will cut out that last para-graph. You must write your goodbye on the other side of the paper, dear.'

He did so unwillingly, grumbling and arguing, but I felt better when I saw him do it. I left him to seal up his letter and went along to the kitchen to ask the head waiter for the picnic tea which he was packing up for us to take to our much-loved river. I was surprised when, before we set out, Lady Warr sent Yvonne, who was also up in the hotel with us, to tell me that I was wanted.

I sighed but went along quite cheerfully; I was growing used to these summons al-though since we had been up here, Monica Warr had certainly been more reasonable.

She was lying on her bed in one of her

expensive negligées with the shutters closed to keep out the sun and a shaded lamp burning beside her. How I hated her dark and perfumed rooms. I always felt that something must be wrong with people who could never bear to let in the daylight.

To my immense surprise she handed me Conrad's letter.

'I had a few words with Con just now, Miss Bray, and he told me he had written to his father. I mentioned that I would like to see how he was getting on with his writing, and so we opened the letter. Might I just suggest that you are going a little too far in allowing him to add such a postscript.'

Nonplussed I stared.

'I don't understand. What postscript, Lady Warr?'

She twisted her lips into an expression of disbelief.

'Oh come! Con says you read it, and made him cut out something about my doctor. He didn't tell me what. You might like to explain. But you must have seen the whole of it.'

I scanned the letter, then turning it over, saw to my dismay that the boy (innocently enough I am sure), had added words that were certainly calculated to put me utterly in the wrong. I could feel myself going bright scarlet as I read them. Oh, the *silly* little boy:

Shelley's a sport. Lots of love and kisses and Shelley sends you a huge kiss too.

I returned the note to her ladyship conscious that my hand was shaking, yet deep down inside me I wanted to laugh. It was so funny; just a seven-year-old boy's unthinking nonsense, and I knew perfectly well that my denial that I had countenanced it would not be believed. It wasn't. I denied categorically and for several moments that I had dictated that bit about the huge kiss. Finally, exasperated, I snapped:

'Oh, really, this is too absurd, Lady Warr. As if I would be so … so disrespectful as to send my employer a *kiss!* Surely you can't possibly believe that. I left Con to put the letter in the envelope and he added those words without my approval.'

She tore the letter in pieces.

'Then it shall not go since you do not approve of it being sent,' she said in a nasty voice, 'and Con can write another more sensible letter. But I would now like to know what *you* cut out of it. This letter of Con's seems to be *very* troublesome, doesn't it?'

'Yes, it does,' I said hotly. 'The children usually write as they feel.'

'And presumably Con felt that you should send his father a kiss.'

I gave a sigh.

'*Please* Lady Warr, must we begin that again?'

She interrupted:

'Very well. Let it pass. But I insist on knowing what *you* cut out of the letter. What did my nephew have to say about Dr Valguay?'

'Nothing very pleasant,' I said, and was annoyed to find myself still trembling, 'that is why I didn't let it go. I told Conrad that I didn't like people who told tales.'

I saw Monica Warr's hard blue eyes staring as though trying to penetrate my thoughts – as though my coolness and the way in which I always refused to be browbeaten by her, drove her to the pitch of exasperation. She repeated:

'*I insist on knowing.* Dr Valguay is my friend. My very dear friend. Sir Austen's to,' she added hastily.

That was not so. On one occasion poor old Sir Austen had let drop the fact that he couldn't stand the French doctor. But it wasn't my affair. We now had a short rather stormy argument about the line that Conrad had written concerning Lucien. I refused to repeat it.

'It was his private and personal letter to his father, Lady Warr, and he realised that what he had written was a mistake even if true.'

That reply of course drove Lady Warr to a

frenzy. She sat up and snarled at me:

'I shall send for Conrad and ask him.'

'I beg you not to do that as it would be bad for him. Children should not be involved in adult disagreements.'

'Oh, you and your theories – you detestable little schoolmistress!' she shrieked at me, now quite out of control.

Sir Austen came running into the room. At once Lady Warr burst into tears and involved him, accusing me of being rude and unco-operative. Sir Austen, poor old pet, hadn't the least idea of what this was all about, but his loyalty and love induced him to sit beside the bed, hold the hands of the sobbing woman, and reproach me.

'Hush, hush, my poor darling,' he kept saying to her, 'you know it's bad for you to upset yourself like this. Miss Bray, my dear, you really must be more considerate.'

I stayed silent.

Dr Valguay was sent for. He gave me a knowing look and with that hateful smile twisting his mouth, offered to give her ladyship an injection. She must calm down or she would have a heart-attack, he said.

I stood helpless while both the men looked at me as though I was the sole cause of Monica's hysteria. Suddenly I felt thoroughly unhappy. I rushed out of the room and left them all. For a moment I found it hard to gain my own control. I did not want the children to be upset. Yet I felt in that moment as though I wanted to pack and leave the Hôtel de Montagne. Run away from them all. But the very idea of never seeing Esmond Torrington again was so painful I could not bear it.

I felt that any misery that I was asked to endure through Lady Warr was worth the candle.

I took the children for their picnic and put a severe stop to any questions that Conrad shot at me. And I did not reproach him for adding that postscript without showing it to me, because I knew he had meant no harm. I even recovered my sense of humour by wishing that the 'huge kiss' had gone to Esmond!

But Lady Warr wasn't going to leave well alone. Having slept off her attack of hysteria she wheeled herself down to the children's bedroom to say good night to them and then, very softly and with a fond smile, said to Conrad:

'What did my darling boy write in his letter that Miss Bray had to take out?'

I almost ran out of the room. Conrad sulkily refused to answer. Lady Warr having failed in her endeavour, wheeled herself out of the room and beckoned to me to follow. She then accused me of turning her nephew against her. Before I came, she said, he would have confided in her and never sulked. By this time I was so tired of the whole petty affair that I gave her the information she asked for.

'He called Dr Valguay a "sneak", Lady Warr, if you must know, and I told him it was not the way to talk about the doctor behind his back.'

Monica Warr stared at me and then laughed.

'Was *that* all?'

'Yes, but surely you would not approve of him running the doctor down to his father,' I said coldly.

'It's *too* ridiculous. How can Dr Valguay be a sneak?'

'He was,' I said drily. 'He told you about Kate paddling. Conrad is now learning *not* to tell tales, and he thought that it was wrong of the Doctor to have repeated what he saw, to you.'

'Well, *I* shall tell Conrad that he was wrong to call Dr Valguay a sneak only because Lucien was quite *right* to tell me that you went against my wishes. Good night, Miss Bray.'

She wheeled herself away. I looked after that chair feeling quite hopeless. How would I *ever* be able to train the minds and characters of my young pupils with such an influence to undermine my teaching? A storm in a teacup, yes … perhaps … but all these little storms were only building up into the positive hurricane of hatred that Monica Warr was waiting to let loose upon me.

That weekend it had been arranged that I should take a day and night off. Yvonne would look after the children and give them their meals when their aunt was resting.

It just happened that Robin was on leave. It was the one weekend that he could come and see me. He had been sent to Paris on an exchange course with two French airmen and had seized the opportunity of a 'flip' down to the Côte d'Azur. I'd found a room for him in a cheap *pension* in Monte Carlo and Lady Warr, although she hated the thought of me having any fun, could not refuse to give me the little holiday. But I felt suddenly sad when little Kate burst into tears as she kissed me goodbye and told me she did not want me to go.

'Now, darling,' I said, 'try to be good and do as Aunt Monnie tells you. I'll be back tomorrow night.'

Lucien Valguay saw me off on the bus.

'Maybe it is not a br-rother but a boy-fr-riend, whom you go so blithely to meet,' he said with his crafty smile.

'That's just your horrid mind,' I snapped and climbed into the bus without giving him a backward glance.

I hadn't been away from the children since I arrived in Monte Carlo. Much as I was going to miss them I felt suddenly free and rather glad to be rid of Lady Warr's malice for twenty-four hours.

I was longing to see my adored brother, and of course, spend this evening with him. We would have so much to tell each other.

I went straight to Arc-en-Ciel. Bertrand and the old cook were there, and I would of course be sleeping in my own room. There were also some things that Lady Warr wanted me to pick up and take up to her tomorrow.

As I reached the lovely villa, standing in its enchanted garden, my heart gave a wild mad leap. I saw the familiar white and coffee coloured Rolls outside the door, and I *knew that Esmond was here.* He had quite un-expectedly come home.

8

'My goodness me!' exclaimed Esmond, 'how dreary everything looks!'

I had just met him in the hall. We were wandering through the villa as though examining it for the first time – like two interlopers, I thought with some amusement.

'Monnie's always so meticulous about wrapping everything up in her absence,' Esmond said with a laugh.

I had to agree that the place had a melancholy air; all the lovely sofas and chairs covered in dust sheets and the jalousies shut and locked. It was curiously cold after the heat outside, and dark, too. Esmond took my arm and led me towards the studio which he had already opened up to the sun and air.

'Let's have a cup of tea,' he said, 'Louise is in the kitchen. She and Bertrand were having a nice siesta when I turned up, but I soon woke them and I must say they've given me a great reception – as though I'd been away for years. They are a dear couple.'

I made no answer. I was too thrilled by the touch of his hand under my elbow. His reception of me had been flatteringly warm.

'Well, well, if it isn't our little Shelley Bray! I *am* pleased to see you, Shelley. But where have you sprung from? Why aren't you up in the mountains?'

I had told him about my night off, and Robin flying down from Paris to be with me tonight. Now he seated himself on the piano stool and lighting one of the cigars he liked so well, he grinned up at me like a boy who had been found out in some escapade. He looked a mere boy today, I thought, his usually smooth dark hair ruffled, coat off, shirt-sleeves rolled up, tie loose.

'I must go and have a bath,' he said, 'I've been driving since dawn.'

'You weren't expected back till next week.'

'We had to cut the tour short. Unfortunately there was an outbreak of some curious fever that laid half the orchestra low. We just couldn't carry on.'

'You're sure *you* haven't got it?' I asked anxiously.

He laughed and tapped his forehead.

'I don't think I'm ill but if I do drop down at your feet, Miss Bray, you shall nurse me back to health and strength. Perhaps that's why the angels sent you down from Mont Viso.'

'Oh, I hope not,' I stammered. 'I mean I hope you won't be ill.'

'I won't. But it's been a tough assignment conducting in that heat.'

'I wish I'd been there to hear some of the concerts!' I exclaimed.

'We had one very fine night,' he said dreamily. 'It was an intriguing programme, well received. I gave them Sir Arthur Bliss's *Colour Symphony* – do you know it?'

I shook my head.

'You must hear it – I've got a first-class recording.'

He went on to tell me that he had included in that programme Brahms Symphony No.4 in E Minor, and ended with the Finale from *The Twilight of the Gods*.

'Rich, gloomy and magnificent,' he said, with a puff of his cigar. 'But what scoring! I never conduct Wagner without being amazed by those scores.'

'I love Wagner,' I told him shyly, 'I'd give anything to be able to hear *The Ring*.'

'What you must do is to go to Bayreuth some time to the Festival.'

'I don't suppose I ever will,' I said sadly.

He eyed me, his handsome brilliant eyes were kindly, full of the warm friendliness which I found so wonderful. I could never understand why he should take the slightest interest in such an insignificant person as myself. Suddenly he said:

'Our Shelley is looking extremely attractive.'

'*Attractive*,' I repeated incredulously.

'You've got a real Indian tan. You look

delightful. And your hair's much shorter.'

I couldn't get over the fact that he noticed it. I admitted that I had had a lot of hair cut off before going up to Mont Viso.

Then he asked after the children – delighted to hear that they were enjoying themselves so much and amused at some of the anecdotes I repeated to him. I had no intention of telling him about Dr Valguay. We came of course to the subject of dear Monica's health and then Esmond rather surprise me by saying:

'I sometimes think that fellow Valguay does her no good. There's a lot in this mind-over-matter business, and I always did think it a pity she has such faith in Valguay. Personally I think him a phoney. And one of the specialists she had years ago actually told me that if she made an effort she might have gone on walking.'

I made no reply. There was so much I *could* have repeated but I did not wish to make trouble. Smiling at me, Esmond rose from his seat and said:

'Well – have you been getting bullied?'

I blushed.

'Of course not.'

'I expect you have,' he said. 'But you take everything very amiably and make no trouble. You are an amazingly self-reliant, composed little person.'

'That sounds awfully priggish.'

'Not at all,' he said, 'on the contrary. You're just what is needed at Arc-en-Ciel. There have been far too many people throwing temperaments around. Oh, but I'm sure you have your moments, too,' he added, 'I don't suppose you always feel as cool or calm as you appear.'

'No, not always,' I said in a low voice.

'I'm glad your brother's coming to see you,' he went on, 'it'll be nice for you to spend an evening with one of your own family.'

'Yes, I'm dying to see Robin!' I nodded.

Then I asked Esmond what he was going to do this evening. He answered that he had no idea. He had made no plans. He was actually free, for once, owing to this premature end to the session as guest conductor in Milan. He rather thought, he said, of flying to London tomorrow. He had no definite engagement to tie him down until the first of a new series of concerts in Monaco next week.

'You won't come up to see us in the mountains?' I asked wistfully.

'I might,' he said, 'if I can stand that fellow Valguay.'

We both looked into each other's eyes then and burst out laughing. We understood each other on the subject of Lucien Valguay.

After a cup of tea he went to his own room to bath and have a rest as he had been motoring so long in this heat. I also went to my room where I found myself thinking not so much about Robin's arrival, as of Esmond's unexpected presence in the house.

I only began to be anxious about Robin when darkness fell and he still had not arrived. The 'maestro', refreshed and dressed for the evening, called me in to his studio for a glass of sherry. I, too, was dressed, I had expected Robin hours ago. We were supposed to be dining out together.

'Something delaying your brother?' asked Esmond handing me a glass.

'It looks like it,' I sighed.

At that moment Bertrand appeared. He drew a telegram from the pocket of his baize apron.

'It has just come, mademoiselle.'

The moment I took the piece of paper from him, I knew what it was. Robin wasn't coming. Sure enough the wire was from Paris.

Ordered back to England. Terribly disappointed.
Robin.

Esmond must have seen my expression.

'Not bad news, I hope?'

'My brother has been ordered back to England. He can't come tonight after all. The telegram has been very much delayed.'

'Oh, I *am* sorry!' exclaimed Esmond. 'You poor little thing. What a disappointment, and after coming all the way down here in that confounded bus, too.'

I smothered my disappointment as best as I could.

'I hope there'll be a bus back tonight,' I said.

'Nothing at this late hour. I'll run you up in the morning in my car.'

I felt my disappointment over Robin vanish.

'Oh, but you can't ... you want to go to London ... surely I can get a bus in the morning...'

'My dear self-effacing little friend,' he said with a twist to his lips, 'do you never think of yourself?'

'But you said you wanted to go to London,' I stammered, 'and I don't mind the bus.'

'I've changed my mind. I shall drive you up to the Hôtel Montagne. I'd like to see the children.'

'Thanks awfully, that'll be wonderful,' I said breathlessly.

He glanced at his watch.

'Meanwhile you've come all this way for an evening out and here you are dressed up and nowhere to go. How about a spot of dinner with me?'

I was speechless. It seemed too good to be true. An invitation to dine with him, *him!* Heavens, what a dazzling idea! I dared not even begin to think what her ladyship would have to say about this. And suddenly I didn't care. Nothing mattered in the world except that he was asking me to go out with him tonight.

'I imagine you've never had what I call a real Casino evening,' he said. 'A deadly bore if done too often, but not unamusing if taken in small doses. We'll have dinner at the Hôtel de Paris on the terrace, then I'll take you in to the Sporting Club to watch the gambling. A shocking spectacle … all those millionaires winning or losing in a positive fever. But interesting for a bit. Personally I never gamble.'

It sounded enthralling to me. Not only the gamblers would be in a fever, I was already in one, I told myself, my heart galloping like mad. I drank my sherry and felt on top of the world, hanging on every word that Esmond spoke. The last bus back to Mont Viso had gone. I couldn't get one if I wanted, and Esmond said he wasn't going to drive the car another ninety miles at night; so here I was, and here I would stay.

He didn't even bother to book a table. The great Mr Torrington was such a personage in Monaco; there would always be a table for him. When finally we drove in the Rolls down towards the Hôtel de Paris, I felt as though I were in a marvellous dream.

He had interrupted me just before we left the villa when I had suggested that he might

162

like to take somebody else out.

'The invitation has been issued to *you*,' he had said quite crossly. 'You've done a lot for my children since you've been here, Shelley, surely I can give you dinner as your brother has not come.'

I argued no further. This was indeed my night. One that might never come again.

A glorious warm evening with a full moon silvering the Mediterranean. In the Place de Casino, the beautiful beds of geraniums which were floodlit looked an indescribably brilliant colour. Down in the harbour there gleamed lights from the portholes of all the sleek white yachts that so regularly put in at Monte Carlo.

I stole a glance at the fine profile of my companion. He looked very debonair. I thought how unglamorous I must seem in my one and only grey silk dress with the yellow flowers.

'I'm afraid I'm not very suitably dressed,' I faltered.

He gave me a quick look.

'You wore that dress for my concert and I thought how charming you looked in it then. Don't fuss,' he said.

Rebuked I sat back and said no more.

Monte Carlo seemed like fairyland tonight. The dinner at the Hôtel de Paris was marvellous. Esmond was received like a prince – the head waiter, bowing and smiling, led us to a table on which there were shaded lights and gorgeous carnations. Even in September which was not strictly the season for the 'best people', this restaurant was full of exciting looking people. Some of the girls wore fabulous clothes and jewels and I should have been envious of them except that I am not of an envious disposition. But it gave me a thrill when Esmond on one occasion pointed out one slender model girl and said: *'That* would suit you, I think.'

'That' was a short dinner dress of some sort of silver tissue, tightly moulded, and absolutely plain. With it, the girl wore a wide turquoise choker and big turquoise earrings. She was certainly terribly smart.

'I couldn't imagine myself in that sort of get-up,' I said.

'*I* could,' he said, 'and it would look particularly well with your rich tan at this moment.'

He spoke casually. I don't suppose he began to realise how I reacted to his show of interest in me. Nor how I was marvelling that I, the little governess and employee, should be sitting here, *vis-à-vis* with him, being treated like an honoured guest. More than that, like a friend, for he called me 'Shelley' now, all the time, and spoke to me with that warmth and simplicity typical of a great man.

I've still got the menu of that meal – my

very first meal with Esmond Torrington at the Hôtel de Paris. While he was talking to some man who came across to speak to him, I slipped it into my handbag like a sentimental schoolgirl bent on securing a momento. I know it by heart.

Saumon fumé
Tourte de ris de veau
Pommes dauphin
Petis pois
Crêpe flambée au Grand Marnier

Never shall I forget them making the *crêpe flambée* in a copper pan on the spirit stove beside us. Two waiters hovering with all the ingredients – the sifted sugar – the butter – the brandy and liqueur – the little pancakes finally being placed in the bubbling liquid, giving out an appetising odour. Then the whole thing was set alight and finally I tasted what seemed a most fabulous dish of an unearthly flavour.

I think Esmond was amused by my attitude and the way I savoured each morsel.

'Your eyes look like saucers, you funny little thing,' he said almost tenderly. 'It really is refreshing to take somebody out who has never done this sort of thing before.'

'Well, I certainly never have!' I said. 'I've eaten far too much, but oh! it was scrumptious.'

Esmond sat back and laughed. He signalled to the waiter and ordered coffee and a cigar.

'I thoroughly enjoyed it, myself,' he said. 'And your pleasure is infectious.'

Now, suddenly, for no reason at all, except perhaps that Esmond had made me drink a little of the iced hock that he told me was his favourite wine, and I felt slightly more courageous and talkative than usual, I broke out:

'Please tell me more about yourself and Milan before the poor orchestra got that infection. Was it *marvellous?*'

'Marvellously hot,' he smiled.

Then I dared to mention the name of the Comtesse de la Notte.

'Lady Warr told me that she is one of the most beautiful women in the world.'

I found myself watching him – and, idiot that I was, being glad that he did not change colour or look particularly interested. He said:

'That's one of Monica's exaggerations. Sophie is extremely attractive, but I would not call her the most beautiful woman in the world.'

I felt idiotically pleased. I went on:

'She has a little girl the same age as Kate, hasn't she?'

'Renate, yes, rather a spoiled morsel. Poor Sophie doesn't know how to handle her. Incidentally they are both coming to Monte

Carlo next week. The Comtesse is exceptionally musical. She wants to attend the concerts I am giving.'

I nodded. I didn't feel so pleased when he added:

'She usually stays with us for a weekend at Arc-en-Ciel. I can see you'll have your work cut out with Renate added to your schoolroom.'

I told him that wouldn't worry me, but I must say my spirits drooped a little at the thought of the attractive Comtesse staying in our villa. Yet why should it *concern me?* Even if the beautiful widow eventually got beneath the mask and appealed to the essential man in Esmond Torrington, why should I care?

I knew that I did.

But this was *my* evening.

The next few hours in the Casino – Esmond took me to the Sporting Club – fascinated me. After watching for a while I don't think I felt any more inclined to gamble than Esmond did. It seemed to me an awful waste of energy and time. The players all got so worked up about their winning and losing. But I certainly held my breath when one wealthy Greek ran a bank of several thousands of pounds, lost it on the turn of a card, shrugged his shoulders, and made another bet. Money seemed to be no object here. As for that tiny ivory ball clicking around the roulette wheel, that fascinated me, too. Once Esmond leaned forward and put five hundred francs on the number 10.

'For you,' he whispered to me.

It turned up... I heard the croupier's nasal announcement.

'Le dix.'

All eyes turned to Esmond. He had won an incredible amount of money, I thought. Flushed and excited, I began to protest as he started to stuff the notes into my bag.

'Bravo! Beginner's luck,' he murmured.

'I can't take all that,' I gasped.

'You won it,' he smiled. 'Don't argue.'

A woman who was sitting at the table, smiled up at Esmond.

'Good evening, Mr Torrington. You don't play in here very often,' she said. She had a metallic American twang. 'You were real lucky.'

'Not I, but my friend,' said Esmond and introduced us.

'Mrs Van Sylk – Miss Bray.'

I saw Mrs Van Sylk eyeing me with interest. I expect she was wondering what on earth the great Esmond was doing in the Sporting Club with a young badly-dressed girl like myself. Somehow I knew in that moment that she would report on this incident to Lady Warr in time to come. Her eagle eye had watched him push the notes into my bag.

Esmond led me away from the roulette and after watching the big baccarat table for a while he suggested that we sat out on the terrace and had some more coffee or a cooling drink.

'I can't stand that atmosphere,' he said.

I told him that I didn't think I could, either. Elated at my success – all that money, won through him – I insisted on giving him back the original stake, which he gravely accepted.

'Very right and proper,' he nodded.

The *salle de jeu* had been thrilling, but it was much more so to be out here in the velvet night, in the blaze of white moonlight, alone with *him*.

Because I was so profoundly interested in him I manoeuvred the conversation around to his life as a conductor, and begged him to tell me about those early years.

He opened up on the subject quite readily. I heard how he had started by learning the 'cello as well as the piano when he was quite a small boy. His mother had been a singer in her time. He resembled her. Monica was more like his father who was a fair blue-eyed man with Nordic blood. That was where Monica got those cold blue eyes, I thought, but Esmond's mother came from Wales. Wales, which had bred so many musicians and dark-eyed, dark-browed men.

I heard how Esmond had gained a diploma in his early youth, then decided that he wanted to conduct.

'I spent hours,' he said, 'playing the great orchestral works and conducting them as I thought they *should* be conducted, with the little baton which my mother gave me. My father disapproved of the whole project, but I showed no sign of liking anything else so well as music, before my parents died. Then – we had always lived in London – Monica saw to it that I went to a Swiss school because of my health, and, as I think I've told you once before – I owe a lot to her original support and enthusiasm.'

That made me feel that I liked Monica Warr a little bit more (but not much), I thought wryly. I heard how Esmond met one of the most famous Austrian conductors in the world, and how this man had been so impressed by the boy's talent, he had taken him to Vienna University. On his return to London, Esmond formed an amateur Orchestral Society and conducted it himself.

'After that,' he said, 'I began to acquire a working knowledge of all musical instruments and to study the famous established conductors. I founded my own symphony orchestra when I was about twenty-seven. Since then I think I have been lucky – I've never looked back.'

I could feel my eyes growing big and bright as I listened, and looked at him.

'It isn't all luck. It's your own genius that has got you where you are,' I said.

'You flatter me, my child,' he laughed.

'But you have such an amazing control of your orchestras!' I exclaimed. 'Everybody says so.'

'I wish I had the same control in my own personal life,' he said suddenly, in a low voice, and flung a cigar stump into the bushes over the balustrade.

I said nothing. We could hear from the distance the strains of a waltz they were playing in the Casino dance room. I could not tear my gaze from Esmond's face, so pale, so sculptured, in the light of the Mediterranean moon.

'Funny,' he went on, 'you always lead me to talk about myself. Why?'

'I – like to hear.'

'You never talk about *yourself*.'

'There's nothing to talk about. Mine has been such a dull ordinary life compared with yours. You are a great and successful man.'

'What is greatness? What is success? *"What doth it profit a man if he gain the whole world and lose his soul?"*' he quoted.

'But you haven't lost yours.'

'You seem to know me better than I know myself...' He turned his brilliant eyes on me, smiling. 'Sometimes I think I *have* lost it.'

'I know how you feel,' I dared to say. 'But you shouldn't think about what's happened in the past. I know you remember sad things but you have so much that is wonderful now, and so much in your future.'

'You're quite right,' he said abruptly, 'I have nothing to grumble at, and since you came, I've felt sure that my two children will grow into worthwhile citizens. Soon Con will be at prep. school and you, I hope, will continue to look after Kate; and if I can feel they are going to turn out well, I shan't feel that I've let their mother down.'

(Veronica again!... I bit my lips.)

'I'm sure you've never done that and never will,' I said.

'You always make me feel good, Shelley,' he said gently. 'You seem to have a high opinion of my character. Thank you, my dear.'

I could not answer. There seemed nothing for me to say. He added:

'I don't mind admitting to you, my dear kind little friend, that the light of my life went out when my wife had that terrible accident.'

Again I caught my breath.

'I'm sure that it did,' I whispered.

'*She* was the most beautiful woman in the world, if you like,' he said.

'She looks like it from her portrait.'

'Yet what is death–' he went on, 'except the end of suffering and the beginning of a long sleep. The real horror of death lies not in the end of one's physical being but in the end of love and faith, and all that you prize most highly.'

(Oh, poor Esmond, I thought, my heart is torn for him. *She* must have hurt you so badly before she died. *That* is your tragedy.)

Now he said in a hard voice:

'What's the use of dwelling on the past. You're quite right, Shelley. But when you suggest that the future holds great things for me – maybe it is so far as far as my career is concerned – but not my personal life which is what really matters, don't you think?'

I did think so, and I agreed with him, but I went on recklessly.

'You're so young still, Mr Torrington. You may find another woman one day to mother the children.'

He stared at me blankly. I felt a little fool ... as though I had said something very tactless, and spoken quite out of turn. I felt my ears burning. But he laughed aloud.

'If you're suggesting that I might marry again – never!'

I don't know what I felt – glad or sorry. But I did remember Monica Warr telling Lucien Valguay that she thought Sophie de la Notte would make a wonderful wife for Esmond. It looked to me now as though Monica was going to be disappointed.

Esmond rose to his feet.

'The children are happy as they are with you, and their aunt, behind them. Especially *you*,' he said. 'You've more than taken a mother's place with them.'

I was enraptured to hear him say so. Now his mood changed again. He took my arm and walked with me back to the Rolls which was parked outside the Casino.

'It's past midnight. I think it's time we turned in, don't you?'

'Yes, of course,' I said.

Fumbling with my bag I dropped it. It had a weak clasp and all the French franc notes fell out. Apologising, I knelt down to pick them up. He knelt too and accidentally collided with me knocking his head against mine. One of those silly embarrassing accidents. It was quite painful and yet I felt no pain. I giggled. But he lifted me up and said:

'I must have hurt you. That was a damned hard knock, you poor child!'

'It didn't hurt, it didn't!' I said frantically.

I was right in his arms then, held suspended for a moment for a fraction of time during which the moon and the great Mediterranean stars seemed to revolve and form a glittering kaleidoscope above me. I could even feel his strong heart beats against my breast. I knew that I was desperately, *madly* in love with him. I thought he was the most marvellous man in the world. I couldn't guess what *he* was feeling except, with my usual inferiority complex, I presumed he had just about had enough of me for one evening. I was absolutely stunned when he ruffled my hair, kissed it and then kissed me on both cheeks, in true French fashion.

'You really are a darling, Shelley. I'm so very glad you came down to look after us all. Stay with us, won't you?'

The touch of his lips on my cheek had thoroughly unnerved me. I had all that I could do to prevent myself flinging my arms around his neck and kissing him back. To have heard him use that word *'darling'* ... was unimaginable bliss, although it meant nothing... I knew he just said it casually and kindly, rather as he would to one of his own children. But I must have turned white and he must have noticed it, and noticed, also, that I lapsed into complete silence and looked altogether strained, because he was tense and silent until we were in the car climbing the hill on the way back to Arc-en-Ciel.

Then he spoke:

'I hope I didn't offend you by embracing you just now.'

'No, *no*, of course not!' I said, 'I ... I *adored* it.'

I could feel him relax. He laughed.

'There's quite an emotional side to the cool practical little teacher, isn't there?'

'Oh, I *know!* I must try and curb it,' I said breathlessly.

'Nonsense,' he laughed, 'It shows you're human. I can't stand robots.'

My heart began to sing again.

'I've had such a marvellous evening.'

'I've enjoyed it too, Shelley.'

'Thank you a thousand times,' I breathed.

'Thank *you*,' he said in his courteous way.

On this formal note we parted. But that night I lay in my bed with the moon pouring down upon me through the open slats of my jalousies and I felt wide awake, restless, almost feverish. I re-lived every moment of that evening, and recalled everything that he had said. But when I remembered the touch of his lips and the clasp of his hands – for no reason at all, I turned my face to the pillow and wept, bitterly.

9

They say one pays for everything in this life. I certainly paid the price for that wonderful evening with Esmond. But I didn't care. During the night, I had wept. But in the morning I was exalted again, because he was so friendly and so charming. He drove me up the mountain side in that wonderful car which climbed and purred so smoothly; and all the way we talked. He told me more about himself. Talked music. Talked art and poetry, and when I made a few shy observations, turned his fine brilliant eyes upon me and said:

'You have a good brain, Shelley. In a way it's a pity you've had to become a teacher. I admit the excellence of your P.N.E.U. system, but teaching in any form must be a bit of a drag. Deep down inside you aren't you a little more creative and impulsive than you appear on the surface?'

I looked up at the bright blue sky and the verdant green of the mountain side. It was a beautiful, sparkling morning. I was drawn from my shell to talk to him freely. I said to him:

'Once I thought I could write. I suppose

it's silly but I wrote masses of poetry when I was young.'

An amused smile curved his lips.

'And now you are so old!'

'Well, I'm not a teenager any more,' I laughed back. 'Most of the poems I wrote when I was in my teens.'

'A lot of very young people pour their souls out in poetry. We have our Keats – and now another Shelley!...'

He laughed gaily and I with him on the play of my name. Oh, it was a blessèd happy drive up to the Hôtel de Montagne. Yet I knew somehow that once we got there the shadows would close in on me again and that I would lose him. *Paradise Lost,* and Lady Warr standing outside the gate, grimly, holding the key.

Just before we turned into the hotel grounds, Esmond said:

'One day you must come out with me again, Shelley. I thoroughly enjoyed last night. You must show me some of your verses, too. I'm never one to laugh at creative work, you know.'

'It's terribly nice of you, Mr Torrington, but... Oh, I'd never dream of showing you my feeble poems. I have none in France, anyhow.'

I saw him frown.

'Mr Torrington! How stiff and unfriendly that sounds, but I suppose you must stick to it for the sake of discipline, eh?'

Discipline!

'Yes,' I said. I would never dare address him as Esmond, yet I was enchanted by the delicate compliment wrapped up in the suggestion that he would not mind if I did.

'Will you promise me something?' he suddenly asked.

I made the answer that I remember my father always made me when I was a child.

'I never promise anything till I know what it is, or is that being too terribly cautious?'

'You're right to be so,' came his reply, and I could see that once again he was amused, 'You know, too, there is a French saying ... it's from Rousseau, if I remember right... *"Le plus lent à promettre est toujours le plus fidèle à tenir"*.'

'Oh, my French is much too bad to understand that!' I gasped.

'*"The slowest in promising is always that most faithful in fulfilling"*,' he translated, and added gently: 'I'm sure that applies to you. You are the faithful type.'

I could feel the blood scorch my cheeks. Never before had he spoken to me quite so tenderly; as though *we knew each other well*. I was dazzled and so full of joy because of that little moment, that I could hardly speak.

But after that ... the deluge!

The Dragon was in her chair waiting for us on the verandah. I did not know it but her brother had telephoned her from the villa early this morning, and she already knew about Robin not turning up. She looked like a thundercloud. Neither Sir Austen or Dr Valguay were with her. They appeared a little later, having taken a walk together. It was just before lunch.

I could see Monica literally forcing her furious face into a grimace of smiling welcome for her brother. I heard her voice as he bent to kiss her:

'What a wonderful unexpected visit, my dearest Esmond.'

'Yes, as I explained on the phone, practically the whole orchestra was laid low by this infection,' he said, 'and it wasn't the slightest good going on. Never before had they had such a general case of fever among the chaps. It was really pathetic. They tried to carry on at rehearsal and one by one they fell by the wayside.'

'So you stayed at Arc-en-Ciel last night,' she said, and now her eyes gimlet-like, turned to me as though trying to probe into mine. 'Good morning, Miss Bray,' she said in a freezing voice.

'Good morning, Lady Warr,' I answered.

'You will find the children in their bedroom,' she said. 'They are getting tidy for lunch. Yvonne has had a lot of trouble with them. They have behaved very badly.'

'I'm amazed,' I said impulsively, 'they've

been so very good lately.'

I saw Esmond's warm wonderful eyes turn in my direction. He had seated himself in a chair and was mopping his forehead with a handkerchief. The drive had made him hot.

'There you are, Miss Bray! You see how much your gentle influence is needed. Knowing Yvonne she probably drove them crazy. She is an aggravating type.'

'Really, Esmond!' protested Lady Warr with an ugly flush, 'Yvonne is the most devoted maid.'

'To you, dear,' he said, 'but not to the children. You know they never did get on with her.'

I could see Monica beginning to lose control.

'Who else can be expected to look after them if their teacher takes a day and a night off? *I'm* as you know, tied to my chair, and Lucien says it just must not happen again. I get too worried. I'm not as well as I used to be...' She stopped, gulping, trying I was sure not to show herself in her true colours to her brother.

I said:

'I'm terribly sorry I went away yesterday, Lady Warr, but I thought my brother was going to meet me.'

'But he didn't turn up,' she said.

Now I saw Esmond give her a quick frowning glance as though of disapproval.

181

'No, it was a great disappointment for Miss Bray.'

Lady Warr buttoned up her lips. She had plenty more to say but it was not to be in front of him. She dismissed me with a wave of the hand. As I left them I heard her:

'Tell me all about darling Sophie. It must have been wonderful for you to have her staying in Milan...'

I felt dismissed and reproached. 'My little hour' was certainly over. But I had a rapturous welcome from Conrad and Kate. Trying to disentangle myself from their arms and get away from their sticky kisses, and touched by their fervour, I said:

'Aunt Monnie says you two haven't been very good. Now you promised me before I left that you would be.'

'I hate Aunt Monnie,' said Kate, tossing her curly head.

I turned to Conrad. At least I was gratified that he did not immediately 'sneak' upon her. He was beginning to learn, I thought, but he looked moody and once the welcome was over, I could see that he was sulking and obviously worried about something.

I didn't question him, but it all tumbled out while he and Kate were in my room watching me unpack my night-bag. Conrad was the spokesman with Kate occasionally putting in a *yes it was* or *no, it wasn't.* Yvonne had apparently forbidden them to do any of the things which they liked doing while Lady Warr rested yesterday. She was supposed to have read to the children, instead of which she had made them lie on their beds and keep dead quiet, and not even allowed them to look at their books, because they had annoyed her during the morning. To do absolutely nothing is the one way to court trouble from small children. Didn't I know it after my training! Kate became mischievous and Conrad rebellious. When they saw their aunt at tea time Yvonne accused them of doing things they hadn't done (so Conrad assured me).

'She jolly well told lies,' he said, his handsome face mutinous.

'Hush,' I said, 'that's not the way to speak, Con.'

'Well, you jolly well told me that liars should be punished, so I put out my tongue at her,' he said.

Kate giggled.

I sighed.

'Con, my dear, you *know* that was an ungentlemanly thing to do.'

'Well, Yvonne isn't a lady,' said Conrad with some perspicacity.

His aunt of course had seen the tongue and despite her preference for him, sent him to bed for the rest of the day. (Oh, I thought, Lady Warr and her punishments!) Now Kate piped up:

'Aunt Monnie said you weren't doing Con any good, Miss Bray.'

I clenched my fingers but tried not to let either of the children see what I felt about *that*. I tried to remember that their father was satisfied, and that was all that mattered. But it wasn't.

Somehow I managed to work the children back into a better frame of mind and tried to square up everything for them, but after lunch, my turn came. Esmond took his children off in the car for a drive higher up the mountain. He would have taken me too I know, for he said so, but his charming sister said that she 'needed me', so in his courteous way he had backed out of the invitation.

In Lady Warr's bedroom she fixed me with a baleful eye and subjected me to half an hour's cross-questioning. Why hadn't my brother come? Why hadn't he let me know before I started out for Monte Carlo? Wasn't it a bit odd that I shouldn't have known about Robin until the very last moment? Why had I accepted Mr Torrington's invitation to go out to dinner? It was all very improper.

'Improper,' I repeated incredulously, having said nothing until now.

Monica's chubby horrid little hands, glistening with the jewels she loved, plucked at the silk of her bedspread. Her eyes were like blue stones.

'Well, I don't mean that anything *improper*

184

took place. Obviously not. Mr Torrington would not have the slightest interest in you nor stoop to such behaviour, but you had no right to stay down there alone with him.'

I literally stared at her, floundering.

'Lady Warr, what did you expect me to do? Walk out because Mr Torrington was in the villa and find myself a room in a hotel?'

She had no logical reply to this and made none. She went on:

'My brother told me it was very awkward for him but he *had* to suggest giving you a meal. You should have refused. You took advantage of your position.'

The nagging went on … interspersed with nasty malicious suggestions. I listened fairly calmly, determined not to be 'drawn'. By this time I had realised that this woman was a psychopathic case. She was almost insanely jealous of any female who came in contact with her brother. Even a nonentity like myself. And I was absolutely certain that Esmond had not said those unkind things about *having* to ask me out. He was no hypocrite. But what really goaded me was Lady Warr's continual suggestions that I *had known* all the way along that Robin would not be meeting me and that I had engineered the night alone at Arc-en-Ciel with Esmond.

Now she touched on the subject of the money Esmond had won for me at the Casino. Mrs Van Sylk, the American, had telephoned her as quickly as she could about this.

Monica said:

'I am told that my brother won twenty or thirty pounds and put it in *your* bag. I don't know how you could have allowed him to do such a thing.'

'I tried to make him take it back,' I protested, 'although he originally staked the amount for me and if I'd lost I would have paid him.'

She twisted her lips into an unbelieving smile which infuriated me. At that moment I decided to send the whole of that Casino win to a local charity rather than spend one franc of it on myself.

Of course I knew that with Esmond behind me, I need not really fear this woman. I could go on regarding her as a 'case' and be tolerant. Why allow myself to be upset because she never said a kind or decent word to me or showed one spark of gratitude for anything that I did for her little niece and nephew? Why care because she accused me of silly things like coquetting with Dr Valguay or making trouble with Yvonne, or causing an 'atmosphere' at Arc-en-Ciel? All the things of which she, herself, was guilty.

But one couldn't stand too much, and now she was beginning to nag again and to hit me where it hurt – not because I was anything but innocent but because her nastiness somehow besmirched my deep romantic love for Esmond Torrington.

'I think it's all very peculiar you going down to Monte Carlo and your brother so conveniently not turning up.'

'This is fantastic!' I exclaimed. 'How could I know that Esmond was leaving Milan before the scheduled time? Even his secretary, Monsieur De Vitte, didn't know…'

'Ah!' she pointed a finger at me, 'so you call him *Esmond* now, do you?'

I felt the perspiration break out on my forehead. I was angry with myself for being so stupid as to let that name slip out. I lost my temper.

'Oh, you are vile! Beastly to go on like this and try to make something wrong of a completely innocent episode.'

'How dare you call me names?' Lady Warr's voice rose dangerously high.

'How dare you make such insinuations!' I returned breathing hard and fast. 'My brother *did* put me off at the last moment. I have the telegram. I'll go and get it and show it to you. I'm glad I kept it. It came from Paris but it was delayed. Betrand said so. And I did not know about Mr Torrington coming back any more than you did. *He'll* endorse that. What is all this building up to? What are you accusing me of? What am I supposed to have done that is so wrong?'

I stopped.

I saw her shaking; her fingers tearing at the coverlet. I saw the pretty pink baby face contort into a grimace of rage and misery. Misery because she knew that she was getting the worst of the argument. But I felt far from victorious. I felt sick to the very bottom of my heart. *I hated her.* Like little Kate, I *hated* Aunt Monnie. She had spoiled my beautiful evening with *him.* Spoiled everything in a vulgar, spiteful way. And by virtue of the very fact that I loved Esmond so much, I felt slightly guilty at the memory of the joy I had felt in his warm sweet companionship.

Usually it was Aunt Monica who burst into tears. This time it was me. I heard my voice, choking:

'This is the end. I'd better leave. Everything I do seems to be wrong in your eyes. I love the children but I can't stay here any longer.'

'Miss Bray...' began Lady Warr, 'if you make trouble between my brother and myself...'

But I did not wait to hear the end of her threat. I rushed out of her room and did the sort of human thing that I might have warned the children not to do. *I slammed the door.* Then I heard Lady Warr screaming:

'Lucien! My heart ... Lucien...'

I saw Dr Valguay emerging from his room wearing shorts and a singlet. His fair hair was wet and he looked as though he had just had a dip in the hotel swimming pool. He collided with me in the corridor. When I tried to escape, he caught and held me.

'*Tiens! tiens!* What is all this about?'

The tears were streaming down my face. I struggled with him.

'Let me go.'

'*Doucement, doucement,*' he said smiling, and holding me a little tighter. 'What is the little bird weeping for? Who has upset her?'

'Lucien!' Lady Warr shrieked his name. It was as well, I thought, that most of the guests were out on the terrace lying in their chaises longues, and there did not seem to be anybody else indoors. I could not bear the close proximity with Dr Valguay. I beat my fist on his chest.

'Will you let me go, please?'

'It's the old cat, isn't it?' he murmured against my ear, 'I know her tantrums. I'll soon silence *her. Tiens!* How soft you are...' His fingers smoothed my cheek. 'How much more feminine the little schoolmistress seems when she is crying like this ... and how very *very* desirable.'

Without warning he brought his lips down on my mouth and kissed me almost savagely.

I can remember to this day how I hated that kiss. I had never had much experience of men, and Lucien was the last for whom I could feel the slightest sensuous response. I could have *killed* him. But he was strong and he obviously enjoyed kissing me. He didn't let me go easily. There were no further screams from Lady Warr. The doctor obviously knew his patient and was not worried about her heart. He just held me in that vice-like grip and, of course, it was my bad luck that poor old Sir Austen chose that moment to return from his walk and come down the corridor almost soundlessly on the rubber-soled tennis shoes he was wearing.

As he reached us, I caught sight of his face. It expressed shocked surprise. By this time I was absolutely speechless. I could imagine how I must appear to Sir Austen … my hair disordered and my face scarlet. Obviously he misunderstood. And that wretched Lucien made things worse by releasing me and saying to Austen with a little bow:

'*Pardon, monsieur,*' and added in a most oily voice with an oily laugh: '*C'est l'amour!*'

'Oh, you wretch, it isn't!' I began, 'it isn't at all.' But Sir Austen gathered his features together in a smile, shook a coy finger at us, and passed on.

Lucien tried to seize me again.

'You are exquisite. I adore you. If you will marry me I will make you Madame Valguay tomorrow.'

I screamed at him.

'I wouldn't marry you if you were the last

man on earth.'

His laughter pursued me as I hurried to my bedroom, where I flung myself on my bed and lay shaking, reduced at last to the feeling that I had been beaten by these people – beaten into leaving the children whom I now loved so much, and into leaving *him*. I loved Esmond as a great poet once put it: *'With a love that was more than love.'* But this time I was determined to go. I was not going to lay myself open to any further insults from Lady Warr, or from her doctor. His conduct had become intolerable. I couldn't even feel gratified because he had asked me to marry him.

When I got up from the bed again I wiped my face and scrubbed my lips to try and remove the memory of his kisses. A few moments later Lucien Valguay himself knocked on my door. I was glad that I had locked it. After various preliminaries, he said:

'*La* Monica sent me to fetch you. She wants to see you.'

'I don't want to see her. Go away, please.'

'You must, she is not at all well.'

'Then give her an injection,' I said, feeling beastly.

'No, no, this time it is genuine,' Valguay called to me, 'she says she lost her temper with you and wants to apologise. She is far from well.'

'I don't accept that.'

'I, too, apologise,' he continued, 'I know I had no right to kiss you just now but you looked so sweet. I'm madly in love with you. Why won't you marry me, Shelley, and let me take you away from all these people? I have a lovely villa. You'd be the wife of the best-known doctor on the Côte d'Azur and – listen – Lady Warr approves. She has just said so. Sir Austen told her what he had seen and she was delighted. I was quite surprised...'

He went on talking in this vein. I sat up, my teeth clenched, listening with a growing sense of confusion and dismay. I felt as though a net had been thrown around me and I was being hauled out of my nice safe harbour into a whirlpool. I knew in my bones, that Valguay and Lady Warr were in league against me. I knew that Sir Austen, silly nice old man that he was, had miscon-strued the whole scene and that he would repeat it to Esmond. They were all trying to make me admit that I was having a love-affair with Dr Valguay. I felt awful, and angry to an extent that could not be measured. But it was an impotent rage. It left me with a feeling that I just did not know what to do next.

Of course I realised now as after other scenes with Monica Warr, that she felt she had gone too far, and once having recovered herself was loth to be the cause of my leaving. She did not want to fall out with her brother. But this time I could not forgive her. Her tirade against me had been too vicious.

Finally Lucien Valguay went away, baffled.

Then Lady Warr wheeled herself along the corridor and started to call to me outside the door. She asked me to let her in. I kept telling her that I didn't want her apology and I didn't want to stay with her or in her brother's employ a moment longer. I imagined that she felt rather desperate because she began to wheedle me.

'Don't be the cause of trouble, please. You aren't really like that, Miss Bray. You're a kind little thing. Surely you don't want to cause trouble,' she kept saying.

But I didn't care at that moment what trouble I caused. I just wanted to get away from them all. Lady Warr began to talk in a way that infuriated me afresh.

'Poor Lucien's so upset that Austen saw you two kissing ... but I never dreamed that you and Lucien... I mean, I'm only too pleased, my dear. You have my blessing!'

I sprang to my feet. I was trembling.

'Oh, go away Lady Warr. Please *go away* and stop saying such things. Your doctor kissed me against my will, and I have no intention of marrying him. I'm going back to England tomorrow.'

'The invalid' had been sitting outside my door arguing with me for about three quarters of an hour. By now I suppose she was tired, because she said:

'Oh, very well.' Then there was silence.

I began to collect my clothes together in a sort of frenzy and packed my suitcases.

In the middle of this I suddenly noticed for the first time a little vase on my dressing table. There was no water in it. The water had been forgotten, and there were only four dead-looking flowers. Underneath was a note which I examined. It had been written by Conrad. It said:

Welcum home we luv you.

That broke me. I could see that the flowers had been gathered from somebody's waste paper basket, but it was a gesture and from a boy who had bitterly resented me when I first came. And now I was going to leave him. How could I even *contemplate* deserting those children who had nobody to teach them sound common sense or stand by them in their father's absence? I asked myself. He had entrusted them to me yet I was preparing to abandon them.

I took the withered flowers out of the vase. I held them in my hands and I cried uncontrollably for a few moments. I then came to the conclusion that Miss Bray had done enough crying and that it was time she pulled herself together.

I was drenched through with perspiration. I felt hot, clammy, awful. I went along the corridor, took a bath and returned, telling myself that I must unpack my trunk again and stop being dramatic. I would go on looking after Con and Kate, no matter what I suffered.

I slipped into a pair of cotton jeans with a blue and red Italian striped sleeveless cotton top which I had bought in Cannes. I sat down at my dressing table, and was just about to repair my face and try to make myself look presentable before Esmond and the children came back, when I heard a voice outside my door (everybody seemed to be coming to my door today, I thought wryly). But this time it was a voice that made my heart leap and the colour fly to my cheeks.

'Are you in there, Miss Bray? Shelley, are you there? I want to speak to you for a moment.'

I walked to the door and opened it. Esmond stood there. His face was brown from the sun but he looked grave and unsmiling.

'Can we talk for a moment, please, Shelley?' he asked.

'Yes, of course,' I stammered.

I saw his gaze travel around my room and rest on the open trunk, and the litter of clothes and tissue paper on my bed.

'So you *are* leaving,' he said.

'No ... yes ... that is I was...' I began.

I felt an idiot, absolutely unable to answer him coherently.

He looked me up and down. I thought he must be thinking that I was a sorry sight with my hair still unbrushed and my nose shiny and my eyes bunged up with weeping. But he muttered:

'Always trouble in this family. Nothing but these damned scenes. When will they ever end?'

I remained silent. I didn't know what he meant, but abruptly he suggested that I should take a walk with him in the garden. He wished to discuss my departure, he said. *Oh, God,* I thought, *now he is going to tell me to go!* The children were with their aunt in the dining-room, he said, having their tea.

'I'd like to speak to you alone,' he said.

So I found myself with him down beyond the swimming pool in a sort of attractive English rose-garden that had been made with a rustic seat and one of those marble statues of which they are so fond on the Continent.

A simpering silly-looking nymph, I thought, on a pedestal, coyly hiding her breasts with crossed hands. (It's funny how little details like that strike you even when your mind is full of feverish conjecture, like mine.) Esmond bade me sit down.

When he, too, was seated, he leaned forward, locked his fingers, and with a scowl that reminded me of his small son, he said:

'I've had a bit of a shock. My sister tells

me that you have given her notice and that you wish to leave us at once.'

'Well, it's like this...' I began, but he interrupted:

'I also understand from my brother-in-law that you are on rather shall I say, *intimate* terms with Dr Valguay.'

'No, that *isn't* true!' I exclaimed.

He did not look at me. He went on:

'I must say I had rather imagined you did not even particularly like Lucien Valguay.'

'I don't– I–'

'My dear,' he interrupted yet again, and this time cocked an eyebrow and gave me an unbelieving look. 'Austen saw you locked in an embrace. Was that how you show your dislike?'

All my sense of injustice and indignation flared into revolt. I sprang up.

'This is the sort of thing that is being levelled at me by all of you and I won't stand for it!'

'I don't understand,' said Esmond slowly, 'Were you or weren't you kissing Valguay?'

Now even to him, my adored one, I became explosive and resentful:

'I don't see that it's anybody's business even if I *had* been kissing Dr Valguay of my own free will. As a matter of fact, I wasn't. He forced it on me–'

'Ah! So it's like that,' broke in Esmond more softly, and strangely enough his brow cleared – or at least it seemed strange to me because I don't see why it should matter to him one way or the other. 'I wondered,' he added. 'Only Austen seemed certain that you were enjoying it.'

'I wasn't!' I breathed, *'I wasn't!'*

'And my sister said she thought you had some secret understanding with Valguay.'

'It isn't true.'

'Then why have you suddenly decided to leave?' he asked, watching me intently. 'My sister thought it was because you intend to marry Lucien Valguay.'

'Oh, it isn't *true!'* I repeated desperately, feeling the whole thing piling up on me again.

'My dear, please believe me, I regard it as your affair if you *want* to become Madame Valguay. I'm really rather surprised that our Lucien means business. He's a noted philanderer. But of course you're a very unusual and charming girl and perhaps…'

'Please stop it,' I interrupted, and I think I must have looked white and so upset that Esmond became conscious of my distress. For he, too, stood up. He said:

'I feel I ought to warn you … you're so very young, despite all your wisdom, and all the things you teach my children, you aren't experienced. I couldn't bear the idea of you being led away by a fellow like Valguay unless marriage is really his aim – and yours

– just as I don't want you to leave my children unless it *is* to get married.'

I had the greatest difficult in maintaining mastery of myself.

'Oh, heavens!' I exclaimed, 'can't you understand. I don't *want* to marry anybody and least of all Dr Valguay. Don't you believe me? Can't you see it's all a put-up job?'

Now he looked puzzled.

'Put up by whom?'

I looked away – straight into the silly face of that silly nymph. I wished *I* could be turned to marble and stand there in her place, unable to feel *anything* … unable to be hurt, through hundreds and hundreds of years.

'Oh, it doesn't matter. I don't know what I'm saying. Please let me go. Let me go home.'

'You mean to England?'

'Yes, perhaps it would be better.'

'I'm sorry,' he said, 'I can't tell you how sorry. I just don't know what the children will do without you.'

I thought of those withered flowers on my dressing table. I thought of returning to south Norwood, to that deadly life I had left behind me. I thought of leaving *him,* and of the children's distress when I told them that I was going. In a voice of despair, I said:

'I won't go. Please let's forget everything that has happened. I'll stay.'

Esmond had been standing with his face averted from me. Now he swung round again, and I could hardly credit the pleasure that I saw in his eyes. He really was pleased, I thought, *really!*

'Shelley, I don't want you to stay against your will, but I honestly would hate to lose you,' he said. 'The children did nothing but talk about you, this afternoon, and describe their work and the new charming life that you have made for them. Since their mother died they've had nothing like it. She adored them ... poor Veronica...' He broke off, and drew the back of his hand across his temples in a weary way that went right to my heart.

'I won't leave,' I said quickly, 'Lady Warr doesn't like me, I know it, and sometimes I have felt it might be better if I left, but I don't *want* to go – I swear I don't.'

'Then please stay with us, my dear,' said Esmond and held out both hands with so impulsive a gesture that I, on an equal impulse, placed mine in his.

'Poor child, you're trembling,' he murmured. 'You look thoroughly shaken.'

'I'm all right,' I muttered, but despite myself clung on to his hands with all my strength. It was as though after swimming in stormy waters, feeling myself about to drown, I had touched a rock to which I could hold and save myself.

His fine face, strangely altered, strangely

moved, came closer to mine.

'Do you know, Shelley, I don't think I would like to see you marry Lucien Valguay. As Monica's physician he may be all right, but as your husband – no, never!'

'He never will be!' I said, feeling suddenly light-headed and crazy. 'I couldn't love him if he was the last man on earth. I told him so.'

'But you *could* love. It's in you to love,' said Esmond in a low voice.

I nodded. I dared not speak. And then it happened. He drew me into his arms and he kissed my mouth; not fiercely and greedily as Valguay had done, but with tremendous tenderness. Oh! it was the sweetest, most wonderful kiss that any girl could imagine either giving or receiving in this world. Still feeling quite crazy, I surrendered myself to its sweetness. My lips moved under his – I knew that I loved Esmond Torrington to distraction, no matter what he felt for me, no matter if this was no more than a kiss from a man who felt suddenly full of emotion and was relieved because he wasn't going to lose what he prized – the right companion for his children.

But just for that moment the world stood still for Shelley Bray – I could have shouted aloud to the mountain-tops:

'I have been in his arms. I have felt the touch of his lips. I could die for him!'

Just for that moment, ridiculous though it may seem, I felt that the great Esmond, the maestro, the conductor who led the finest orchestras in Europe and was world-famous, belonged to *me*.

Then I crashed from the pinnacle of ecstasy. He moved back from me. He took my wrists and *pushed* me away, almost as though angry with himself for that moment of intimacy. He said:

'I shouldn't have done that. I think we're all a trifle off our heads today. It must be the mountain air.'

I gave an hysterical laugh.

'Yes, that's what it is. They say it's like champagne up here, don't they?'

He looked sterner than I had ever seen him. Only much, much later on, did I know that he, like myself, was struggling to hide what he really felt. He said:

'Come along. Monica's very upset. Just tell her that you won't walk out. I know she doesn't want you to. And as for Valguay, I'll inform him that if he tries any more funny stuff on you, he can get out and stay out or attend my sister in another house.'

'Oh, I'll tackle him!' I said quickly, nervously. 'Please say nothing to the doctor. It will only cause more trouble.'

I couldn't of course guess what was in Esmond's mind, but it struck me then that that kiss from him was something he regretted, and that the sooner *I* put it out of my mind the better. Not that I ever would, I thought. Oh, not that I ever would or could. To love him was to *live*. But I would have to learn to live apart from him. I was no child – no silly, sentimental Victorian, blushing and putting the wrong construction upon a single kiss. He had just meant to be kind, that was all, and he didn't want me to leave his children. That was final.

I set my lips and said:

'I'll behave myself in future, and please forgive me for letting my feelings run away with me.'

'*Your* feelings?' he asked, and I thought he eyed me strangely now.

'I mean ... oh, I don't know what I mean,' I stuttered, 'but this is where I must start being Miss Bray again, the practical sensible teacher. Please will *you* tell Lady Warr that I'm going to stay. I'd rather not face her just now. Tell her I'll try to be more what she wants and I'll never leave the children while they want me; that is, while *you* want me to stay with them.'

He frowned. He seemed to me to be repressing something ... to have lost all that spontaneous boyish gaiety which had been so glorious to watch while I was with him last night. He did not look again in my direction, but lit a cigar and walked with me in silence back to the hotel.

10

NOVEMBER.

I had now been governess to Esmond Torrington's children for nearly six months. Half a year, I kept telling myself incredulously, and despite all the storms that blew up so regularly, I seemed to have weathered them. I was still at Arc-en-Ciel.

In the schoolroom, I sat one afternoon correcting some sums that I had given both the children for a 'test' yesterday. They were resting. The work was not bad. Conrad's was generally rather untidy and smudged, but correct. On a little tray stood a pile of numbers made with counters – small Kate's way of learning her sums. She was much more orderly.

There were times when I worried about Conrad. He was a far more disciplined agreeable child now than when I had first come here but still subject to outbreaks of defiance, and he even slipped back at unfortunate moments to telling lies or being unkind to Kate. Such times were made more difficult for me because of Lady Warr's interference. If she got to know about the trouble, she took Conrad's side. Kate had learned to be no more demonstrative to her aunt who held the fact against the little girl with lack of understanding and petty vanity that amazed me.

But I was really beginning not to be amazed too often by Monica Warr. I knew her too well by now. That Monica whom Esmond only glimpsed in flashes, and then, busy with his full life, forgot.

But living with her as I did – perpetually suffering through her tyranny and petty malice – I realised what a jealous, revengeful woman she was.

I finished correcting my pupils' work and walked on to the terrace for a moment. I felt strangely limp and exhausted in spite of the fact that it was cooler these days in the Midi. Perfect weather, in fact. The blistering heat was over. I had also had to cope with the mistral once or twice – those humid days of mists and winds that made one feel cross and tired, and kept the children indoors.

Lady Warr was always worse during such weather. She rushed around the villa in her wheel-chair, picking faults generally, not only with me but with everybody. Sometimes when I heard her nagging at her husband, I wondered how poor old Sir Austen stood it so cheerfully. He never failed with his *yes, darling'* or *'no, darling'*, and she took full advantage of his devotion.

Since we came back from the mountains, I hadn't seen quite so much of Dr Valguay for which I was thankful. Maybe he had decided that I was 'no go', or maybe, without telling me, Esmond had said something to him. Not that Lucien showed it to me, for when he did come to see her ladyship, which was two or three times a week, and I happened to run into him, he still tried to induce me to meet him alone. He embarrassed me by those long passionate glances from his sensual eyes. Once or twice Lady Warr asked me openly if I would not like to go to a concert or dance with the doctor and was livid because I politely but firmly refused.

Yes, there were always little 'scenes' between dear Monica and myself. She was determined not to stop showing that she hated me, and she never seemed to get over that night out that I had with Esmond instead of meeting my brother. However, Robin did eventually get leave and came to see me.

It was in October. Lady Warr was forced to let me off for a day or so because I was bold enough to invite Robin to the villa and introduce him to her. He asked her to give me a holiday. She was treacle-sweet to him. She put on one of her 'brave little woman' acts. Afterwards, when Robin took me out to lunch he said that he thought my boss was 'rather charming'.

'Must have been a good-looker, too, before she got so plump through being confined to that chair,' he said.

'You can call her anything you like but she's never *ever* charming,' I said dryly.

'Oh ho! I know my Shelley. What's she done to you?' He grinned at me across the table in the little café where we had just had a dish of *escargots* which I had learned to enjoy. 'You don't like her ladyship, do you?'

'Didn't you guess it from my letters, Rob?' I asked him.

'I suppose so, but I didn't think you positively *dis*liked her.'

'I always write cautiously. I think letters can be dangerous.'

'But surely you can write the truth to your own brother,' said Robin.

I smiled at him fondly. It was rather fun being with my brother again. He looked so clean and fresh and thoroughly English in his grey flannels with an R.A.F. tie. It was like old times having a meal with him and discussing life. But whereas I have always been introspective and analytical – Robin was a happy-go-lucky boy without much depth in him. A good sportsman, he was more interested in games and flying than in people. He really wasn't interested in analysing Lady Warr's character, but because he was deeply attached to me, he was interested in whether I was really happy here or not.

'Of course that villa is smashing – absolutely Hollywood,' he said. 'You're living like a Princess. And the kids seem very attached to you but you don't look really happy to me. *Are* you?'

'Oh, yes,' I said on a rather high false note, 'why not?'

He lit a cigarette and stirred his coffee.

'I don't know. You've changed.'

'In what way?' I asked, rather nervously.

'Well, in a funny sort of way. Of course, living in the South of France with rich people like these has given you more poise and you're jolly smart, even in your jeans. Your hair's beautifully cut. Shorter at the back now, isn't it? You're looking very attractive, my dear Shelley, if a mere brother may say so.'

'How much do you want to borrow?' I parried, teasing him as in the old days when he flattered me.

'No – seriously. You look, very, very nice, Shelley, and there's a sort of *new* look about you. But it's a sad one. Have you fallen in love?'

I had been praying that he wouldn't ask me that but as the hammer hit the nail on the head, I felt the old tell-tale blush sting my cheeks. Robin was quick to notice it.

'So you have! Well, jolly good luck to you. I'm rather keen on a little blonde whom I met at one of the dances in the mess the other day.'

'Tell me about her,' I said hurriedly.

He said there was nothing to tell except that he had fallen for this girl, Pattie was her name, and he would be writing to me later to let me know whether it was serious or not. He didn't intend to get officially engaged or married, he said, until he was further ahead with his career. There was plenty of time. He was having a whale of a time now. Flying fascinated him. But he had often thought that *I* was wasting my life – just teaching kids. What a dreary sort of routine job! He *wanted* me to meet someone I liked and get married. But not a Frenchman, he added, with his youthful grin.

'For lord's sake don't cotton on to one of these hand-kissing chaps and go right away from me and live in France for the rest of your life.'

'I assure you I won't marry a Frenchman,' I said, 'although I have met some very fine ones at Arc-en-Ciel.'

'That chap that I met going out of the villa just as we were going into it – he gave you a saucy look, I thought.'

I shuddered. Of course the 'chap' had been Lucien. I had had to introduce him to Robin. Then as Robin got nothing more from me about the Frenchman, he rather relentlessly turned the focus upon my employer.

'What sort of a fellow is the Great Conductor when he's at home?'

Now I felt all my muscles tense. I tried passionately to keep calm and pull the wool over Robin's eyes.

'Oh, delightful,' I said casually, 'and of course it's a great thrill to live in the home of such a celebrity. One basks in the lime-light.'

'Is he young?'

'Older than us but well under forty.'

'Have you fallen for *him?*'

I thought desperately:

I won't tell Rob. I won't own to it even if I've got to do the one thing I'm already preaching to the children that they *mustn't* do.

So I lied, crazily:

'Of *course* not.'

Mercifully, Robin stopped probing. He paid the bill and we wandered down to the *plage* where he wanted a dip.

After that pleasant interlude with my brother, life seemed to go on much the same at Arc-en-Ciel. But Esmond... Esmond whom I loved so crazily and whose sole embrace I could not put out of my mind even though the long weeks went by ... I saw far too little.

After the Monte Carlo concerts he always seemed to be away. He was touring Europe. He had a short season in Venice. He was a guest conductor in Holland. He was due to come back for the opera season here, where *Tosca* was to be performed. A week ago he had taken a short rest, but he was madly busy – always shut in his studio with opera soloists or members of the chorus or orchestra, or down in the town for rehearsals, or dictating letters to Monsieur De Vitte.

I saw him only at meal times with the children. Once or twice he drove us down to the *plage*, but Lady Warr saw to it on all occasions that Sir Austen came too.

Rather bitterly, on this, the last day of November, I considered the fact that I had not seen or spoken to Esmond alone since we were up at Mont Viso. With one exception – when he happened to come out in the garden and found me picking some flowers. (I now did all the flower arrangements at Arc-en-Ciel.) He happened to be strolling around, and I found myself beside him.

He was kind and charming but I thought he looked very tired. As he looked down at me, I felt as though my knees would give way and I'd sink to the ground – he affected me so powerfully. But I managed to talk lightly and casually about the progress Con and Kate were making in their lessons. Esmond said nothing very personal until we walked together back to the villa, then he asked:

'All going well? Valguay behaving himself?'

I looked away from him and breathed a,

'Yes, thank you.'

'Aren't you losing weight?' he asked with a sudden frown. 'I'm sure you are. You look very much thinner to me.'

I thought it was wonderful that he had noticed this. I managed to laugh.

'Funnily enough I was thinking the same about you.'

'Oh, I'm worked to death,' he said with a brief smile.

'I've followed all your tours,' I went on. 'I bought the papers and read the reviews. They said in Venice that your interpretation of Beethoven's Ninth was "titanic" – that was the word they used. And in Holland they said you brought out the most "magical tones and harmonies".'

He stared at me, wide-eyed.

'How did you get hold of all that stuff?'

'I – I was interested,' I stammered. 'I just found the various papers and got one of the interpreters at Cooks to translate the musical reviews for me.'

He gave me his sweetest and most friendly smile now.

'How very flattering. Bless you!'

Why should he bless me? I did not know. But I treasured the words, fearing to have this magical moment spoiled by Lady Warr. I ran quickly into the villa before she could come out and find us together. The next day he went away again.

When he came back it was to warn us that the Comtesse Sophie de la Notte and her small child, Renate, were coming to spend that next weekend at Arc-en-Ciel. He was bringing them from Paris. That meant tomorrow.

I stood looking out at the garden on this bright December afternoon, and felt a pain in my heart ... remembering how triumphantly Lady Warr had announced to me this morning that I was to make sure that the guest room looked its loveliest. And that I was to buy the most beautiful flowers in Monte Carlo for her suite.

I know I had absolutely no right to feel anything at all, but I was conscious of deep depression as I had marshalled Thérèse and Bertrand and supervised the preparations. A high polish for the floor ... glorious red carnations for a vase on the table in front of her verandah windows. Roses for her dressing table. Exquisite embroidered linen for her bed. And, of course, Louise had been detailed to serve up a very special dinner tonight for the guest.

Renate, the Comtesse's little girl, would share Kate's room.

I had never felt my position more keenly than that next morning at lunch time when Esmond and Sophie de la Notte arrived.

In a way, I had wanted to meet this admiring musical friend who followed Esmond around on his tours, just to watch him conduct. It was so much the sort of thing *I* would have liked to have done, I told myself sadly. She was supposed to have come here earlier in the year but had cancelled the visit for personal reasons, but now here she was.

'You will take over Renate entirely and make her very happy here and there will be schoolroom meals for you and the children all this weekend,' Monica Warr had announced to me with a rather spiteful smile, I thought.

Well, I did not mind being banished from the dining-room or the salon and having my meals with the children; that was my job and I was perfectly happy to be alone with them. What I suffered from was the anguish of being banished from *his* presence. Ordinarily, when he was at home, I did at least see him at meal times or whenever he chose to send for the children. This time Con and Kate were allowed only to greet their father on the terrace and welcome Renate; then Aunt Monnie said they were to 'fade'. I had already been primed by Conrad about what he thought of the Comtesse's little girl.

'She's more of a baby than Kate even, and she's a cry-baby, too, and last time she came she broke one of my Dinky cars and pulled the hair off Kate's best doll. And she can't speak English.'

I retaliated:

'Well, you can't speak French fluently, my boy, so don't be too critical. You're quits, and whether you like Renate or not you must remember that *you* are the host and she will be your guest so you must be nice to her.'

Kate had been troublesome ever since she heard Renate was coming. She was even rude to me, and when I threatened a little punishment she burst into tears. I then found out that it was all jealousy. She kept sobbing:

'Pwomise that you won't love Renate better 'n me.'

I laughed and kissed her and promised. The trouble cleared up. The stars shone out of Kate's eyes again.

Jealousy! Oh, heavens, I thought, *I* was the jealous one. I felt the green-eyed monster tearing at me when, on the morrow, with the children on either side of me I watched Esmond hand his lady guest out of the car.

Looking at Sophie de la Notte I failed to understand why he had not fallen in love with her long ago. She was wonderfully chic – a true Parisienne. Slim, elegant, in a Balmain tussore silk suit and wearing impeccable white gloves, and carrying a white bag. No hat, only a tiny black lace veil on a shining ash-blonde head, cut rather short in the latest fashion.

As the Comtesse drew nearer me I heard her rippling laughter and rather low-pitched husky voice. She talked in rapid French with many gesticulations of long fingers. I saw her pale aristocratic face with red, curved lips, and heavily lidded, heavily fringed blue eyes. Beautiful, soignée, poised – all the things that I was not. Despite dear brother Robin's assurances, I had the biggest inferiority complex of my life that day; standing there in my much washed cotton frock – just a little governess!

Renate looked less attractive than her mother. Presumably like her father, thin and small and dark with that sallow peaky little face that you so often see on Continental children. She wore a very short blue pinafore dress of the Austrian type, with white embroidered blouse, and she, too, had on white gloves like a true little Parisienne. She was holding on to Esmond's hand.

I looked at Esmond. Perhaps I was wrong but he appeared to me to be radiant today. He was laughing and talking gaily, also in French.

Then Lady Warr wheeled herself forward and gave the Comtesse a theatrically warm welcome.

Esmond turned to me with his usual kindliness.

'How's our Miss Bray?'

'I'm fine, thank you, Mr Torrington,' I said, tight-lipped.

He introduced me to the Comtesse.

'Sophie – you haven't met our Miss Bray. Very much our right hand now at Arc-en-Ciel, isn't she, Monica?' turning to his sister.

'Yes, of *course*,' said her ladyship, her smile becoming glacial again. Now she told me, peremptorily to take Renate and her bag, and retire to the schoolroom.

'Oh, Daddy, can't we lunch with you?' began Conrad.

I could see Esmond wavering, but before he could answer, his sister announced that it would be much better for the children to be altogether in the schoolroom today. We were having different meals anyhow.

'See you later then, kids,' said Esmond.

But for the rest of that day we didn't see him. We were driving alone with the chauffeur down to the *plage*. I knew that Sophie de la Notte was staying with Esmond. They went off to his studio. Just before tea I heard him playing records. I pictured him sitting on his sofa beside her. I imagined her big blue eyes feasting on his face. I even hurt myself by imagining him melting towards her and gathering her in his arms, *as he had once gathered me,* only much more seriously.

Perhaps he would become engaged to Sophie before this weekend ended. Who was to know?

I listened outside the studio door just for a second, anguished, trembling, despising myself for being so weak, so unutterably foolish. I heard the strains of the César Franck Symphony. A new recording – conducted by Esmond himself. It was just as the first side of the record ended. I could hear Esmond's voice:

'They played that well, didn't they, Sophie?'

And hers in French, which I understood:

'You have remarkable control of your orchestra. Such a fine balance. It's so vital. Oh, *mon cher ami,* there is just nobody to touch you!'

I waited to hear no more. What right had I to eavesdrop? I went back to the school-room. Gritting my teeth I told myself to put an end to the emotional folly which was threatening to ruin my whole happiness, and make a nervous wreck out of me instead of a well-balanced girl.

I pulled Meynell's *Farm Animals* out of the bookcase and with fingers sadly shaking, made some notes and decided to read various scraps of this to the children when they were in bed tonight.

I had trouble all the afternoon with Renate. I could speak enough French to cope with her, but she was a spoiled little thing with an unusually cruel streak for one so young. She would not co-operate or play with Kate, and she took a delight in upsetting the soldiers that Conrad started to assemble on his fort later that day.

Finally she seized a soft Koala bear that was a particular favourite of Kate's and started to dig out its button eyes. Kate set up a howl. I took the bear away from Renate. She rushed at me and grabbed it, shrieking:

'*C'est à moi! C'est à moi!*'

'It's *mine!*' bellowed Kate.

I tried to take it away from Renate. She dug her nails into my arms and actually drew blood on one wrist in a frenzied temper. Conrad saw this and the boy was suddenly seized by the chivalrous desire to defend me.

'Look what you've done to Miss Bray, you little beast!' he yelled, and before I could prevent him, he hit her across the cheek.

I do not think Renate de la Notte had ever been struck before. She stood still, holding her breath, turning quite white, then she flung herself on to the floor and screamed until she was actually sick. Nothing I could do would console her, and she went on being sick which happens to a lot of children if they are really upset, and inclined to be hysterical. I was furious with Conrad.

'A big boy like you to hit a little girl, shame on you, Con!'

'She did it to you,' he said sullenly.

'Thanks for defending me, but you never should have hit her,' I said.

Renate made a bee-line for the school-room door, and tore out, yelling: '*Maman! Maman! Maman!*'

The Comtesse, followed by Lady Warr in her chair, came rushing down the corridor. The mother clasped the child in her arms and kissed and questioned her. What Renate said then was obviously unflattering to me for the beautiful Sophie fixed me with an eye almost as cold as Lady Warr's and asked in very good English:

'Will you please explain, Miss Bray? I am most upset. The poor child says you have been very cruel to her and that you hit her.'

I tried to think of some retaliation without bringing Conrad into it. Esmond had arrived on the scene now. I knew that the boy greatly valued his father's good opinion and would not want him to know in what an ungentlemanly way he had behaved. I saw his frightened eyes. Esmond looked rather vague, but Lady Warr expressed 'absolute horror'.

'My dear Sophie, how can I *possibly* apologise to you. Your poor *sweet* little girl! *Really*, Miss Bray!'

Renate continued to wail. I could understand some of the things she was saying. Grossly exaggerated allegations against me. The Comtesse with an arm around her child looked at me indignantly.

'To have hit her – she says it was such a blow that she fell upon the ground and only because she wanted to play with one of Kate's toys. And she has been sick, I can see

– how shocking!'

I began to stammer, but Lady Warr interrupted:

'Miss Bray is very much at fault. I'm afraid she has a very much higher opinion of Kate than I have. Kate is a naughty, mean child.'

This brought a howl of protest from Kate.

I felt absolutely awful. There was a general 'schemozzle'. Everybody talked at once. Sophie then turned to Esmond.

'C'était épouvantable! Maybe I had better take Renate away from the schoolroom and look after her myself.'

'I'm sure there is some mistake–' Esmond began.

Lady Warr fearing that Sophie was so offended that she might leave Arc-en-Ciel altogether, took the Comtesse and the weeping Renate away from the schoolroom trying to comfort them. Esmond was left with me. I did not dare meet his gaze. I looked at Conrad. The boy had not yet spoken. I could see that he was dead white. He looked at me now and then away and began to bite his nails. The highly-strung little boy was obviously in a state of nerves, struggling with himself as to whether he should own up to the fact that it was he who had hit Renate or not. I found myself hoping that good would triumph – for the sake of his own moral progress. But his courage seemed to fail. For the life of me I could not 'sneak' on him even at this cost to myself. I had been so success-ful in making him believe that one should never sneak under any circumstances, I did not want to start the doubts up in his mind all over again, just in order to clear myself.

Esmond spoke to me rather more coolly than usual.

'I think Renate can be a bit troublesome, but I suppose you lost your temper. That's not like you.'

I said nothing for a second. I bit hard on my lips. Then I stammered:

'I ... the whole thing got out of hand ... she was, in fact, trying to tear up one of Kate's favourite soft toys.'

'She scratched Miss Bway,' piped Kate.

Daring to look at Esmond now, I saw him frown.

'All very unfortunate,' he muttered, and turned and walked away.

Miserably I looked after him. I could bear being falsely accused by Lady Warr, but not by *him*. I knew that I had lost his good opinion, and that he thought of me now as a bad-tempered young woman who could quite viciously strike a five-year-old girl. It might even make him agree with his sister that I should be dismissed; that I was no longer fit to look after Kate.

Yvonne came to collect Renate's clothes. As she went out with them, she gave me what I thought a dirty look. Possibly she knew that I was in disgrace, and was pleased.

The rest of that day was truly wretched. Conrad never spoke a single word and avoided looking at me. But he did not eat his supper, I noticed that. And he kept whistling very much out of tune. Conrad always whistled like that when he was upset. Sadly I watched him. I knew that the struggle between cowardice and courage was still going on inside him. Kate, too young either to understand or care what was happening, played happily by herself. She refused to let her Koala out of sight and now and again muttered that Renate was *howwid*.

None of the grown-ups came near the schoolroom again that night. I felt desolate as I ate my solitary supper after the children were in bed. Perhaps I had been rather too quixotic and I ought to have defended myself, but I did so want the confession to come from the boy himself. I wondered what was passing through his young unformed mind. When I went to say good night and tuck him up, he was crying, but he turned his face from me and refused my good night kiss. I said:

'Would you not like to tell your father what actually happened, Con?'

'No, I wouldn't,' he said sullenly. 'Renate's a beast and so's Aunt Monnie and so's everybody.'

I could see that he had a grudge against

the world, and I could also see that he was ashamed of himself but refused to admit it. So I left him.

That night I went to bed feeling heart-sick. I could not bear to remember how coldly Esmond had spoken and looked at me. I knew that he had gone down to the Casino tonight with the Comtesse. The pangs of jealousy were on me again. I could hardly bear them.

Not for the first time I felt like running away from Arc-en-Ciel.

Much later that night – after I had fallen into an uneasy sleep – I heard a knock on the door.

I switched on my light, and seeing that it was half past three, sprang out of bed, put on a dressing gown and opened the door. I wondered what on earth was the matter. To my absolutely astonishment, I saw Esmond standing outside holding Conrad by the hand. The boy was in pyjamas. His face was tear-stained but he grinned at me sheepishly.

Esmond looked very tall and rather pale in his handsome dark red silk dressing gown, and scarf. He was not smiling, but his face wore the old gentle, tender expression.

'Miss Bray ... Shelley ... we owe you an apology,' he said.

'What's all this about?' I stammered.

'Con has just come to my room and woken me up and told me the truth. I think it was weighing on his conscience heavily

224

that he did not own up at the time.'

'Oh, Con!' I said turning to the child.

He flung himself into my arms.

'I told Daddy you were a sport and didn't sneak on me.'

'And I,' put in Esmond, 'told Conrad that the finest thing anybody could do was to take the blame for somebody else rather than *be* a sneak. Even though in this case I think you were a little too good to him, your training has borne fruit. You see, he came and owned up in the end.'

'Thank you, Con darling,' I whispered in the boy's ear.

Esmond held out his hand to me.

'Thank *you*, Shelley. I shan't forget this and I'm sure Con won't either. It's been a wonderful lesson to him.'

I felt nervous but I was deliriously happy again and full of pride in my pupil. Just imagine, I thought, the little chap waking up and rushing along to his father's room to clear my good name. Bless his heart!

I felt Esmond's firm warm fingers around my hand. I saw him look down at me with a gratitude that I did not feel I really deserved. He said:

'I will see, of course, that the Comtesse and my sister know about this, too, in the morning. They will be told that nothing more is to be said to Conrad. I want no more punishment. I think he has suffered in his way, quite a lot.'

I kissed Con again and bade him run along to bed. Then Esmond said to me:

'My word, what a difference your teaching has made to my small son. If he grows up dishonest or a coward, it won't be *your* fault.'

'I'm glad he told you about it himself,' I said.

'So am I, but I could wring that little Renate's neck,' he said with his quick sudden smile. 'I understand she drew blood.' And he took my wrist and examined it. But I snatched it away.

We began to laugh. I was reassured. All was well between *him* and me – that was all that mattered. I fed richly on the crumbs that were thrown at me. They appeased some of my intolerable hunger.

'Dear little Shelley, good night, and thank you again,' he said.

That next morning Lady Warr (obviously forced into it by her brother) sent for me and expressed her admiration for the way that I had 'handled the situation'. Sophie de la Notte, later on, apologised.

Between them the children had confused her, she said, and she had thought quite the wrong thing, and falsely accused me. She hoped I would forgive her and forgive Renate, and take her out again.

Of course I did and had my work cut out

to keep peace between the three antago-
nistic children. But I managed it. And
although Esmond and Sophie drove into
Cannes together to see some musical
friends, and I envied her passionately and
did not see Esmond again alone for the rest
of that weekend, I had my memories to
sustain me. Memories of what he had said
to me in the early hours of the morning.

11

Esmond was away all the rest of December, until Christmas Eve when he returned from England. He had been giving a series of concerts at the Festival Hall, up in Liverpool and Manchester; all the leading musical centres. At first it had been suggested that we should all go to London and stay at the Torringtons' house in Eaton Square, but Lady Warr vetoed this. Her health was not good, she complained, and she did not wish to exchange the sunny Riviera for the fogs and chills of London. (She did not want to leave her precious Dr Valguay either – I knew that – he was far too ready with his tranquilisers and sleeping pills and to agree that she 'suffered'; whereas her medical adviser in town might well have disagreed.)

The weather remained sunny but colder, crisper, down here on the Côte d'Azur. I think the children benefited from it, and I certainly enjoyed more energy than I had done during the summer. On the whole, December had so far not been a memorable month, apart from the usual skirmishes with her ladyship and various attempts to escape from Lucien's amorous eye.

Then came Christmas. I always used to love Christmas even after my parents died, when I and my brother were alone. I liked to share it with the children I was teaching at the time. But now I had my own two special pupils to cherish and we spent happy hours making paper chains and big scarlet bells; silvering pine cones; and fashioning pretty festive centre pieces for the table.

The schoolroom table seemed always to be laden with tinsel and red satin ribbon and all the paraphernalia of 'Noël' as they called it over here. *Père Noël* – Father Christmas – was just as real to Conrad and Kate as he used to be to me. Their excitement grew more and more intense as the 25th approached. There was much talking about the size of the stockings that would be hung up, many notes, asking *Père Noël* for the presents they wanted, were written and sent up the chimney. We had a log fire burning in the schoolroom now as well as the central heating.

I must say the villa was very warm and extremely agreeable to live in during a season that for me, as a rule, meant the agonies of cold and chilblains and all that the once hard-up Miss Bray of south Norwood used to have to endure.

I enjoyed these Christmas preparations. I was heartened by the children's delight. But deep down inside me I was still rather sad and lonely. I could not stop thinking about

Esmond and missing him. This was the longest he had ever been away from home. The days dragged. I would have given anything in the world to be able to write to him as his children did. The only news I got was through them. Monica, ever spiteful, seemed deliberately to withhold his name from my hearing and never mentioned any of the news that came in his own letters to her.

Every morning I scanned the English papers – particularly *The Times* – for the music critic's page. In that way I knew a *little* of what was happening in his particular sphere. I was thrilled because one review described him as *Torrington the Great*. There was a photograph of him too – handsome, immaculate, in white tie and tails and with a carnation in his buttonhole – as I had so often seen him; baton raised, just before the opening of some Overture which he was conducting.

The review said:

Not for years have we heard Beethoven's Fifth so superbly played. Every man in the orchestra seemed to respond to the dynamic personality of this superb young conductor. He extracted all the nobility and grandeur of the work, keeping a fine balance that we shall long remember.

I cut out the photograph and the review like a silly sentimental schoolgirl, I suppose, pasting it in my scrapbook where there were already so many 'scraps' about Esmond Torrington.

When at last on Christmas Eve he came home, I felt more than an ordinary thrill. With the children hanging on to either arm, he came buoyantly into the schoolroom laughing and talking to the pair of them. I saw his fine bright eyes smile warmly at me.

'Hullo there! Back at last. Merry Christmas, if it isn't a day too early, and how is our Miss Bray?'

'I'm fine,' I said, 'and I hope you are too.'

'A bit tired, but we had a wonderful tour and nobody need ever say that old England isn't the most musical country in the world. How nice you look...'

Just those few words of praise but enough to set my heart beating, my spirits soaring, and to make me feel that it was worth while having spent hours of my spare time making this dress for the winter. A wheaten-coloured wool, with a wide, studded tan leather belt which I had bought, rather extravagantly, in Cannes.

I blushed even harder when Esmond noticed that belt.

'What a waist, too – the belt suits you. A most Victorian looking waist. What is it – eighteen inches?'

'Certainly not. It's twenty-two inches,' I found myself giggling and relaxing as he teased and flattered me. Oh, it was good to have him back! He walked around the schoolroom, examining the monster scarlet bell we had made and hung over the table; admiring our colour schemes, and stopping in front of the little crêche which the children and I had taken great pains to create. We had removed some of the books from a shelf and formed a niche and put in it a little crib and some of Kate's toy animals on real straw, with cardboard figures of the Holy Family. Bertrand had helped me to fix a bulb up over it all, so that the tableau could be illuminated.

'How absolutely charming!' exclaimed Esmond.

'It's the Baby Jesus in the crib,' exclaimed Kate who was in a fever of excitement. 'And I made the donkey, and Con and I can sing *While Shepherds Watched*. Shall we sing it to you, Daddy?'

He picked her up in his arms, put her on his shoulder and smiled at me.

'All the Christmas magic and you are the magician, Shelley. Come along to the studio, all of you.'

(Just now and again that Christian name slipped out, despite his efforts to remain formal and disciplined. How I loved it!) I hoped that Lady Warr would not come trundling down that corridor in her chair to spoil it all. Fortunately the nurse, who always visited her at this time, and Yvonne were giving her ladyship a bath so she couldn't possibly be up for another hour.

We all trooped into Esmond's studio. He flung himself down on his couch and laced his long fingers behind his head. He sighed:

'It looks dreary in here after your Christmas festoonery. Now what about these carols?'

'Play for us, Miss Bray. Play for us,' said Conrad. 'Daddy, Miss Bray plays jolly well.'

'Nonsense, Conrad,' I began.

'I see you have a firm admirer in my son these days,' smiled Esmond. 'Well, go ahead – play for them.'

'In front of you!' I gasped.

'My dear child, I'm not going to criticise. I've had my fill of critics, and we're all off-duty. Open the piano.'

Then Conrad, always unpredictable (and I certainly never anticipated that anything like this would be running through his mind), said:

'Mummy used to play carols for us with one finger. Miss Bray does it with five fingers on each hand.'

Silence. The dreamy relaxed look on Esmond Torrington's face was replaced by that sinister mask that I could never explain. But his lips smiled.

'Yes, yes,' he said vaguely.

'Do you *'member* Mummy playing the

carols?' persisted Conrad.

Hastily I put out a hand and caught his arm.

'Come, help me open the piano.'

Conrad wriggled away from me. He was nothing if not obstinate.

'Do you *'member*, Daddy?'

'Yes, I do,' he said abruptly. 'Now go and sing your carols.'

But the magic had gone. I felt nervous and distressed as I sat down at the big concert grand and played the opening bars of *While Shepherds Watched*. It was a glorious instrument to touch. I remember so well that day when the Duchesse Secundo di Freitas had drawn such beautiful music from it. Kate and Conrad now did their stuff and sang their carol quite creditably if not always in tune. Esmond, keeping his face averted from us, called for an encore – without real feeling, I thought – with none of his former gaiety. They also sang *Good King Wenceslas* and *Away In A Manger*. Esmond applauded and appeared to try and pull himself out of his sudden depression. He fetched a suitcase, opened it up, and found some parcels which brought squeals of interest and excitement from his children, but he said they weren't to be opened until tomorrow. They were for Christmas. And now he handed a biggish parcel to me.

'For you.'

I caught my breath. The joy I felt must sparkle in my eyes, I thought, as I looked up at him and stammered my thanks.

'You shouldn't have ... I didn't expect ... oh, *really!*'

'It's nothing,' he interrupted. 'A trifle. But you've been so very good to these kids. They've benefited more than you know by your teaching and companionship.'

'Thank you again,' I said my pulses racing, and my fingers clung to the long rather flat parcel, wondering what on earth it could be. But it was from *him.* I didn't care now if nobody ever gave me another present.

With my precious parcel under my arm I prepared to leave the studio. Conrad then unfortunately brought his mother's name up again. He hadn't done so for months. I presume the whole association of ideas must be connected with Christmas. He remembered the last Christmas with *her.* He said:

'Miss Bray plays better'n Mummy, doesn't she, Daddy?'

'Much better,' said Esmond coldly, and seeing my distress, added in a low voice: 'Don't let it worry you,. He doesn't do this often.'

Conrad was picking up the parcels he had just dropped.

'No, he doesn't, but I'm sorry...' I began.

'There's nothing to be sorry about,' interrupted Esmond. And then as though to try and put things right: 'It's quite natural for the boy to speak of his mother. He just seems to have been unusually dogged about it today. I think it's because the first Christmas after she – died, he particularly missed her.'

'It'll fade. I don't suppose he'll mention her at all next year,' I said hurriedly.

The children ran out of the room. They went to place the presents from their father amongst those already stacked under the tree in the salon. Lady Warr had organised this. Presents from the tree were apparently distributed with royal formality by Monica to everyone after lunch – not before.

Esmond pulled one of his favourite cigars out of his pocket and pierced the end of it. His brows were contracted. Now I could see how very tired he looked. He said:

'Children are lucky. Their memories are seldom bitter. They have simple minds. They forgive and forget quickly. I wish we older ones could do the same.'

I kept silent, as always when I knew that he was referring to, or thinking about, Veronica.

'Perhaps,' I said gently, 'children do not harbour unhappy memories with any bitterness because they are not usually introvert – like so many adults. They pour things out and so the trouble seems to grow less.'

Esmond began to walk up and down the

room lighting his cigar. He was still frowning.

'There are some things one *must* keep locked away. You might understand my feelings more fully, for instance, if I could be more frank with you. But I can't.'

'Please don't try – don't worry about what *I* think or feel, anyhow,' I said hastily, 'I'm perfectly happy.'

'Dear little Shelley – are you?' Now he turned and gave me the full sweetness of his smile. 'I hope so.'

'Very happy,' I said, and it was true at that moment. I was – I was on fire with happiness because he was sharing some of his own thoughts and feelings with me. He murmured something in French. My quick ear caught it.

'"*Le bonheur semble fait pour être partage.*" Racine said that. You prove it.'

I translated in a whisper.

'"*It seems that happiness is made to be shared*".'

'Yes,' he nodded, 'and you give out so much of yours to all of us.'

I was quite nonplussed. I did not like to say so but I felt mighty sure that Esmond's sister would not think that I gave out any happiness at all. However with Esmond's kind words ringing in my ears, I retired, and followed the children into the salon.

I looked for a moment at the tree which

stood in front of one of the windows. A very handsome glittering tree. We hadn't been allowed to decorate it. Her ladyship had sat in her chair, issuing instructions to Yvonne. It was a brilliant but conventional Christmas tree, hung with expensive ornaments and loops of silver tinsel. A most richly dressed silver angel was fixed on the top and it was all lit up by electric candles. Underneath, lay a mountain of parcels wrapped up in scarlet tissue with stiff cellophane ribbon or white cellophane wrappings with coloured strings and bows. Presents for everybody in the house, including the staff. Even one for me. I saw my name written on a label in her ladyship's familiar loopy hand. Rather cynically I told myself it must have hurt Monica to *have* to give me a present. But Christmas was really the children's time, and all I really cared about was that it should be wonderful for them.

I did not see Esmond again that night. There was a 'grown-up dinner party' and I retired to my room and to bed. However, Lady Warr took pleasure in telling me before I went that Sophie de la Notte was coming (without Renate this time) for another weekend quite soon.

'My brother is a changed man when she is here. I do so hope … but you know what I hope, don't you, Miss Bray?'

'Yes, indeed,' I said quietly.

I left her, as usual, feeling sad, angry, deflated.

My parcel from Esmond remained unopened. I could not and would not untie the knot until tomorrow morning. It was a very masculine brown parcel tied up with ordinary string; *heavy*, nothing glamorous. But to me it was more valuable than its weight in diamonds. *What could it be?*

I woke very early, long before the time for the children to come to my bed and start opening their stockings, which I had promised as their treat.

It might, perhaps, have been six o'clock. But I could no longer sleep. I put on my light and sat up in bed with an excitement I had not known since I, myself, was a child. I lifted Esmond's gift on to my knee and began to untie the string. It was firmly knotted. I broke one of my nails, but I would not cut the string. I eked out the opening of that present, so as to savour the delight until the very last moment. Then at last the wrappings were off and on the floor and I sat there, transfixed with delight, looking at a magnificently bound blue leather score of *The Dream of Gerontius*. It was something that I had always longed to possess but could not possibly have afforded to buy. In any case, with my usual inferiority complex, I had presupposed that it would be absurd of me even to imagine I had any right to possess it. I knew nothing much about orchestral scores and couldn't follow them very well. I could only try. But of course I knew the music well. Esmond knew I did, because we had discussed *The Dream* when I dined with him that night at the Hôtel de Paris. He loved it, too, he had said.

In my scrap book there were many cuttings about that great work of Elgar's. It had often been conducted by Esmond Torrington during Easter week, in London.

There was a wonderful photograph of Elgar at the beginning; plus the poetic libretto by Cardinal Newman and a full explanation of the whole opus. On the first page – here was the great thrill – Esmond had written:

For Shelley Bray
With best wishes
From Esmond Torrington.

Just that formal signature but I was enraptured. I kept looking at the famous autograph. Esmond wrote in a clear bold hand – the name *Esmond* was firmly written with a Greek 'E', and at the end of the surname, the last stroke of the 'n' curved back and underlined the whole name.

I sat staring at it, clasping the big leather volume in my hands until my fingers ached, and I became conscious of a chill across my bare shoulders. Then I heard Kate's laughter. I knew that the children were on their way in to me. I did not want to share the joy of my Christmas present from *him,* even with them. Hastily I wrapped the bound score up in its paper again and put it under my pillow. And as I did so, I felt how sad and how unfair it was that I couldn't give *him* a Christmas present in return. First of all I couldn't afford to buy a man like that a present that was good enough for him, and secondly, I feared that Lady Warr would 'create' if I dared offer him even the smallest gift. So I had had to content myself with sending him a Christmas card.

After a riotous hour of opening stockings with Conrad and Kate, breakfast. It seemed so strange to me to spend Christmas morning in bright sunlight under a blue sky. Esmond did not join us as he often did when he was at home. I suppose he was too tired, but he came to church with us which I am sure annoyed Lady Warr who, when she saw us about to depart, immediately said that Sir Austen should go too. The poor man stared at her and murmured that he did not particularly wish to go to church, but she said:

'Now please go with the family, Austen. It will do you good.'

'Yes, darling, you're right,' the poor meek man surrendered and got into the car with us.

I had the inestimable joy of kneeling in the

pew close to my adored one. I prayed for him. I prayed that he would soon be happy, *for I knew that he was not.* I knew that the anguish of the past was still tearing at him.

When we came out of church, I snatched a second in which to thank him for his present.

'It's absolutely *gorgeous.* I can't tell you how thrilled I am.'

'I'm glad,' he said. 'I remembered that *The Dream* was one of your favourites. One day I'll show you how to follow the score.'

'Oh, that will be wonderful,' I exclaimed.

I was late at my place at the lunch table. We had turkey and plum pudding – a real English Christmas for the children. I found, just before the bell sounded, that there was a ladder in one stocking and I stopped to change it. As I passed through the hall to the *salle à manger,* I looked up at the portrait of Veronica Torrington – at that proud beautiful face in its frame of red hair; at the enigma of the smile that lifted a corner of her rather big, curly mouth. I thought:

Oh, Veronica, how could you have been *his* wife and not made him happy? What happened? What happened between you two? Oh, Veronica, think of the chance fate gave you. *To be his* ... completely his ... dear God, what *happened?*

But that question was not wholly to be answered yet awhile. But sooner than I expected, I was to discover more than a hint of the dark curtain of secrecy that hid the life and death of Veronica Torrington from me.

12

Every spare moment I had alone that afternoon, I opened my score of 'Gerontius',
studied it, and wondered if the day would
really come when *he* would help me deci-
pher its intricacies. Assuredly there would
come a concert which I could attend in
order to hear him conduct the opus. Then I
would be able to follow it with my very own
score, I told myself happily.

Lady Warr and I were coldly polite to each
other during the giving of the tree presents.
Hers to me was a bag to hold needlework or
knitting. I think she seemed determined to
keep me in my place for she said, as she
handed it to me:

'This should be useful to you, Miss Bray.'

I thanked her. There was another present
for me from Sir Austen. I don't think he was
allowed to spend as much money on me as
he had wanted because he was a generous
man by nature, and I saw him look rather
embarrassed when I opened his present and
found only a small box of chocolates. He
coughed and looked away again. The children, bless them, had each made me something. From Kate there was a little mat

stitched with red wool which she said was for my dressing table. From Conrad a bouquet of very stiff-looking artificial paper flowers. (They were starting to learn to make these sort of things.) They had made some needlework presents under my direction for their aunt. She did not enthuse over them but rather looked down her nose as she kissed them both. Then a frightful thing happened. For Kate drew away from her aunt's embrace, rubbed her cheek, and said in a piercing voice:

'Aunt Monnie's got a whisker. It scratched me.'

Conrad giggled. I caught Esmond's eye, agonised, and was thankful to see him try not to laugh. Sir Austen coughed loudly. Anybody but the woman in the wheel-chair would have passed it off as the tactless remark made by a very small child. But Monica Warr's face had gone scarlet. She looked at the poor little girl almost as though she could throttle her.

'I think you're old enough to have learned not to make rude personal remarks. You're a most unpleasant child,' she said.

Immediately Kate hung her head and began to weep. Esmond moved forward.

'I don't think she meant any harm, Monnie. Don't be cross. It's Christmas.'

'Does Christmas excuse such a disgraceful exhibition?' she snapped. 'But I blame Miss

Bray more than I do Kate. I think it's time she improved the children's manners. They are nil.'

I could see Esmond also beginning to lose patience. He patted the sobbing Kate on the head and told her gently to go back to the schoolroom with her brother and play with some of her new toys. As I followed them I heard Esmond's voice uneasily trying to point out yet again to Monica that the child was too small to realise that she had given offence by what she said. Lady Warr's high-pitched voice retaliated.

'You and I don't agree on the way Miss Bray is bringing up those two.'

I thought:

She *would* try to spoil our Christmas Day. She *would*.

I tried to forget the silly little incident. I told myself that it was time I hardened up and took not the slightest notice of Monica Warr's bad temper. But worse was to follow. Christmas was to be spoiled in earnest for all of us.

Lucien Valguay turned up at the villa at half past six to pay his compliments to his 'very special patient'. He brought her a magnificent present – a porcelain ornament that she had told him she admired in one of the big Cannes shops. Later on, I met him in the hall and he detained me and thrust a small parcel into my hand which I took reluctantly. It was a bottle of French perfume. FEMME FATALE.

'That's *you*,' he murmured in my ear. 'You're quite fatal to my peace of mind. When are you going to relent and be kind to me? I'd like you to drench yourself in my perfume and let me breathe it in, *petite adorée*.'

'Oh, don't be so silly!' I exclaimed rather rudely.

He had given me the present when we were alone. We were standing actually right under the famous portrait of Veronica. Now Dr Valguay's eyes gazed up at it, as mine had done just before lunch. It was queer how the dead woman's personality lived on through that portrait, I thought. It was so alive. Nobody ever seemed to be able to pass it without looking at it, and coming under the spell of those wonderful eyes. Said Lucien:

'It's the scent *she* used.'

I thrust the parcel back into his hand, violently.

'I don't want it, then. Take it back.'

'Now it is you who are being silly,' he said. 'Why shouldn't you be a little like her? Veronica was the true *femme fatale*. One couldn't keep away from her. Oh, I'm not surprised that the gr-r-eat Esmond was jealous.'

I tried to move away from Lucien, feeling myself stiffen with resentment, because he would persist in talking to me about the dead woman. But he caught my arm and pulled me back.

'*She* drew all men to her with her magnetism as well as her beauty. There are many model girls as beautiful but none with that strange ineffable charm. You might not believe it, my modest little flower, but you have some of it. You are not beautiful, but you have wonderful, compelling eyes, and a quiet distinctive charm of your own. What we French call a "*Je ne sais quoi*" – it is maddening!'

'Well, you don't madden me, Dr Valguay,' I said curtly. 'Please let go of my arm.'

He glanced at all the closed doors and, unfortunately for me, there was mistletoe attached to a glass chandelier just above us.

'*Tiens!* But it is Christmas. Am I not entitled to a leetle kiss under the mistletoe?'

'I've no wish to kiss you,' I snapped.

'That's what makes you so attractive. Most women like to kiss me. *She* did...' And he pointed in a dramatic fashion to the portrait of Veronica with a smug satisfied smile on his lips. 'She enjoyed my kisses – but enormously *and* more...'

'You damned liar!' said a voice from behind us.

Lucien released me. I swung round and to my dismay saw Esmond standing by the salon door. He had just opened it and come into the hall – yes, just in time to hear Valguay's last words and see that significant gesture.

Oh, God, I thought, now the fat *is* in the fire.

I never saw a man look more white about the gills than Lucien Valguay. He put a finger inside his collar as though it had become too tight for him. He began to laugh and splutter.

'You have misconstrued, monsieur ... you did not hear what I was really saying... I...'

'Till now I did not suspect that it was you!' said Esmond in a deadly voice. Then he sprang forward, and the next moment his clenched fist with full force struck the doctor on the mouth. His heavy signet ring cut Lucien's lips and loosened his front tooth. Blood trickled from them. Lucien went down on the floor in an ignominious heap. He struggled up again gasping, craven, the epitome of a coward.

'Do not touch me again. Do not dare–' he began shrilly.

But Esmond seemed to be in the grip of an ungovernable rage. Perhaps, I thought, in a daze, this was the crazy violence about which I had heard, although I had never before seen it in him. A dozen thoughts tumbled through my mind. *He was jealous.* Lucien had suggested by his words and his smile that he had been Veronica's lover; he had said that she had *enjoyed* his kisses. Esmond had not suspected Lucien, but now he did. It was too horrible. Yet in that dreadful moment I was conscious of one overwhelming fear – that my beloved conductor's sensitive and important hands might suffer. His right one was already bleeding. *Was* it his blood or Lucien's? I didn't dare think. But I saw Esmond hit Lucien again, and this time the doctor set up a loud, unmasculine scream for help.

'*À moi!* Lady Warr! Lady Warr! Sir Austen… *Bon Dieu! Sauvez-moi!*'

Again and again, Esmond hit the Frenchman, saying nothing. I hardly recognised my beloved with that wax-white face, those furious eyes, and clenched teeth.

I began to sob:

'Oh, don't … don't hit him any more … please…'

Monica and her husband now appeared on the scene. Her ladyship had just changed into a dark purple velvet house-gown trimmed with white mink and was wearing a great many pearls. She had wheeled herself down the corridor at a great pace, having heard Valguay's shrill cries. As she came into the hall, followed by Sir Austen, she looked with stricken eyes at her physician cowering on the floor with a handkerchief to his face. Blood was pouring from both his mouth and his nose.

'He is insane,' he sobbed, '*il est fou!*'

Under the delicate tinting, Monica Warr's face had turned a sickly ashen colour. She was obviously shocked. She wasn't pretending now. She gave her husband a hand. He gripped it and kept patting it and murmuring to her:

'Keep calm, my darling, keep calm. We'll sort this out. Keep calm.'

'Your brother is mad!' repeated Lucien in a croaking voice. 'I must go home immediately.'

Monica Warr stared at Esmond. He stood there looking up at the portrait of his dead wife. He did not seem to be with us any longer, I thought. Poor unhappy Esmond ... he was staring up at that wonderful face as though seeking for an answer to all the ugly questions that flitted through his brain. He had not even bothered to wipe the blood from his right hand. It dripped on to his light grey suit.

'Esmond!' screamed Lady Warr. 'What have you done? You *must* be quite out of your mind.'

'Yes, my dear chap ... what the devil ... I mean ... under your own roof,' began Sir Austen. 'What possible reason had you to attack the doctor?'

Then Esmond turned, gave them a long look – all of them and finally came to rest on me.

'Shelley,' he said in a toneless voice, 'will

251

you please instruct Bertrand to take that portrait down tomorrow and put it in the attic. It is not to be hung again and I forbid Veronica's name ever to be mentioned in this house again – by any of you,' he added ominously. Then he walked away – down the corridor towards his studio – out of sight.

'He is mad, *vous voyez!*' Lucien Valguay muttered into his handkerchief.

'Oh dear, oh dear!' Lady Warr began to cry now. 'Poor Lucien!'

'I've had enough of this house. I have been grossly insulted,' said Valguay, and brushing back his disordered hair with a theatrical gesture, marched to the front door, opened it and walked out, slamming it behind him.

I could neither move nor speak. I was too shocked. I thanked God that the children were in their rooms, in bed. Sir Austen began:

'My dear Miss Bray, kindly tell us…'

'Austen, I wish to speak to Miss Bray alone,' broke in Monica.

'Yes, my darling.'

He left us. The woman in the chair turned the wheels and moved into the salon. I followed her.

Once it seemed so beautiful, I thought, with all the lovely flowers, and so restful with the softly shaded lamps which I always admired – the great yellow velvet shades with silk fringes which had been made in

Paris. But this evening I saw no beauty – and no peace. Only ruin – and the decay of hope. The final death blow had been struck this evening at a man's love and faith in the woman he had adored.

I could even feel sorry for Lady Warr tonight. I could see her hands trembling. I said:

'Can I fetch you some brandy, or something, Lady Warr?'

'No, thank you,' she said and put her handkerchief across her lips and stared at me over it. 'Kindly sit down and tell me exactly what happened out here. What started the … the fight?'

'There was no fight,' I answered quietly.

'Why did my brother hit Dr Valguay? What started it? I have a right to know. I shall never forget the way he screamed. Poor Lucien … it was horrible…' she choked a little… 'What did he do? I wish to know.'

'Lady Warr, I don't want to be drawn into it. Please don't ask me.'

'Don't you make things worse by upsetting *me* now,' she said shrilly. 'I'm the mistress of this house. I have a right to know what happened. What were you doing in the hall anyhow? Why weren't you in the schoolroom?'

I did not sit down. I stood, clasping and unclasping my hands, feeling cold and nervous. *My thoughts were with him.* What agony was he undergoing, there alone in his studio?... And this, dear God, was Christmas night ... (peace and goodwill ... *dear God!*)

'Miss Bray,' said Lady Warr, 'I know you do not like me any more than I like you and it would suit you to torment me but don't you understand, *I must know what happened.*'

That at least was frank, I thought. I could almost admire her for her new honesty. I said:

'Very well. I will tell you. After the children were in bed, I had meant to go for a walk in the grounds and get some fresh air, but Dr Valguay stopped me in the hall. He gave me a bottle of perfume for a Christmas gift. He said it was the same perfume *she* used to use.'

'Who used?' demanded Lady Warr.

'The late Mrs Torrington.'

I could see Monica wince. Her hands gripped the sides of her chair tightly. Her diamond rings glittered in the lamplight.

'Go on,' she said.

'I told him that I didn't want the scent and then he tried to kiss me under the mistletoe.'

'That was no crime,' said Monica impatiently. 'What next?'

'I told him I did not want his kisses. He pointed to Mrs Torrington's portrait and said that *she* used to enjoy them. *Enormously* was the word he used. Then he added *"and more"*. Mr Torrington heard it.'

I broke off. I felt sick and somehow a little frightened. I heard Lady Warr mutter under her breath:

'Good heavens!'

When I looked at her again she seemed strangely shrunken and without any of her usual bombast and self-satisfaction. She, too, looked frightened. I thought: 'It takes a terrible thing like this to pierce through this woman's conceit and egotism...'

'Miss Bray,' said Monica after a pause, 'tell me frankly. Did my brother ... say anything to Lucien before he hit him?'

'Yes,' I replied, 'he called him a damned liar and said he had not suspected Lucien of such villainy.'

'What?'

'I do not know,' I said, frowning.

'But you have drawn your own conclusions?'

'Yes,' I said in a low voice.

'And I must draw mine...' muttered Lady Warr. 'Oh, that mad brother of mine to lose his self-control like that. Lucien will never come here again.'

'Would you want him to?' I asked in an astonished voice. 'After the doctor suggested that he ... that he and Mrs Torrington–' I stopped, ashamed.

'Well, what of it,' she interrupted me on a high hysterical note, 'maybe it's true. Lucien Valguay is attractive to women. And maybe he wasn't the only man to attract Veronica. She was a bad lot, *I knew her*... I'm quite sure she led Lucien on and that he was not to blame. I'm sure that my brother knows that too, but would die rather than admit it. He was always infatuated with her. *Infatuated* ... like Lucien ... like all the men ... she took them all away from me. I hated her. I still hate her. She's dead, yet now she has taken my beloved physician away from me too.'

She began to sob. I recognised the signs... Monica Warr was going out of control. I thought it was time I sent for Sir Austen. She began to beat her clenched fists against the side of her chair. Her face was ugly and distorted.

I said:

'Lady Warr, I don't know how anybody could call such a snake as Dr Valguay, a *beloved physician*.'

Those words were out before I could restrain them. But I could feel my utter contempt for Lucien Valguay, and my deep sorrow for Esmond, rising in me. I did not mind what Veronica Torrington had done. I only knew that Esmond had loved her and that she was the mother of Conrad and Kate and that I could not bear to think that she had dishonoured them – and with a man like Valguay.

Lady Warr screamed at me:

'You've always been hateful to poor Lucien. You've told tales against him to Esmond and tales against me, too. *You* have helped to promote this scene tonight. You're a wicked girl. You're after my brother ... everybody's warned me...'

But that was too much. I put my hands over my ears and ran out of the salon. I ran down the corridor. Everything had happened so quickly and it had all been so dramatic and horrible, I could not think clearly. But I did know for the hundredth time since I have lived under this roof that I wanted to run away from Lady Warr's hatred.

Then the studio door opened and before I could turn into my own quarters, Esmond appeared.

He had changed into a travelling suit, carried a light-weight coat over one arm and a brief case in the other hand. He barred my way. I could see how pale he was. His whole face was granite-hard.

'I wanted to speak to you, Shelley,' he said. 'I am driving down to Nice now to catch the next plane to Paris. Then I shall go over to London. I am going to open up my house there.'

I looked up at him. I knew that my eyes must be big and scared. I asked:

'When will you be back?'

'I'd rather never come back,' he said grimly, 'but I've got to. I've got to be here for a concert early in the New Year.'

I nodded miserably. I thought:

Everything's ruined. He was to have stayed here for the Christmas holidays.

'I'm sorry for what happened just now,' he went on. 'It wasn't a very pleasant thing for you to witness ... but I ... lost my temper.'

'I think I understand,' I whispered.

'No,' he said with a short ironic laugh, 'you don't. I don't suppose anybody does. And I don't intend to stand here and explain. Think what you must. All I do ask is that you should try to eliminate from Conrad's mind in whatever way you think best, the memory of his mother – *completely.*'

That seemed terrible to me. Impulsively, I began:

'Oh ... no ... *please!*'

'Do as I say, Shelley,' he interrupted in a harsh voice, 'and don't argue or try to use any of your child psychology. Just do the best you can to eradicate her memory. I could not stand hearing Conrad talk of her again. And for God's sake, *stay* with the children. No matter what my sister says or does, please stay with them. You're all they've got to stand between them and this bloody world.'

I gulped. I had never heard him use that word, common enough to some people. I saw that he was still under the grip of deep emotion. He added:

'I leave them to you without a single anxiety. Promise you'll consent to stay with them for my sake as well as theirs.'

I felt the tears start to my eyes as I raised them to him.

'You know that I will.'

Again he apologised for that ugly scene.

'My sister will be told of course that as long as she remains under *this* roof, Dr Valguay will not be allowed to attend her.'

I nodded.

'And make sure that portrait is down before I come back,' he said roughly.

I struggled with my tears. He looked so grey and so bitterly unhappy, I could have thrown my arms around him and tried to comfort him as I would have done his small son in a time of stress. Then he put down his coat and brief case, and took me in his arms.

'Don't cry, my dear,' he said. 'What is past, is past. One can never put back the clock. I'm facing up to that fact for the first time, perhaps. Please don't cry.'

But I was sobbing with my face against his shoulder now, clinging to him for dear life. I felt him kiss the top of my head, not once but many times, then he said:

'God bless you, Shelley. Thank you for everything.'

He walked away. I heard the front door

shut and the sound of the Rolls moving away from the villa.

I felt utterly bereft, ice-cold as though some ghastly shadow had suddenly fallen upon Arc-en-Ciel and blotted out all the sunshine, all the happiness, for ever.

I went into my own room, picked up my score of *Gerontius* and clasped it against my breast. My tears had dried. But I read as through a veil those terrible poignant words that Gerontius sings:

> '*I can no more; for now it comes again,*
> *That sense of ruin, which is worse than pain.*'

I understood that feeling. Not mine, but Esmond's. For him the loveliest memories of a once-adored wife had been ruined by Lucien Valguay.

I found it almost impossible to get back my sense of balance and well-being, although, as you always have to do when you are with children, the effort has to be made to keep them from noticing that anything was wrong. For the rest of that evening I could at least be alone. In the morning the questioning and the chattering would begin.

Boxing Day. The day when all the presents would be brought out and looked over again and 'thank-you' notes had to begin, in the schoolroom.

I kept wondering when Lady Warr would

send for me but she did not. I did not in fact see her for several days. Sir Austen came to the schoolroom the day after Esmond left looking harassed and without his usual friendly smile. He just said, in a halting voice:

'Oh, Miss Bray ... I ... er ... I don't think ... explanations are necessary, but ... er ... my wife isn't at all well. Dr ... er ... Valguay ... has been called away and an older man whom we know in Monte – Dr Raphael – is coming up to attend to my wife. Will you keep the children as quiet as possible? Er ... thank you very much.'

I asked no questions. I made no comment on that stuttered announcement. I knew only too well why Dr Valguay was having to retire in favour of another physician. And I knew that Monica Warr would not care to see me for the moment. She had been too humiliated.

I felt almost sorry for her that morning.

13

The New Year passed. February and March went by, then came April – the glorious Mediterranean spring. For reasons of her own Lady Warr chose to ignore me during that time. She pretended to be (or was) ill enough to keep to her room quite a bit. Once or twice I saw the new doctor, Jules Raphael – a nice little man with a pointed beard and pince-nez, carrying his little black bag and looking absolutely typical of the French doctors one saw in English plays. He had neither Lucien's looks or smooth social graces, but my goodness! I preferred Dr Raphael, and we always said, *'Bon jour'*, to each other most pleasantly when we met. Once I ventured to ask him how her ladyship was and he answered:

'Pas mal troublé, vou savez…' He tapped his forehead but smiled his reassurance. It was as I thought; a great many of Monica's ills were mental.

It seemed far too long before I saw Esmond again. I had carried out his request to me to have his wife's portrait taken down. I stood by, feeling miserable, while Bertrand mounted a ladder and unhooked the famous oil painting. With Thérèse's help (for it was a very big heavy frame), we carried it to the attic which ran right over the villa, and was used for storage. Bertrand kept shaking his head.

'*C'est triste, c'est triste,*' he kept on saying. Of course he had been here when Veronica was alive.

I found a large dust sheet and covered over that beautiful intriguing face. I, too, shook my head. I still did not see *how* she could have done it. Lucien instead of *him*. It didn't make sense!

We found an oil painting – a still-life of flowers and fruit by a contemporary French painter, to hang in the place of the portrait. I did not want Esmond to come back and find a gap over the hall fireplace; besides which the deep claret-coloured paper with which the hall was decorated had faded where the portrait had hung.

Esmond returned to conduct in Monte Carlo and nothing of importance happened. He went away again.

Came a cool April morning when Lady Warr sent Yvonne for me.

'Milady wishes to see the children.'

I tidied Kate, made Conrad wash his hands and took them into their aunt's bedroom.

It was, as usual, overheated, and stacked with flowers. I could see the faithful husband's work here. Sir Austen as usual hovered anxiously in the background.

'Don't let the children tire her, Miss Bray–' he began.

'Stop fussing me. I'm quite all right now, Austen. Go for a walk,' snapped Monica.

'Yes, my darling,' came the usual reply.

The children were staring curiously at their aunt. I, also. Monica Warr was a good actress. I could not believe that she was really ill but she gave a very nice impersonation of a fragile invalid, despite her plumpness. *And*, I had heard behind the scenes, she was eating huge meals. She had used less make-up than usual although her lashes had been darkened, and there were mauve shadows underneath her eyes which gave her a languid look. She wore black ... a chiffon pleated negligée. I could see how very pretty she must have been and why her husband and brother were so fond of her, whatever she had become in recent years.

She glanced towards me – a strange hostile look, but said not one word. She talked to the children, trying a little more effectively than usual to interest herself in their doings. She soon dispensed with Kate, but held out her hand to Conrad and murmured:

'Poor Aunt Monnie has been so ill.'

Like any small boy of his age, Conrad had neither understanding nor sympathy with grown-ups' illnesses, but repeated the words

I had fiercely whispered into his ear as we walked to the room.

'I hope you're better, Aunt Monnie.'

'You dear thing!' she said, and patted his cheek. 'Ask Uncle Austen to give you twenty francs and you shall buy yourself a book or some sweets.'

'Can I have twenty francs, too?' asked little Kate.

'People who ask, don't get,' began Lady Warr, then as she saw Kate's rosy face crumple, hastily said: 'You shall have *ten francs.*'

I could see that she did not want tears or scenes today. I tried to speak to her.

'I am so sorry you have been so ill, Lady Warr.'

She avoided answering by closing her eyes and pressing a hand to her breast.

'I have my palpitations again. I must rest. Children, you can go back to the schoolroom. Come and see me again tomorrow.'

She did not address me. I was made to feel in disgrace although I did not know what I had done. I suppose her ego had been badly deflated by the ugly scene at Christmas, and because she was ashamed and furious she had to have *someone* to whip. That of course must be Miss Bray.

I returned to the schoolroom, and told the children to get on their shoes. We would go down and walk through the famous Exotic

Garden, and perhaps have a peep at the museum which was a bit above their heads, but they seemed to enjoy it.

Passing the Hall wherein Esmond so often conducted, I saw the posters advertising the forthcoming concerts with the name ESMOND TORRINGTON in big letters under his photograph. He was to be here again during the month of May.

The children hopped about excitedly and pointed:

'That's Daddy!'

I looked hungrily at that fine intelligent face and wondered how I could wait for his return. Arc-en-Ciel was like a morgue without him.

That night I had promised to take kind little Thérèse to the cinema. It was a rather stupid lurid film but Thérèse enjoyed it and her pleasure communicated itself to me. She was the sole one of the staff besides old Bertrand who was always unfailingly polite and attentive to me. I felt that this was little return for her. Just as I was turning into the gates of Arc-en-Ciel after Thérèse left me, I saw a familiar figure step out of a car near by and approach me.

It was Valguay.

I would have passed on without talking to him, but he caught me up.

'Do you hate me so much that you won't even say a word to me, Shelley?'

'I don't see what we can possibly have to say to each other,' I retorted.

He gave a smile that was more of a sneer, but there was nothing of the suave, on-top-of-the-world, play-boy doctor about him tonight. He looked rather abject, I thought. He said:

'At least you can tell me how Monica is. You may not believe this but I was very attached to her.'

Attached to the wealth and all the perks you got, I thought rather unpleasantly, but I told him that Lady Warr had not been well, but was better now. Lucien made a few disparaging remarks about 'that fool Jules Raphael' – the two men cordially disliked each other – then started to sneer about Esmond.

I felt my face flame with resentment.

'Good night, Dr Valguay,' I said.

He caught my arm.

'Wait! Once when we spoke together, *chère petite,* you told me that you valued justice more than anything. Do you think that *I* have been justly treated?'

'Not only justly, but inadequately,' I said. 'If I had been Esmond Torrington I'd have done worse than knock you down.'

Lucien gave a low laugh.

'Aren't you a little hell-cat? And what have I done to deserve your scratches? Where you are concerned, all I did was to honour you with a proposal of marriage.'

'Coming from such a dishonourable man I no longer consider it in that light,' I said.

'*Tiens!* Is this the English idea of fair play – to hit a man when he is down?'

'You are not down, Dr Valguay,' I said, my lips curling. 'No doubt you are still busy with your large fashionable practice and you will soon find another lady of title to be your special patient. But if you *feel* at all "down", I am delighted. You did an unforgivable thing.'

'Little fool,' he said, 'surely you must realise that I did not mean monsieur to hear what I said.'

'I'm sure you didn't. It was unfortunate for you.'

'He had it coming to him,' Lucien muttered. 'Why should he suppose that a woman with Veronica's *allure*...' he gave the word its French pronunciation ... 'should be content to spend her time waiting for him to come back from his musical tours.'

I felt myself beginning to shake. I did not want to listen to this sort of talk, or have any further details of what happened between Veronica Torrington and this hateful man thrust before me.

'Good night, Dr Valguay,' I said again and turned and walked through the gates. I heard his voice following me.

'Your precious conductor is not going to

have it all his own way. I am sueing him for assault. It is in the hands of my *avocat*.'

I waited to hear no more but hurried through the grounds to the villa. I did not for a moment suppose that Dr Valguay would bring such a case against Esmond. I hoped not. A well-known man like Esmond would not want a scandal.

I wondered whether to mention this to Esmond when he next came home. But I could not bring myself to open the subject when he first got back. The mask had fallen again, shuttering his face, hiding all his feelings. Esmond these days was harder. He was also nervous and restless. He did not spend as much time as usual with the children, but rushed into the schoolroom to pat them on the head and say a few words, then rushed out again.

He made no bones now about calling me 'Shelley'. In front of the whole family, too, and if Monica Warr noticed it and was angry, she said not a word. Things had changed, I thought, at Arc-en-Ciel. Emotions were not running riot quite so much on the surface. People seemed to be holding themselves in check. Perhaps it was just as well. Although, at times, I wondered uneasily if it was the calm that precedes a storm, and if another shock was waiting to shatter the calm of this lovely Mediterranean home.

Lady Warr recovered completely and

forsook black chiffon for more colourful clothes, and her bed for her wheel-chair again. She never said a word to me that could be called 'personal', and spoke to me only when it was necessary – as though in this way she would show her dislike; but she knew she could not altogether cross her brother's wishes and dismiss me.

There was, of course, a return to the old narking and criticism of my methods with the children or their work. And there were one or two little 'incidents' over Kate whom I tried to protect fiercely from her aunt's intolerance.

I did not see Esmond alone, and when we met at lunch time, or if he accompanied us in the car for an outing, he remained formal if pleasant, and never looked me in the eye. I felt, somehow, that all the old warmth and real friendliness had gone. I presumed that he was behaving like this on purpose; yet I was mortally hurt. Night after night I went to bed thinking of him, feeling more and more empty in my heart and more and more hopeless about the future. I did not see that there could ever be any place for him in my life other than that of a much respected employer. But I loved him passionately; with every fibre of my being. I was happy only when I was in his presence – and unhappy, too. Dear God, how unhappy! Perhaps fortunately for me, he was often away from the villa working.

Sophie de la Notte came again for a brief weekend in May, without Renate. Once again I had to watch from a distance as Esmond escorted her to a concert or out to dine. Once again I was just the little teacher shoved in the background. And once again I tried not to give way to the appalling pangs of jealousy that shook me every time I saw them or pictured them together. Since that affair with Valguay I wondered whether he would not decide now to marry again and put the beautiful Comtesse in Veronica's place.

I learned in time that Dr Valguay intended to sue Esmond for assault.

I was told by Esmond himself, one morning at the beginning of June, that he could not take the children out as promised because he was having an urgent meeting in Cannes with his *avocat.*

Then at last he suddenly came out of the reserve which had been unbroken since his return from London. He called me into his studio and confided in me.

'I'm in the middle of a legal dispute, Shelley,' he said.

'I hope nothing to worry you,' I murmured. I did not mention that Valguay had already warned me of this.

'Our friend Valguay is trying to twist me. Threatening a case of assault because I hit him and he had to spit out one of his precious teeth.'

I nodded.

'I want no nonsense of that kind,' went on Esmond abruptly. 'I'd quite willingly fight that gentleman anywhere with my fists, but I'm not very keen on a newspaper brawl and a vulgar display of all our names in the cheap press. It would bring my late wife's name into it too, and that is totally undesirable.'

'I understand,' I said, feeling awkward and unhappy as I looked up at his frowning face. Always frowns these days. Gone that delightful smile. He went on:

'For your ear alone, Shelley, I'm not anxious for such a case to be brought up, not only because of its repercussions on my own family, but you would be dragged in as a witness too. That would be very disagreeable to me. I don't see why you *should* be pulled into our personal troubles at Arc-en-Ciel.'

'Oh, you know I'd do anything – say anything I could to help you,' I broke out impulsively.

Now he gave just the hint of the old smile.

'You're very sweet. But I think I can settle this business out of court. I've just learned through various investigations on the part of my legal advisers that despite his smooth ways and all the women who are supposed to adore him, Lucien is in debt. I think my sister, poor misguided soul, was one of the mainstays of his exchequer. Now he's feeling the draught. So I'm pretty likely to be able to get a settlement and close the matter, by paying him off.'

'Thank goodness for that,' I breathed.

'I've also decided,' said Esmond, 'to sell this villa.'

'*Sell* Arc-en-Ciel!' I repeated dismayed. 'Oh, but it's so beautiful.'

He walked to the window and looked out at the trees. There was no sun today. It was a humid, misty April morning, although the startling exquisite colours of the spring flowers were already adding new beauty to the gardens.

'Once I like it very much and I thought perhaps I could stay here after my wife died. Now I know I can't. It's curious, Shelley, but for the first year or two I was rather *numbed* by it all. It is as though I have just come to life and most unpleasantly.'

Then I acted on one of my rather rare impulses. A flood of feeling seemed to break loose in me.

'Oh, Esmond,' I said … and at the time I don't think I even noticed that I dropped the respectful 'Mr Torrington'… 'Esmond, do try to put the past out of your mind. It isn't good for you to go on harbouring it. I know it's all been reawakened by that horrible Lucien and you must feel very hurt but–'

273

'Not so much hurt,' he interrupted, 'as degraded. It's *degrading* to think that Veronica...' He broke off and I could see him biting his lip.

I went on desperately:

'It may not even be true. You don't *know* ... it's only what that man hinted...'

He swung round. He was in the grip of some acute nervous tension and it snapped. I could actually see the sweat on his forehead. His handsome face was contorted as he spoke again.

'I knew that something was wrong between Veronica and myself. I guessed that she was going out with someone else but not Valguay. Good God, not *him*.'

'But you don't know. You can't be sure,' I argued, scarcely knowing why.

'What can you know?' he demanded in such a fierce voice that I felt really afraid.

I began to stammer:

'I don't believe it can be anything like you imagine. No woman who was married to you could ever really want to be touched by Lucien Valguay. It was just that she was lonely, perhaps, or bored. You were always away. The children perhaps, were not enough for her. Children are not enough for some women. She may have liked Lucien as an escort but not ... not ... oh God!' I broke off floundering and scarlet. Yet fascinated, I still looked at Esmond and watched his face change from white to red and red to white again. His eyes were brilliant with a kind of suppressed rage and despair. Then he started to laugh.

'Listen to her! Listen to our little Miss Bray ... our little teacher trying to analyse the situation. Why don't you do it by mathematics, Shelley? Your theories – my suspicions – Valguay's rotten allegations are all insoluble. And the only one who really knows the truth perhaps is old Nannie, who became her confidential maid and was always with her. Perhaps Monica knows too but she won't tell me. Nobody has really told me. And the whole thing is driving me mad ... *mad*, I say!'

I could see him shaking from head to foot. I put out both hands and caught his arms.

'Please, please, Esmond, don't feel this way. Don't let it upset you too much. Love must be different from this, surely! There must be trust too. You must trust Veronica in death as you did in life.'

I stumbled over those words, little understanding really what prompted me to defend the dead woman in such dramatic fashion unless it was just in order to wipe that look of misery from Esmond's adored face.

He stared at me for a long time without speaking. I wondered if I had said too much and offended him. Then he seemed to recover his equilibrium. When he spoke again it was in a low steady voice.

'Thank you. Thank you for those few words. There's a great deal of truth in them. You're always a stickler for the truth, aren't you, Shelley? I don't think Conrad has told a lie since you came here. Well, I'm not going to lie to you now. And let me tell you: *I don't love Veronica any more*. You're quite right. Where one loves one must trust. Anyhow it's not my love for her but my pride that's taken such a toss. And in that I'm wrong. Pride is one of the deadliest of sins. You're always right, little Shelley. Now run along and forget what we have said and I'll go to my *avocat* in a slightly more calm and practical state of mind.'

I stepped back. I twisted my fingers behind my back feeling very nervous. As he passed me he looked down at me with that half-tender, half-mocking smile of his.

'You must think we're all a bit touched at Arc-en-Ciel, Shelley? Well, perhaps there is a crazy shadow over this place and that's why I'm going to put it up for sale. We will all go back to London this autumn anyhow. I'll be conducting at the Festival Hall right through the winter. We'll stay here till then, and after that *fini*.'

I nodded, I felt that I had nothing else to say, but as he passed me he bent and dropped a kiss on my hair.

'My little friend and counsellor! What

would the children and I do without you these days?' he murmured.

I felt a lump in my throat choking me. I could not for the life of me have moved or spoken. After he had gone I went back to the schoolroom and because the children were disappointed that their father could not take them out, I arranged another treat.

I did not see Esmond again that day. After his visit to Cannes he was driving up to Grasse to see some English friends.

During this period of intense feeling – reducing me at times to tears – I went back to my teenage habit of finding expression in poetry. I wrote the first verses I had produced since I became a teacher.

I was inspired, if one might call it that, by a symphonic poem recently composed by a friend of Esmond's and dedicated to him. Esmond had conducted it and had a special recording made. A few weeks ago he had played the record to me and the children. I had found it immensely sad and beautiful. The composer had called the work: *'Désespoir'* – 'Despair' – a melancholy title, indeed. But it appealed to me in my emotional state and I wished, with passion, that I had been the composer.

These were my humble verses:

I would, I would I were the one
Who wrote that sad sweet score;

That he to whom it is inscribed
Should love me more.

I watch him raise the baton in his hand.
I guess the secrets of his heart.
I understand:
O, cease to play! Sweet orchestra, depart,
Lest I should hear your music all my life
And break my heart.

Not very good, I thought. Very bad in fact. But he would never see it. I folded the verses and put them in one of my drawers and forgot about them. A few days later – Esmond was having a brief rest and spending the day in Grasse – Sir Austen and Lady Warr were out. They had taken the children on a treat; I had not been invited! An unexpected visitor came to Arc-en-Ciel, just before tea. Thérèse was off-duty. I don't know where Yvonne was. Louise would be sleeping now. She never came on duty till six. It was old Bertrand who announced this visitor to me. Brought her, in fact, to the schoolroom door. I was sitting darning out on the verandah. The old boy looked anxious. Just behind him came a little old woman in clerical grey with a grey straw hat. I could see snow white hair under that hat. Her face was wrinkled, and she wore gold-rimmed glasses. She looked English, I thought, and for all the world like a good British nannie of the old type. To be sure that's what she was. Bertrand did not speak but she stepped forward.

'You are the governess?' she said. She had that croaking sort of voice that some old women seem to get when they are past seventy. And she had gnarled rheumaticky looking fingers, but the eyes behind the glasses were shrewd.

'Yes, I'm Miss Bray,' I said.

'I'm Con's and Kate's old Nannie,' she said.

I put down my sewing and stood up. I felt surprised. I had rather gathered that she was in England, and not particularly *persona grata* here because she had been such a gossip and made so much mischief. She started to talk, nineteen to the dozen. Bertrand retired.

I bade Nannie sit down. She told me her name was Miss Sleigh, Annie Sleigh, and she came originally from Berwick-on-Tweed. (The burr in her voice was slightly Scottish.) And she had been with the Torringtons from the time that Conrad was a fortnight old.

It just about broke her heart, she said, when she was given notice; but that was all due to Lady Warr who did not like her. Mr Torrington would have kept her on, she was sure. Even if Con and Kate needed a teacher, they could have kept Nannie too. She could have stayed as housekeeper for instance.

'You should have seen how the poor little

things cried when I left,' she said. She had taken off her coat and was seated in a chair fanning herself, breathing rather heavily. She was seventy-three years old yet had walked from the station to this villa. She never stopped talking. I did not get a word in but sat fascinated while she went on and on, taking a big breath between each sentence. She had come especially to see the children and give a parcel to Mr Torrington.

When she left Monte Carlo nearly a year ago she had gone to her sister in Putney but hadn't 'settled'.

Even at her age she had found another job with a new baby. And it was a bit of luck the mother of the baby was French and she'd come down to Juan-les-Pins for a holiday, so Nannie took this train journey to come and see her old charges. She had something very special for Mr Torrington.

'Perhaps something I ought to have given him before I left, but I didn't,' she said. 'I can't say we parted the best of friends, and I kept my parcel to myself. I'm sure I've been a faithful friend to the family and I never used to let those dear children out of my sight, but I didn't get much thanks for it in the end.'

I remained silent. I felt uneasy, I wished that Miss Sleigh hadn't come here, and poured herself out like this. I could see that she was a worthy soul in one way but a menace in another, and I could quite see why she hadn't been good for Kate and Conrad once they passed babyhood. She talked so much and so quickly that I could hardly take in half that she said. She spoke a great deal about the late Mrs Torrington.

'My dear sweet lamb was Mrs Torrington. A more angelic generous lady never lived, I tell you! Her death was dreadful. And it needn't have happened too. It needn't I know. *I know!*'

This was dangerous ground. I picked up my darning again, and said quietly:

'How about a cup of tea, Nannie?'

But Miss Sleigh was not to be put off. She went on rhapsodising about Veronica. Her kindness to Nannie. Nannie had been more than just a nurse. She became Mrs Torrington's friend and confidante. She used to wash and iron her beautiful lingerie and brush her gorgeous red hair, just as she brushed Kate's. And everything was all right between her and Mr Torrington too, until *her ladyship* made trouble.

'I don't mind telling you I couldn't stand the likes of Lady Warr. She did nothing but make trouble for my lady and her husband.'

'Nannie,' I said, my cheeks hot, 'I don't think you ought to be telling me all these things.'

Miss Sleigh tossed her head. She didn't see that it mattered, she said. It was time someone told the truth about that hateful Lady Warr.

'Her and her arthritis and not a thing wrong with her!' exclaimed Nannie tossing her head again.

'Nannie–' I began, but she interrupted.

'I've got my conscience and I'm going to act on it now and it's time Mr Torrington read this…'

From a large black plastic bag which she carried she drew a paper parcel, with the string sealed.

'It's all in here. Her diary,' she said. 'My poor angel used to write in it quite often but she gave it to me to put in my room. *"Nannie,"* she said, *"it wouldn't do for this to get in the wrong hands but I'm going to write down what's happening, because I'm afraid of the future. One day perhaps this story may have to be told,'* so I kept the diary in my room. After Mrs Torrington died, I took it away with me. Now I think it's time I brought it back.'

I looked at the big parcel fascinated. What was in that diary? What secrets had Veronica written that could be unfolded now, nearly three years later … and make any difference? Miss Sleigh put the parcel on my lap.

'You can give it to him. I hear he's away. I'll trust it with you. I had a few words with Bertrand and he says you're the only one here that can be trusted, now. All sorts of goings on there are, I hear. Between Mr Torrington and her ladyship and that snake Dr Valguay ... yes, the three of them...'

Snake. I held my darning needle suspended in my fingers. The very word that I had used. Queer that the old nurse should use it too. She continued.

'I'm not having any wrong said against my dear lady, and if things have been said that shouldn't it's time they knew the truth. It's all in those pages. I've read them, so I know,' she said triumphantly.

'But you had no right to read someone else's diary,' I said indignantly.

Miss Sleigh cackled.

'Och, my dear, I had the right. I knew it all anyhow. My dear angel used to talk to me while I brushed her hair. *"There's going to be a tragedy and I dread it,"* she used to say. She was psychic she was. She *knew*. Mr Torrington suffered after she died, but so did she, worse.'

'Don't go on,' I interrupted. 'I'll give Mr Torrington the parcel as soon as he comes home.'

'Lock it up now then,' said Miss Sleigh harshly, 'or that old cat, her ladyship will get hold of it, she'd burn it for two pins.'

'Nonsense, Nannie,' I said rather irritably, 'you mustn't talk that way.'

But she went on talking vindictively against Lady Warr. If I agreed with many of the things I wasn't going to let the old nurse know it.

She had a cup of tea with me. I really felt rather sorry for her, because she did not see either Conrad or Kate. They did not return as early as expected. Lady Warr came home early – brought by the chauffeur. This I did not know until later either but she had started a bad migraine and for once, not wishing to disappoint the children, had let Sir Austen take them off alone for the promised treat.

Miss Sleigh seemed in no way willing to see her old enemy. She must return to Juan-les-Pins, and her baby, she said. But she threatened to come again to visit her 'two darlings' at Arc-en-Ciel. She also added another warning to me about Monica.

'Don't you let that old cat get *you* in her clutches or she'll do you an injury like she did me and my sweet dead lady. All was well until Lady Warr came to stay here with Sir Austen. Only supposed to come for a fortnight, she was, and stayed the whole winter before my darling had her accident. Said she was too ill to move, but I know it was put on because she didn't want to leave Arc-en-Ciel and Mrs Torrington was too kind to turn her out. Although I used to hear Mrs Torrington say she wished her sister-in-law further. She was making bad blood between Mr and Mrs Torrington ... and Mr

Torrington got the wrong end of the stick, Lady Warr saw to that, I tell you!'

On and on the malicious voice continued. Anti-Monica Warr, Anti-Esmond. She was all for the dead woman.

At last I rose and said:

'I must go. I'll put the diary in my drawer, Nannie.'

I felt really relieved when Miss Sleigh finally departed. What she had said weighed on my mind, like the memory of that parcel in my drawer. After I had rung for the taxi for Nannie and seen her off, I took a walk along the sea front.

When I got back to my room, I opened my top drawer to pull out a handkerchief, and I stared aghast. The parcel containing Veronica Torrington's diary had gone.

14

I shall never forget the consternation I felt when I found that diary was missing.

First of all I thought I must have gone crazy and put it in another drawer, but it wasn't in any of them. I even searched all round my room and under the bed, but I had to reach the conclusion that the diary just wasn't in my bedroom any longer. Someone must have stolen it while I was out.

I had a sudden feeling that Yvonne might know something. I don't know why, it just struck me that she might. I found her in the pantry preparing a fruit juice drink for her ladyship. Trying to keep cool, I asked her in a quiet voice if she had seen a brown paper parcel in my room. I swear that she changed colour and flicked her lashes in a guilty way, but she answered.

'I nevairre go to your room, mees.'

'Oh, yes you do,' I said. 'You go to all the rooms, Yvonne.'

She marched past me almost brushing me out of her way.

'I tell Milady you insult me. *Vous êtes—*' she ended with an uncomplimentary word to me in her own language. It infuriated me to such an extent that I, too, turned and rushed out of the kitchen and reached her ladyship's bedroom before Yvonne. I knocked, but without waiting for an answer, barged in – in a way I would certainly not have done under ordinary circumstances.

I knew now that I had been right in what I had suspected. Monica was sitting in her wheel-chair under a strong light which she used near her dressing table. *She was reading Veronica's diary.*

My heart gave an ugly scared kind of leap – the way it jumps when one is confronted with something really shocking. I knew that Lady Warr had told Yvonne to go and steal that parcel, while I was out. There was only one other conjecture to make – Lady Warr must have come down to the schoolroom and listened outside the door while Nannie was with me. She must have been told by Bertrand that Nannie had arrived. Instead of going straight to bed, she had wheeled herself along to eavesdrop. That was the sort of woman she was. She and Nannie had been such deadly enemies.

I saw Monica shut the book and look at me in a thoroughly startled fashion.

'How dare you come in here without being invited?' she began.

I felt no fear of her in that moment. I answered:

'Lady Warr – the children's old nurse

entrusted that parcel to me, and asked me to place it in Mr Torrington's hands. It was in my drawer. I would like you to explain how you got hold of it.'

Lady Warr's flabby pink and white face went that ugly red that always preceded a rise in temper. She glared at me.

'I don't know what you're talking about.'

'Yes, you do,' I said. 'You have just opened the parcel that Nannie gave me. I presume you listened outside my door, and when you found out about it you sent Yvonne to get it for you.'

Her eyes glittered.

'What if I did? My later sister-in-law's diary ought not to be in *your* possession, that's certain.'

'Believe me,' I said, 'no amount of curiosity would have tempted me to read it.'

'Well, I have just about finished it,' she confessed this openly now, and I could see her beringed fingers trembling. 'And it's a pack of lies. All lies against me and poor Lucien. Trying to put herself in the right and us in the wrong.'

I felt a queer surge of thankfulness when she made that announcement. I said:

'I am sure it is true. I only hope that whatever she has written in that diary will clear her in her husband's eyes. He has suffered cruelly because of his suspicions, and I don't doubt you've helped to make things worse, Lady Warr.'

She screamed at me shrilly:

'Oh, you *wicked* girl – to come here and accuse a poor invalid–'

'Poor invalid you may be,' I broke in hot and angry. 'But not too ill to cause trouble between Mr Torrington and his wife in the past. If Mrs Torrington's diary makes it plain to her husband, he will understand everything.'

Then Lady Warr put back her head and burst into hysterical laughter.

'He'll never read it. I won't let him.'

'But you must!' I protested, and stared aghast at this vindictive little creature who, I was sure, had an almost maniacal side to her.

But now Monica turned in her chair towards the beautiful carved pinewood fireplace which was a feature of her bedroom. A huge log fire burned there. She liked the comfort of this now that the central heating had been turned off. It accounted for the stifling atmosphere. She may have felt cold. I thought the evening very warm.

I realised in a split second that she meant to destroy that diary, and that with it would go my adored Esmond's last chance of learning the truth. That knowledge gave me the courage to act as I did. When with a wild laugh, Monica threw the big leather bound book on to the flames I rushed over, leaned down, and pulled the book out, wincing from the pain as the flames licked my finger tips. Already the pages were curling up. In a panic I threw myself on the floor and rolled the book in the white rug which was spread in front of the fireplace. Then Monica came at me full force in her chair. She screamed:

'How dare you. *How dare you.* Give that back to me. Give it to me I say!'

Yvonne knocked on the door.

I heard, but her ladyship did not. She was in a frenzy. I staggered on to my feet. There followed the most degrading scene in which Monica tried to snatch the smoke-blackened book which was still hot from the fire, and I hung on to it grimly. Come what may, I was not going to let that diary be destroyed by this woman who was maddened by her jealousy of the dead Veronica, of me, of anybody who came into Esmond's life. I think the Comtesse de la Notte was the only person she had ever genuinely liked and looked upon as a possible second wife for her brother.

Certainly she did not want him to read what his wife had written either against herself or her doctor, for whom, I suppose, she had had a sort of passion that had its roots in sex as well as friendship.

Since Lucien's departure she hadn't been able to get hold of all the injections and sleeping tablets and pep-pills that Lucien had dished up for her. The more responsible Dr Raphael had cut them down by half. As I look back now, I am not at all sure that it wasn't an excess of such drugs that had sent Monica a bit round the bend.

Anyhow it was in the middle of this struggle, with the two of us grappling for possession of the diary, that the awful accident happened. At one point, Monica pulled the book so forcibly from me that she dragged me down with it – I being so small and light. There was amazing strength in her ladyship's small chubby hands. As I lost my balance I flung my weight to one side. Somehow or other – I was much too dazed at the time to remember the details – she too, fell forward and right out of the chair. She pulled me and the diary with her. Her head struck the fender. She screamed once, then there was silence.

Yvonne heard that cry and rushed in. She saw the body of her mistress lying in a heap on the rug. Blood was pouring from the top of the ash-blonde head. To add to the general confusion, Yvonne dropped the fruit juice drink she had brought in. It smashed on to the polished floor. Then she turned and fled out of the room, howling:

'Oh, bon Dieu, bon Dieu. Elle a tué madame! Sir Austen, Sir Aus-ten!'

But of course he was not there. He was still out with the children. I knelt down beside Monica feeling absolutely sick. In heaven's name, I thought, I had never meant such a dreadful thing as this to happen, even for the sake of recovering Veronica's diary.

Trembling from head to foot, I took one of Lady Warr's hands and put my fingers against the pulse. For one ghastly moment I could feel no beat. I really did believe she was dead. Then I laid my ear against her breast and heard the throbbing of her heart, so I knew that she was alive. What followed was a nightmare. The whole bedroom filled with people. Yvonne's panic had communicated itself to the rest of the staff. God alone knew what she told them but they all came in, looking first at her ladyship's body, then at me, with horrified eyes, as though I really did stand there, *a murderer.*

Nobody spoke. They just huddled... Louise, Thérèse, Lili, Bertrand and an old apple-cheeked woman who washed up dishes.

Somehow I recovered myself and became practical again. Sternly I ordered them all to leave except Bertrand who helped me lift Lady Warr on to her bed. The poor old man was badly shaken. I examined the cut on Lady Warr's head. There was a nasty swelling high on her forehead under the hairline, already in evidence and blood seeped through the dyed blonde curls. There is always a lot of blood from a scalp wound. I knew that, for I had passed a first-aid exam, and had learned a bit about such injuries. Yvonne had crept back, weeping and moaning, I told her to be quiet and fetch me a bowl of water and find some lint and cotton wool. Lili, I bade telephone at once for Dr Raphael.

Monica did not open her eyes. She was deeply unconscious. It was as well, I thought grimly. I wished to God that Sir Austen would come back. The responsibility was too great. And all those staring horrified eyes had made me feel guilty even though I was not so in the strictest sense. In her rage, it was Monica herself who was responsible for this accident.

Lili returned to tell me in a breathless voice that Dr Raphael had gone to some hotel further down the cost to attend a visitor and would not be back for a couple of hours. The blood was soaking steadily through Monica's dainty frilled pillow. I could not staunch it. I was so anxious for her that I thought that there was only one thing left to do. Send Bertrand next door for the hateful Lucien. At least he was a doctor and knew all about Monica. He would just have to be brought into the house again. I felt that he would probably be at home – and he was.

He returned with Bertrand, carrying the smart cream parchment leather case which I always used to think so 'pansy'. He gave a shocked look at the woman on the bed and the blood-stained pillow and turned to me for an explanation as he took Monica's wrist between his fingers.

'Attend to her now. I will explain later,' I said curtly. 'Please stop that bleeding.'

Now Yvonne, her face convulsed with hatred of me (she shared that feeling with her mistress) burst into loud sobs.

'*Mees* tried to keel my lady...' Then realising that she was speaking to one of her countrymen, added a flow of French which I could not understand.

Lucien shut one eye and looked at me somewhat ironically with the other.

'There seems to have been what you English call "a rough house" here. Did you try and do the old girl in?'

Sick at heart, I turned from him, wishing that I had not had to bring him back to Arc-en-Ciel. But what could I do? I'd tried to trace Esmond. Nobody knew the name of the friends he had gone to see in Grasse. I could not allow Monica to bleed to death.

It was lucky that by the time Sir Austen and the children returned Lady Warr had recovered consciousness. The bleeding had been controlled. Her head was swathed in a capelline bandage which gave her a queer, unnatural look. Deathly white and still in a state of shock, she lay in bed in a darkened room. Lucien sat beside her, his arms crossed.

'I will stay till she feels better,' he said. I think in his way he was really quite fond of the woman. I thanked him coldly.

And now he asked me what the 'rough house' had been about.

'I prefer not to discuss it with you, Dr Valguay,' I said.

'Still the same char-r-r-rming Mees Bray!' he sneered.

I did not reply. It was then that the car returned with Sir Austen and the children. The latter I dealt with hastily. I put Conrad on his honour to see that he and his little sister went to bed immediately, and said that Thérèse would bring their supper to them and read one of the little French stories which they were beginning to understand.

I then had to make a few explanations to Sir Austen. He began by rebuking me for calling in Dr Valguay.

'I'm shocked, Miss Bray. You know it was Mr Torrington's wish that—'

'I am sorry, Sir Austen,' I broke in, 'but I had no option. Dr Raphael is at the Eden Roc. I thought it better to call in even Dr Valguay rather than that your wife should lose any more blood.'

'I suppose that is justified,' said Sir Austen doubtfully. I could see that he had had a severe shock. I felt sorry for him. The poor kind harassed old man had been such a slave to his 'invalid' wife for so long and put up with so much of her craziness, and he ended by thanking me courteously for what I had done.

He seemed to know that the friends whom Esmond had gone to lunch with were called Neal – a charming English family with teenage children, who loved music. He wanted to see their newly acquired home. But when I telephoned Les Aspres, it appeared that Esmond had already been there and gone again; he was they said on his way back to Monte Carlo.

Now Sir Austen came out of his wife's room. He approached me in the hall and spoke to me more sternly than he had ever done.

'Miss Bray, this needs more explanation. My wife said that you deliberately pushed her out of her chair and fought with her in order to get something that you wanted. Miss Bray, I can hardly believe it but it must be true if she says so. Miss Bray, I am absolutely *horrified*. I don't know *what* to say!'

He didn't, poor dear. Heaven knew what that awful woman had been telling him but it was obviously not the truth.

I thought of the diary for which I had fought in so tigerish a fashion. It was now safely locked – yes, locked up this time in a suitcase under my bed. I really felt rather thankful that the charred cover and brown curled edges would prove what I had to say about Monica trying to burn it, but I felt too weary, too utterly sick at heart tonight to explain anything to Sir Austen. Besides I just could not disillusion him in the kind of 'suffering angel' he *thought* Monica.

I did not meet his accusing gaze. I said:

'If you don't mind, Sir Austen, I would rather make my explanations to Mr Torrington himself when he comes back.'

'Very well,' said Sir Austen, 'if that is how you feel. But this is a most serious thing. I just do not understand it. You who are so kind to the children and to all of us … to treat my poor wife so shamefully … a helpless cripple … good heavens! Were you out of your mind?'

'Please Sir Austen,' I pleaded, 'let me wait and tell Mr Torrington my story.'

He took off his horn-rimmed glasses, polished them and replaced them on his nose. He looked as confused as he must feel, poor man. He sighed heavily.

'Very well. But meanwhile I must ask you not to come near my wife's room.'

'No,' I said, 'I don't wish to – I assure you.'

'She is afraid of you,' he added, 'my poor darling!'

I thought oh, yes, afraid of me but not because I might harm her physically. She is afraid of what I might reveal to her brother through that diary. But I was going to give it to him. I felt no mercy for Lady Warr now, or for Lucien Valguay. They had done harm enough. I still did not know what lay in those pages, but I was sure from what the old nurse had told me that it would be best for Esmond that he should read it.

I said good night to Sir Austen. He left me without replying. For the first time in his distress he forgot his impeccable manners. I walked out on to the terrace, not wanting to face the children just yet. My mind was in a turmoil and my head ached violently. I needed some air. As I stood there on the terrace, I wondered, ironically, how the world could be so beautiful. The stars were glorious. The Mediterranean was turned to shining silver. Lights flickered like golden tapers along the coast. Yet this lovely world contained such people as Monica. Her venom, both while Veronica lived and after she had died, seemed to have entered the veins of the whole family and poisoned them.

Dr Valguay came out of the front door carrying his smart bag. I presumed that his work was done. He saw me and came up to me.

'She is sleeping and should have a good night now. There was a lot of blood but the wound is not serious, but she will really have a little pain and headache this time to complain about...' He laughed unpleasantly. 'You must have pushed her very hard, to cause that fall, *ma chère petite*. Did she drive you so far with her taunts?'

I clenched my hands as I looked up at the face which I thought had grown more than ever debauched since I last saw it.

'I did not push her.'

'No? She just *fell* out?'

'Your sarcasm doesn't amuse me.'

'She says you tried to murder her.'

I gave a nervous angry laugh.

'That, of course, is ridiculous.'

'*Bien!* Then what happened?'

Suddenly I looked him straight in the eyes. I said:

'Earlier today, Dr Valguay, I had an unexpected visitor – the children's old nurse, Miss Sleigh.'

I saw his long womanish lashes flicker.

'That old *crapoule!*'

'*Crapoule* or not, she had in her possession a diary written by the late Mrs Torrington right up to the day she died. Miss Sleigh asked me to give it to Mr Torrington. Lady Warr knew and stole the dairy out of my drawer then tried to burn it.'

Now I saw him change colour.

'*Pas possible! Mais c'est incroyable!*' he murmured.

'I burnt my fingers as you will see...' I held out my hands. The balls of my fingers were blistered and angry-looking.

He stared, obviously too surprised and rattled to find it as easy as usual to speak. I went on:

'I shall see that the diary *is* given to Mr Torrington. Good night.'

'Wait,' he said, and pulled at my arm. 'Come back. Tell me what was written in the diary. Was *I* mentioned?'

'I believe so,' I said (rather spitefully I am afraid, meaning to upset him, and it did). His jaw positively dropped. But I went inside the house and shut the front door. He made no effort to open it and I knew that he had gone. I made a bet with myself that before Esmond got back, the smooth-tongued Lucien would be away from this part of the world – and stay away. My guess was right. At a much later hour, Esmond actually tried to get in that house but failed. It was locked and shuttered except for an old caretaker who said that *monsieur le docteur* had gone and left no address.

I steeled myself to face the children, tell them their usual bedtime story and listen to their chatter and description of the outing they had had with Uncle Austen. But I am afraid I took in very little of what they told me. Following that fight with Lady Warr I had kept calm and been busy. Now reaction set in. I felt cold and apprehensive. I dreaded it, yet longed for Esmond's return.

He did not come early. He must have taken a detour and gone to visit other friends on the coast after he left Grasse. I lay on my bed, swallowed a couple of aspirin and tried to cure my headache, but I kept thinking about that awful tussle with the woman in the chair and the blood ... and all those servants thinking that I had tried to murder her. I thought dismally:

What in God's name will Esmond think? What will he say to me?

The pain in my sore fingers became worse than the one in my head. I put some cream on a handkerchief and wrapped up both hands and lay down again. So weak, so miserable did I feel that the tears began to trickle down my cheeks. I think I must have dozed off, then suddenly I was roused by a knock on my door. Esmond's voice, stern and abrupt, uttered my name.

'Shelley! Shelley, will you please come along to my studio at once. I must speak to you.'

The hour had come. I combed back my hair, hastily powdered my face and put on the skirt which I had taken off, and a black woolly sweater. Then I unlocked my suitcase and took out the charred diary.

Trembling with nerves I carried the thing that was the cause of all the trouble into Esmond's studio.

15

Sir Austen was in the studio with his brother-in-law. Both men turned and looked at me as I came in. I know I hadn't bothered much with my appearance and that I must look rather frightful. I was certainly very pale. I hadn't even put on any lipstick.

I glanced at Sir Austen.

'How is ... Lady Warr?'

'She is sleeping, thank God.' He answered very coldly. 'Dr Raphael has been and I've told him all that I know. He will, of course, come again first thing in the morning.'

'It was a pity he wasn't here at the time,' snapped Esmond.

'I certainly did not like Valguay coming into the house,' sighed Sir Austen.

'He wouldn't have set foot in it if I'd been here – I'd have broken his neck for him,' said Esmond.

Now I looked at him. His face was like granite. He was, as usual, a model of sartorial elegance, wearing the customary buttonhole which looked strangely out of place in this atmosphere which was so full of unease.

Sir Austen coughed.

'Well ... Miss Bray says she wishes to

make her explanation to you.. I'll leave you alone, Esmond.'

He walked out of the studio and shut the door.

Esmond balanced himself on the edge of his desk, a half-smoked cigar between his fingers. He gave me a long enquiring look.

'You must see for yourself that what I have come back to here this evening, has shocked me tremendously. I could hardly believe my ears when Austen told me about my poor sister.'

I stared stonily at the floor.

'Yes,' I said, 'it must have been awful for you.'

He got up and came towards me.

'Shelley. This doesn't make sense. What in God's name prompted you to do such a thing?'

I raised my head and looked up at him with some bitterness.

'You have been told, I presume, that I pushed Lady Warr out of her chair – that I tried to kill her.'

He laughed without humour.

'That's a little too dramatic. I can only presume that you lost your temper sufficiently to warrant you making an attack, and an accident happened. The chair turned over.'

'You believe that?' I asked incredulously.

'I do find it hard to believe, knowing you,'

he admitted.

'I'm thankful for that much,' I sighed, relieved.

Now suddenly his brilliant gaze wandered to my hands which I suppose I was holding a little awkwardly.

'Good God, what are those blisters? Have you burnt yourself?'

'Yes,' I said quite drily, and handed him the diary. 'I got burnt trying to snatch this out of Lady Warr's fire.'

He took the charred book slowly. He stared at the initials 'V.T.' and I saw the muscles on the side of his cheeks tauten.

'What *is* this?'

'A diary written by your … by your late wife.'

'I know the book,' he said in a low voice, 'I gave it to her for her appointments. I had those initials put on.'

'She used it as a diary,' I said.

'How did it come into your possession?'

'Miss Sleigh brought it this afternoon.'

'Miss Sleigh,' he repeated, staring at me in surprise. 'The children's old nurse.'

'Yes.'

'But she lives in London.'

'She has come to Juan-les-Pins,' I said, 'with a French-woman who has just had a baby and who engaged her in London.'

'Nannie came here and gave you this book?' he asked incredulously.

'Yes.'

'How did *she* come by it?'

'Veronica ... Mrs Torrington,' I corrected myself, 'didn't want it to be seen by you at the time and asked Nannie to keep it for her, each day after making her entries. Then when Mrs ... when Mrs Torrington died ... Nannie took possession of it. But Nannie said it weighed on her conscience and she thought you ought to read it.'

'Why is it half burnt like this?'

'Your sister tried to throw it on the fire in her bedroom and I retrieved it,' I said. 'She then tried to get it back in order to try and destroy it again, and pulled me down so that I fell on her. She tumbled out of her chair and hit her head on the fender. I swear that to you, Esmond, by all that I hold holy. I swear it on my most *sacred* oath – by your *children!*'

He stared at me with bemused eyes. The poor man was obviously reeling back from this – the second blow delivered to him this night. He whispered:

'I believe you, of course. I must. I know that Monica has these uncontrolled moments. Besides ... your blistered hands ... this scorched diary ... they prove it.'

I seated myself suddenly on the edge of the sofa feeling sick – unable to stand any more. I put my face in my hands.

'It's been so horrible,' I said in a muffled

voice, 'you don't know what I've been through. I've taken all the blame so far, but you *know* I would never willingly do anybody any harm. I'm not a violent person.'

'I am sure you are not, Shelley, but Sir Austen doesn't understand and I could only know what he told me.'

'Nobody knew about the diary except Miss Sleigh.'

'But how did my sister get hold of it, when it was given to you?'

I explained how I guessed that Monica had overheard Nannie telling me to put it away in my drawer, and told Yvonne to steal it.

He said in a slow voice:

'My sister seems to have behaved very badly. I wonder what was in this diary that she was so reluctant for me to read.'

'I don't know,' I said, my face still hidden. Now I felt his hand on my bowed head. His voice was gentle again.

'Poor child. Poor Shelley. This has been frightful for you. Of course I see now, Monica's accident was not your fault. But why did you feel this diary was so well worth saving?'

I raised my face – the tears were tumbling down my cheeks.

'Because,' I sobbed, 'Nannie told me that it would make it quite clear to you that your wife was not to blame for anything that happened, and that your sister … and her doctor brought all the original trouble about. Oh … I don't really know what I'm talking about. It's all still a mystery to me, but I felt that whatever happened, you *must* read what your wife had written. I thought it would help you. I thought… *Oh, I don't know.*'

I choked and began to weep copiously again. I felt Esmond's arm go round me. He sat beside me, and drew my head on to his shoulder. He stroked my hair – very quietly, very tenderly. He said, for the second time:

'Poor child. Poor Shelley. You *have* been caught up in a maelstrom in this house. And so you burned your fingers and got yourself accused of a wilful attack on Monica, in order to save the dairy for me. It was plucky of you, Shelley. Very plucky.'

I could not answer. I stopped crying and just clung to him, pressing my drenched face against his shoulder. It was such bliss to feel the warmth and kindliness of his embrace. At least, I thought, I was forgiven, by him. He had exonerated me – without questioning my story. But after a moment I felt him draw away from me. I looked up timidly, my handkerchief pressed to my lips. I saw him open the diary and flip through the pages, his brows contracted, his face very severe and wearing a slightly uneasy expression … as though he dreaded what he might find out. One or two thin brown flakes frayed away from the diary and fluttered on to the floor. I could smell the pungent odour of scorched paper. An unmistakable smell.

Now I saw his expression change and became alert and deeply watchful. He began to read aloud:

'MAY 12TH. *Con's birthday. We had a lovely party. Darling Es flew back specially from Paris where he had to return. Con three years old. Growing up. Very intelligent, I think. But the day was spoiled by Monnie. She always spoils my happiness if she can. She hates me and shows it, but never to Es. She puts on an act for him and Austen. Always moaning about her arthritis and being so ill, playing on their feelings. She knows Esmond owes her a debt because of what she did for him when he was young. She is a fiend that woman. I hate her and I am afraid of her too. She is jealous because Es loves me so much. I feel that one day she will try to do me an injury.'*

Esmond's voice broke off. I saw him brush his lips with one finger, nervously. He turned and looked at me.

'You see. History repeats itself. Monnie must have made Veronica's life a misery, as she has been making yours. I see it all now.'

Being me, and fairly ingenuous, I broke out:

'But why should she be jealous of *me?*'

He made no answer. He returned to the diary.

'No – no. I oughtn't to listen!' I began.

'You're wrong,' he interrupted in a queer voice. 'You are the very one who should. You have become a sort of cat's paw in this wretched game. I can see it all. Monnie and her damned doctor have tried to destroy you – as well as my poor Veronica. You *shall* hear what Veronica wrote. I owe it to you.'

I sat silent, shivering. Yes, my teeth chattered. I listened fascinated, yet feeling guilty, still uncertain that I had the right to hear what Esmond's wife had written four years ago. 'Es' she called him. The shortening of his name somehow sounded so intimate, it roused all my compassion. She had obviously been happy with him and the children, *then.*

'The early part of this diary,' said Esmond, 'seems to contain just snatches of her thoughts about me and the children and how happy she was. Now this: *'Every man I meet seems to fall in love with me.'* She wrote that, Shelley. Yes – she drew men to her like flames attract the moths. In a funny way she was innocent of real harm. But she had a touch of coquetry which is born not made. She couldn't help being alluring, either consciously or unconsciously. I was too busy with my work. I trusted her implicitly, but I neglected her too. I see it all now.'

'Don't imagine things, Esmond,' I spoke to him earnestly, 'just read and learn what must be the truth.'

He began to read aloud the diary to me.

'LATER. *It is winter again. Monnie and Austen have been here six months now – six whole months of hell for me. Maybe I am crazy to put all these dangerous things down in black and white but I had a ghastly row with Monnie last night. I told her very politely that I thought it was time she and that poor fish Austen left* Arc-en-Ciel. *I said it was not good that there should be other people living all the time with a husband and wife. Then she started shooting that unfair line about 'being too ill to move' and that it was wicked of me to try and drive her away from her adored brother and the South of France, and her doctor who did her good. Because I knew that Es loved her, my poor blind Es, I relented and let her stay. But she said something that made me wary. She warned me that if I came between her and Es, she'd come between Es and* me *in a way I'd regret all my life. I began to feel really afraid of her. I often wanted to talk things over with Es but I couldn't bring myself to hurt him. She was always so different with him and he looked up to her. But sometimes I wonder how long I can keep up the pretence. She's a* bitch. *That blue-eyed golden-haired chubby little hypochondriac in her wheelchair is nothing more than a* bitch. *There! I've* used that ugly word, and if one day Es sees it I don't care. I know I shall need vindicating...'

Esmond lifted his head. Our gaze met, I looked away again, hating to see the pain, the suppressed anger, the shocked astonishment on his face.

'Oh, God,' he said, 'I'm certainly having my eyes opened now. If only she'd told me at the time ... my poor Veronica.'

'She must have been very good,' I whispered, 'and brave, to keep it from you.'

'Dear God, how blind can one be?' he breathed.

'Oughtn't I to go away and let you read the rest alone?' I began weakly.

'No,' he said in a harsh voice, 'things have gone too far. You know too much. You've heard me accuse her – and Valguay, too. In God's name let us hear the truth now – you as well as me.'

I sat spellbound, listening to his voice. It was rather horrifying and ghostly to listen to words that had been written by the dead woman. Each entry became shorter now and more poignant.

'MAY 30TH. *Things are getting worse. Monica and I maintain a kind of armed neutrality and give each other freezing smiles when Es is home, otherwise we hardly speak. She is beginning to act the fond aunt to little Con and spoiling him dreadfully. She doesn't seem to care for Kate.*

'JUNE 10TH. *I have nobody to talk to except Nannie. Rightly or wrongly I have started to confide in her because I know she loves me. She doesn't get on with Monnie, either. No one really likes Monica except Yvonne who is a detestable girl, although Es thinks I'm prejudiced. The trouble with Esmond is that he always wants to be nice to everyone and to have peace. He can't bear scenes at home. Poor lamb! He says he has too many of them in his job – what with temperamental prima donnas and musicians!'*

Esmond put in an aside to me here:
'You see? Veronica pities me. I was a pacifist. But you see, Shelley, I never felt all those undercurrents – never really noticed the hostility between Veronica and my sister. I just thought they hadn't much in common.'
He went on turning the pages of the diary, skipping some which seemed to be of no importance. He began again:

'JULY 5TH. *Esmond is away on tour. I hate him being away. Monnie is tormenting me and I feel dreadfully worried and lonely. Sometimes I think Es forgets that I have no parents and that I am utterly dependent on him...'*

I stole a glance at Esmond. I saw him

chew at his lips. Doggedly he continued:

'JULY 20TH. *This new doctor, Valguay, who is attending Monnie seems to be a great success with her and she has been better-tempered since he came on the scene. At first I disliked him. He's the smooth flattering type of Frenchman whose* blague *cuts no ice with me, but he has been very kind in his way, and sometimes we talk together and I enjoy his company. Once or twice lately I've been down to the Casino with him. He can be quite amusing...*

'AUGUST 4TH. *Last night Monica seemed to be more friendly than usual. She told me she was going to try and understand me better and that she realised how much I loved Es, but that she thinks her dear brother doesn't realise it and is putting his career before me. I've always believed that he* had *to, but when his own sister notices how lonely and sad I am, one starts to wonder...*

'God,' said Esmond, 'do you see that? My own sister poisoning my wife against me.'

I nodded. Esmond went on:

'AUGUST 20TH. *Es is still away but I've been quite gay. I left Monnie and Austen down here and went up to the Hôtel de Montagne, and Lucien comes up in his car quite often to play with the children and cheer me up. He now*

313

*openly declares that he is in love with me.
Monica knows it and says she doesn't see why
we shouldn't go on being friends. She says that I
need Lucien's companionship. Last night I went
out for a walk with him and he kissed me. I
knew then that I could never care for him that
way and I told him he mustn't kiss me again,
but he said he would not give up trying. I
suppose I oughtn't to let this friendship go on.
When I got back to the villa I talked to Monica
but she said I was stupid not to let Lucien
console me. I had a right to be comforted she
said, considering that my husband neglected me
so often.'*

I listened to this rather naïve confession
which seemed so incongruous with the
whole sophisticated personality of the dead
Veronica, and I felt in a way that it made her
rather more endearing. It was such a human
and honest revelation of her own weak-
nesses. But it must be hurting for Esmond,
intolerably.

'How can you bear to go on reading it?' I
asked him.

'With difficulty,' he said. 'It's twisting the
knife in my very entrails, my dear. I didn't
realise I was neglecting her. I … I didn't
know that she felt like that. I thought the
children were enough for her as they are for
a woman like you.'

Esmond, *Esmond,* I thought sadly, oh why

are you and most men so blind? Why should you imagine that *I* am content? Yet if those children were mine and you were coming back to me as you did to her – maybe I *would* find it enough.

He went on reading:

'SEPT. 21ST. *Four weeks since I made an entry. It's been an awful month. Now I know what a viper my sister-in-law is. For weeks she has encouraged me to see Lucien and assured me that I was doing no wrong, then suddenly he stopped coming to the villa and she said that it was my fault. That I had been so cold and indifferent and he could not endure it. I told her that I hadn't meant to drive him away and that I missed him and our amusing evenings out. Nannie used to warn me that he was up to no good, but I just thought he was a man hopelessly in love and I suppose I was flattered, besides I did not see Lucien with Nannie's cold disinterested eye. Anyhow Monnie saw my distress and persuaded me to sit down and write a little note and send it next door. She practically dictated it. It was to say I missed him and how grieved I was that he was staying away on my account and would he* please *come back. He came. I was rather foolishly pleased to see him again, and when he took me in his arms I responded. I even fancied myself a little in love. Just a little, only now I know what a fool I was. I've never loved any man but my husband, and thank God I*

315

didn't let things go very far. I was tempted. I could easily have become Lucien's mistress. Yes – I won't spare myself now. I'll admit that I wanted to, but I didn't because of Es whom I knew believed in me – and my honour to my children.'

Esmond broke off. He was shaking. I put out a hand and caught one of his.

'It's too painful for you, oh, please stop,' I implored.

'If it's painful, I deserve the pain,' he said harshly. 'I must have been mad not to see what she was going through.'

'OCT 2ND. *I don't know how I have the courage to write this. I feel sick with shame and despair.'*

'Oh, stop, stop,' I interrupted Esmond, 'don't go on.'

He pulled away from me roughly.

'I've got to. Don't you see that I've got to know. *We've all got to know now.'*

I sat dumb listening, terrified, feeling that a host of macabre shadows out of the dead past were crowding down upon us in that lamplit studio. Terrible shadows with cruel strong wings that beat against us, trying to batter the present out of recognition – and destroy our peace of mind forever rather than restore it.

Esmond, flaying himself, continued to read in that harsh strange voice.

'This is almost the last entry I shall make. I feel I want to end everything. It isn't only what's happened to me but the depths that Monica, Esmond's own sister has sunk to, to try and ruin me. Yes, I know now that she meant to come between Es and me, and in the lowest most abominable way. She won my confidence, then encouraged my folly.

'Three nights ago I told her I was going to have supper in Lucien's villa instead of at home or out at one of the restaurants. I asked her if she thought Es would mind, and she said she knew he wouldn't. I've only been once to La Giocanda – for a cocktail party that Lucien gave for his resident patients. I was told he had an excellent cook. Well I went. We were quite alone. In Lucien's salon, a wonderful little dinner was served. There was a big sofa in the salon at right angles to the fire, shaded lights, and everything seemed very cosy and intimate. I had just that morning heard that Es wasn't coming home as soon as expected, but had to fly to New York to meet some important impresario and fix up a future visit to the States. All I got was a brief cable. I suppose I felt sore and allowed myself to be consoled and charmed by what I thought was Lucien's devotion.

'I am now perfectly certain that he drugged my coffee. I am equally certain that that reptile

317

of a sister-in-law of mine was in the conspiracy with him, and knew exactly what he meant to do.

'Anyhow, after dinner, when the servants had gone, I felt rather drunk and drowsy and lay down on the couch. I came to my senses to find myself lying like that with a silk shawl over me and Lucien kissing my throat, madly, begging me to wake up and return his kisses.

'At the same time I heard the click of a camera. I suppose I'm very innocent but I really didn't imagine that anything so awful had happened, but I know now that he had a camera concealed a few feet away, and controlled it by pressing a bulb. I saw the result the following afternoon. Monica had a copy of that photo all nicely developed and printed. A good big print, too. I couldn't have looked more guilty, lying there on the couch with one hand on Lucien's shoulder, and his head buried against my breast. My hair was disordered. For all the world we looked as though we had just had 'a party' together.

'When Monica showed it to me I was staggered – and sick to the very soul. I asked how it had been done. She told me. It was perfect evidence, she said, and when I asked her to explain, she gave a cruel triumphant sort of smile and said she would show it to Es as soon as he came home. She would tell him that I had been betraying him with Lucien and then he could divorce me.

'Nobody can realise what I went through. I

had been betrayed in the most sickening fashion and I wasn't even guilty, but I knew exactly how it would all strike Esmond who had never liked Lucien and who had openly declared that he couldn't understand why I did. Es is very jealous and he hates me going out with other men. I pictured him half killing both me and Lucien. I went nearly out of my mind. I called Monica every name under the earth, but she only laughed and said I had condemned myself and she would see that I lost the children as well as Esmond. When I said that I would get Lucien to defend me and tell the truth, she laughed all the more. Lucien needed all the money she gave him. He had been gambling and was heavily in debt in Monaco. He would do as she said.

'OCT 3RD. I've been walking up and down my bedroom all night. Nannie has just been in with my early tea. I told her to take care of the children if anything happened to me. She was frightened and said what could happen. I didn't say any more, but I intend to take the Citroen and drive hundreds and hundreds of miles away from Arc-en-Ciel. I just can't face Es. I have given Nannie my diary and told her to lock it up, and that if I died she was to give it to Esmond.

'Now I am alone. I haven't undressed all night. I'm going to find a coat and scarf and go out in the car. I don't care if I have an accident. I don't care what happens. Monica has got her *way. She and Lucien have ruined me. I can't, can't face Es. Or that my children should believe shameful lies against me. But I still love them. I was never unfaithful to Esmond. I hope one day he'll know that and forgive the rest.'*

The diary dropped from Esmond's hands. He got up. My heart beat to suffocation point. Through burning eyes I watched him walk to the mantelpiece, fold his arms upon it and lean his head down upon them. It was an attitude of abject despair. It left me with nothing whatsoever to say, but I could feel a deep sympathy for the dead girl as well as for Esmond's acute grief. I, too, would have been a victim of Monica Warr's mad jealousy if I hadn't fought back every inch of the way. Veronica, his wife, had been in a much more tricky position, and she had been weak. Yes, up to a point she was a weak character, and yet, thank God, strong enough not to have surrendered to the ultimate temptation. At least Esmond knew that, now, too.

The moments went by. I don't know how long it was before he lifted his head and turned to me. He looked years older, I thought. The great man seemed suddenly to have been completely deflated.

'So they drove her to her death,' he said in a low monotonous voice. 'A few hours after that entry she died on the road near Villefranche, driving at break-neck speed.

That was what they said in the verdict. That was what I never understood. Now I know. My sister drove her to kill herself.'

'No, no,' I protested, 'it was an accident.'

'The same thing. Veronica was always rather highly strung and hysterical. She intended to end her life. I am sure of it now. Just as I am sure that she never had anything more than a passing fancy for that unspeakable gigolo who was hired by my sister to ruin her. My own sister. *Monnie...*' He shut his eyes, clenching and unclenching his long fine fingers convulsively.

I got up and stumbled towards him; I could not bear that look on his face.

'Oh, Esmond, don't let it hurt you!' I cried. 'Don't let this vile thing poison your life any further. What's past cannot be undone. Whether Veronica died by sheer accident or on purpose, the verdict was 'death by misadventure', you said so. Even if she was too weak to face you and fight for herself, she can be forgiven, can't she? That final business of the photograph must have been too hideously degrading.'

'It was a criminal act and my own sister is responsible for it,' he said hoarsely. 'Presumably the photograph was torn up and the incident wiped out by Veronica's death and they decided to say absolutely nothing more. Death had done their dirty work for them.'

'Try not to hold it against her. She's been ill for a long time. Physical illness can warp the minds of human beings in a queer way. You must try to forgive her.'

'I never will.'

'You must, you must. It must all be wiped out and forgotten.'

He did not look at me. He looked over my head. I could imagine the way his thoughts chased wildly through his tired brain. He had had as much as he could stand. He said:

'I shall tell Austen nothing except that I have decided to put an immediate end to this *ménage*. You're quite right. If I were to face Monica with this, I … I don't think I'd be responsible for what I did or said. *She* killed Veronica. I'd tear strips off her.'

'Oh, hush, *please*,' I implored him.

'You called her mad. You said that physical illness sometimes distorted people's minds. Maybe you're right. Even after Veronica died, Monica couldn't let well alone. Veronica's death wasn't enough. They brought her poor broken body back here and it wasn't enough. I'll tell you now – Monica hinted that Veronica was going to meet her lover. She said she wanted me to know about it, so that I shouldn't go on grieving. To know that the mother of my children was not worth grieving for would help me, she said. I didn't agree but I believed Monica said it for the best. Now do you see why I couldn't bear Veronica's name to be mentioned in this house. I didn't know facts, but the suspicions had been put into my head. It would just never have struck me that Monica had told me infamous lies, to blacken Veronica's character. But if I'd had any definite idea Valguay was the man, I'd never have allowed him in the house.'

It was then that Esmond turned and rushed out of the villa, feeling compelled to go next door and face Lucien with the facts and punish him further. All I know is that I ran into the night wildly calling him by name and begging him not to do anything rash. The anticlimax of finding the villa closed and Lucien gone was merciful, I thought.

Esmond hardly seemed to notice that I had been pursuing him until we got back to the house. Then in the darkness I stumbled over a stone pot. He heard my cry of pain. He turned, saw me and seemed to become aware of my part in all this. He picked me up in his arms as though I was one of his children and carried me into the studio. He set me down in a chair, walked to a cupboard, pulled out a bottle of brandy, and poured some into a small glass. He brought one also for himself.

'I think we both need this,' he said grimly.

I sipped the cognac, shutting my eyes. I felt emotionally drained and physically exhausted. Then Esmond began to make plans in a very quiet voice.

'I shall speak to Austen – I shan't of course tell him the facts because the poor devil is still fond of her. Let him keep his illusions, but I shall inform him that her accident was not *your* fault. She's all right now. Raphael says so. No lasting harm has been done. The others must think what they like. I'm quite sure you won't care.'

I said that I wouldn't, for indeed, all that mattered to me was that *he* knew. He went on with his plans:

'I shall sell Arc-en-Ciel. I never want to see it again.'

Something, I don't know what, made me remind him of the oil painting that had been taken up to the attic.

'That must be put back in its place of honour. It's only right that it should.'

Esmond put down his glass and stared at me. He gave me a humourless laugh.

'By God, you're a strange child! What an extraordinary thing to think of. It's so like you. I think I told you once before, you think too much of others, and not enough of yourself. You have often tried to defend Veronica. It is extraordinarily touching of you.'

I remained silent. He came across the room, and as he had done not once but several times, picked me up in his arms and kissed me.

'Thank you for everything. I owe you a

very great deal. Too much. Look at these...'
And he lifted my scorched fingers and kissed each one in turn very gently. Then he kissed me on the lips. For all the world I dared not respond with the tremendous passion that I bore him. I held myself stiffly, hardly daring to move or breathe. Then he released me.

'Thank you for saving the diary, too, Shelley. I feel better. In time I shall get over it. I owe Veronica's memory a deep apology. I hate myself for my suspicions – for taking down her portrait–'

He broke off, bowing his head. I stood dumbly listening.

'Now go to bed,' he added, 'it's long past midnight and you look dreadfully tired. We'll meet in the morning. We'll work out something.'

I nodded again. For one moment I felt the unspeakable hunger of my love almost conquer my good sense and my reserve. I could hardly bear not to throw myself into his arms and offer my lips for other, different sort of kisses; for a more fervent embrace. Once I was alone I went down to the very depths of despair. I told myself that nothing could 'work out' as he put it and that I must get away from him and all of them here before, like Veronica, I should be totally destroyed.

It was that night that I made up my mind

to leave Arc-en-Ciel before any of them were up in the morning, and go back to London – some place where they would never find me again.

16

SOUTH NORWOOD.

It sounds very different from Monte Carlo. *It is.* And somehow to me it was not in the least like coming home when I first opened the door and saw the little semi-basement flat again.

That year at Arc-en-Ciel had altered me completely. Fifty-two weeks. Three hundred and sixty-five days of living with *them* could not leave anyone unchanged.

My taste for lovely things, for instance, my knowledge of the world in general had sharpened and improved. I looked rather bleakly round the little lounge wishing that Robin was home to welcome me and take the edge off the frightful lonely feeling, wishing that there were even a dog or a cat here to greet me. But there was no one – nothing.

Robin had used the place from time to time, when on leave. Various friends who needed a bed in town had stayed here. The caretaker, Mrs Binks, a cheerful Cockney, who lived in the back of the building (which was a huge gaunt house that had been built before the First World War) had a key. She was supposed to dust the flat occasionally and see that everything was all right.

But I saw a thin film of dust over everything this afternoon. Poor Mrs Binks of course didn't know that I was coming home. I hadn't had time to warn her. There were some circulars on the door mat. Cigarettes and ash in a tray on the little circular table in front of the gas fire. Evidences that Robin had been here, as there was also an old pipe of his lying by an empty cigarette carton.

I looked at the mantelpiece. At the familiar clock – rather a nice old one actually that had belonged to my father. At the photograph of him and my mother in a faded double leather frame. At a rather attractive print of a Degas ballet scene which I remember I'd fallen in love with when I was about nineteen. It hung over the fireplace.

It all looked so small, after the huge rooms at Arc-en-Ciel – shabby and insignificant. The green coarse linen chair covers were faded and had shrunk after many cleanings. The arms had been darned (by me). The cushions were a disgrace. The carpet had once been good – brought from my parents' home – but that, too, had faded and bore stains that wouldn't come out.

It wasn't even a nice day. Muggy, with a drizzle and lowering skies that threatened more rain. A typical English summer's day, I thought, and for no reason at all began to shiver; not because I was really cold but because of the awful blankness that stretched before me in the future. The fact that I had cut myself away from Esmond. It was as though I had severed one of my own limbs and would henceforth be one of the deformities on this earth. I could never feel really whole again.

As for the children ... already I felt a thousand miles from them and censured myself bitterly because I had run away from them. I had stood in place of their mother. Esmond had given them into my care. But like a coward, feeling that I could bear no more, I had run away. It's funny but I felt ashamed of myself, and it was that sort of feeling that got me down now, rather than the comparison between my little home and the elegance of Arc-en-Ciel.

I walked into my bedroom. I used to think it rather pretty. Robin had distempered the walls a pale blue and I had used bits of an old brown carpet that used to be in my father's study. I had bought myself one of those sofas that turn into a bed. It was as tasteful as my limited funds would allow: with a brown and blue cretonne cover.

There were my favourite books (oh, so dusty!) in a white painted bookcase. There were all the little framed snapshots of my school friends. There were a lot of manuals and pamphlets on education and the

P.N.E.U. system. After a photo of myself, looking rather severe, in a group of P.N.E.U. students.

I felt suddenly frightened:

What was I going to do now? I must get in touch with Robin and talk things over with him. But he had his own life to lead and that blonde girl he was falling in love with. And I had very little money. I hadn't even waited to ask for my salary. Lady Warr used to pay me every month. How could I possibly have waited to ask *her* for anything?

Suddenly I sat down on the edge of my bed, locked my hands and stared at the floor blindly. I don't think I had ever before known what it was to feel desperate – isolated from everything in life that was beautiful, gay or thrilling. I could almost regret that I had lost my head and rushed away from Monte Carlo.

I'd left a note for *him,* begging him to forgive me for leaving the children and to try and understand that I just couldn't go on, because this had all got on top of me.

Under the children's doors I had slipped little notes written in large letters that they could understand. One to Con, and one to Kate, begging them to be good and remember all I had taught them, and that I'd had to go away in a hurry.

But now I began to wonder about all kinds of silly little items; such as that Conrad had a blister on his big toe, and we'd run out of plaster and I had meant to buy some and put a strip on for him. Who would do it for him now? Kate had torn her best white silk knickers which she usually wore with her broderie anglaise party dress. I'd bought some silk, meaning to make another pair. Who now would find the silk and do them? I'd also promised to make the children a chart which was to encourage them to work harder. They were each to have a little motor car to move up to petrol stations that were numbered. Each number marked the progress of the pupil, and the first car to reach the final petrol station – which meant having the highest number of marks – would get a prize at the end of the week. We had laughed over it because we had decided, together, to call the affair our Monte Carlo Rally. Now I would never paint that chart and the Rally would never take place. They would be disappointed.

I hid my face in my hands and sobbed. If in that hour I could have got up and stepped into an aeroplane and flown back to Arc-en-Ciel I think I would have done so, even if it meant facing all the reproachful faces in France. But there was no plane outside my door, and I'd spent as much as I could afford on the journey here by train and boat (I'd crossed last night, by the cheapest route – the night-boat from Dieppe to Newhaven).

I knew I could not face any of them, especially those who thought me guilty of deliberately trying to harm Monica Warr. But I could not forget her or that ugly episode, for my blistered fingers still pained me.

I tried to argue with myself: I'm better at home here even if it's only a horrid little flat in a suburb. It's home! I could never start life at Arc-en-Ciel again.

I hadn't slept much in the ladies' dormitory on the boat. I kept seeing Esmond's face. I kept wondering what would happen to the children. And I wondered if Esmond would despise me for running away.

Arriving home, I felt really ill. The girl who looked at me from my mirror was sunburnt all right, but there were dark circles under her eyes, a look of strain about her mouth. She was thin and feverish. The bright-eyed, curly haired, healthy Shelley who I used to see reflected in this same mirror had vanished. This new one looked years older – no longer a child either in appearance or at heart. There were few curls left. Her hair had been cut short and curved smoothly into the shape of the head by a chic Monte Carlo hairdresser. Her lipstick was a new deep coral pink shade fashionable in Paris with summer tan. This girl might almost be called 'elegant'. How curious, I thought. What a metamorphosis! What a change just *one* year can bring about in a person's life.

After my cup of tea (I was going to miss the *café* and *croissants* that Thérèse used to bring me), I wrote a long letter to Robin and told him what had happened. Then I decided to go along to Miss Arlott's Agency in Warminster Road. She usually found good posts for qualified teachers or secretaries. She might even find one abroad for me. I was beginning to feel I would never settle down in London again. I'd go anywhere save the South of France, I told myself grimly.

Mrs Binks came in, apologising that she hadn't had a moment before. She expressed great pleasure at seeing me again. But she commented on my appearance.

'You don't 'alf look queer, ducks.'

'Why queer?' I laughed. At least here was an old friend; Maudie Binks, her auburn head swathed in a bright scarf, plump legs and arms bare; short flowered cotton overall stretched across ample bosom and protruding stomach. Nothing to look at, but a heart of gold. I felt quite pleased to see her.

'Queer,' she repeated, 'well – not yerself, love, if yer know what I mean.'

'I do,' I said dryly.

'Come back unexpected, didn't yer?'

'Yes.'

'Stayin' long?'

'I don't know,' I said, averting my gaze from her inquisitive eyes.

'Well, I'll come and clean over for yer after

I've done old Paintbrush's flat.'

Paintbrush! That brought a faint smile to my lips. Mrs Binks's name for the lodger in the first floor flat which had a studio in the garden and was occupied by an elderly woman commercial artist. I knew her. She used to ask me up to her studio to see what I thought of some of her work. It was no good. She was hard up but unfailingly cheerful. I always respect people who have to work under difficult circumstances yet never complain.

After Mrs Binks left me, I began to feel contempt for myself because I had spent so much time lately in crying. I must pull myself together. After all, I had chosen to leave my wonderful job. This unpleasant hiatus in which I found myself was unenviable – but of my own making.

Then I began to think of the children again and that silly Monte Carlo Rally and back came the tears. I just couldn't stop crying.

When I first started to write all my experiences, I had meant to finish the thing after my return from France.

But I've taken up my pen again just to add a little more. That 'little' which, in my life, now embraces a whole world … a great devastating area … a sort of canvas stretching to infinity, which was once blank, but across which, suddenly, an unexpected and invisible brush painted a new and glowing landscape; a unique scheme of things woven into a picture of such blinding beauty I hardly dared look upon it. But when I did, it transported me, I became another person altogether – one who had nothing to do with that sad forlorn, confused young girl who wept her heart out in her shabby flat on that June afternoon.

I feel that I have recorded the worst of my life. Now I must tell the best. I want everybody to hear about the sudden miracle that evolved out of all the bitterness and pain.

On the day of my return – it was just after lunch – I received a telegram. I opened it, thinking at first that it was Robin. As I looked at the signature, my heart gave a quite agonising leap. It was from Esmond. Long and typical of the man to whom expense meant nothing.

I do not know your telephone number or even if you have one so please get through to Arc-en-Ciel immediately. You know the number. It is vital. Make it reverse charge. Esmond.

My breath came fast. For the first time since I left France, I felt the colour surge into my face. Not even for a second did I contemplate refusing Esmond's request. If he said it was *vital* – it was. If he wanted to speak to me, even though I'd walked out on him, then I would not, could not refuse. I only hoped that there had been no further tragedy at Arc-en-Ciel.

I kept making all kinds of wild guesses as I snatched up a macintosh and walked to the nearest post office.

The thought of speaking to Esmond brought him so close again it was almost unbearable. There was half an hour's delay on Continental trunks. I hardly knew how to contain myself. Crowds came in and out. I looked at every girl of my age who entered that post office and wondered if their lives were as simple and uncomplicated and ordinary as my own used to be. I almost envied them.

Then I was in the box, my pulses hammering as I heard the familiar confusion of French voices on the line.

'*Ello! Ello! Ici Londres.*' Then Monte Carlo, and Arc-en-Ciel. And Esmond's voice, so clear, so amazingly near, he might have been in that South Norwood post office beside me.

'Is that you, Shelley?'

'Yes,' I replied, 'it's me.'

He spoke angrily now.

'Why the hell did you want to behave like such a little idiot and walk out on us this way?'

I stuttered.

'I can't explain over the phone. I left you a note.'

'I read it. But I don't want to waste time over any more explanations. You've caused quite enough trouble. I'm furious with you,' he added.

'I … I'm sorry…' I stammered. 'I'm sure you don't understand… But I couldn't go on.'

'Rubbish. We can all go on, no matter how much we are provoked.'

I knew that he was right. I myself had felt that throughout the entire journey home, and since I arrived, I felt all kinds of a fool, and a shirker, too. I spoke humbly.

'Please do try and understand and forgive me. I suppose I got in a sort of panic.'

I heard him laugh.

'Miss Bray in panic? That's hard to believe.'

'I was, *I was*, it all became too much for me, Esmond.'

'What do you suppose *I* was feeling? Do you think it was easy for me, or that your running away made things any easier? I've had Con and Kate in floods of tears ever since they woke up and found your ridiculous notes. If that's the P.N.E.U. system it's punk and you're fired.'

I gave an hysterical laugh.

'You can't fire me. I've already left.'

'Listen, Shelley,' he said, 'I'm putting Con and Kate on a plane leaving Nice tomorrow afternoon at four o'clock. Young De Vitte is going to bring them over. You will meet the plane. It lands at five minutes past six. He'll hand the kids to you, and you'll take them back to my house in Eaton Square. You will stay with them until I get back. I believe they are short of staff in London so I am sending Thérèse with De Vitte. She's never been to England and is thrilled to the core. She won't remain but she can tide us over. My butler, Williams, is there and his wife who can cook for you. As soon as I've got through some urgent work here I'll join you.'

He gave me no chance to refuse. I listened to his peremptory orders – Esmond gave orders in the manner of a man who was used to being obeyed without question – I did not know whether I was on my head or my feet. I was really what the French called *bouleversé*. Once I tried to speak and he cut me short.

'You can't have got another job, there hasn't been time, so don't argue with me, please. I know you had a bad time over here, but you owe the children something. They're so damned fond of you. They've only stopped crying because I've promised they will fly to you tomorrow. Are you going to let them down again?'

'No,' I gasped, 'oh, *no.*'

'Right. The Comet gets in at London Airport at six five. Ring up Godfrey Davis and hire a car. Drive the lot of them back to Eaton Square.'

'Yes, Esmond,' I said meekly.

'You've been the hell of a time ringing me up,' came his grumbling voice, 'why were you so long? I've had a lot of work to do and I couldn't go out until your call came through.'

'The telegram must have been delayed. I phoned as soon as I got it,' I said wildly.

'Have you got the time that the plane arrives? Are you quite clear what you've got to do?' he demanded.

'Yes, but–'

'No "buts". Just do as I say. I'll phone through to Eaton Square tomorrow night. I'll have to. I can't trust you an inch now and I want to make sure you're safely there.'

'Oh, Esmond!' I exclaimed, half laughing and crying, 'you *can* trust me. Honestly, I'll never do anything so stupid again.'

'I'm glad to hear it. My opinion of you went down when I found you gone.'

'Oh, *no!*' I wailed.

'You left a couple of letters in a table drawer. Thérèse brought them to me.'

'What were they?' I asked stupidly.

'I had to open them,' he replied, 'I was frantic to find your phone number, and wondered if one of the notes might be from your brother, on your note-paper. But they were both notes from friends.'

'I'm sorry I gave you all that trouble–' I began.

But now with dramatic suddenness, his whole voice changed. Very low, inexpressibly tender it sounded to me – and every word he said is imprinted for ever on my memory.

'A poem fell out of one of those letters. You must have tucked it in and forgotten about it. It's called *"Despair"*. Listen, Shelley, I'm going to read it to you:

'I would, I would I were the one
Who wrote that sad sweet score;
That he to whom it is inscribed
Should love me more.

'I watch him raise the baton in his hand.
I guess the secrets of his heart.
I understand:
O, cease to play! Sweet orchestra, depart,
Lest I should hear your music all my life
And break my heart."'

I was too dumbfounded to speak. With flaming face I stood in that hot telephone kiosk, growing hotter every moment, listening to my own feeble composition. Esmond read it so beautifully that it made it almost sound beautiful.

340

Heavens! I thought, I must have been in a hurry when I put my silly poem inside a letter, and even more of a hurry to miss clearing out that drawer when I packed.

I heard him say:

'Shelley! Why should you break your heart? Do you really want me to "love you more"?'

I struggled to answer. I couldn't. I heard him speak again.

'Shelley, are you there?'

'Yes!' I answered, thickly.

'I *do* love you,' he said. 'With all my heart. Goodbye for now.'

'Esmond! Esmond!' I called his name wildly, but I heard a French voice, then an English one ... operators on the line ... then silence.

I literally stumbled out of that box, and into the street. It was raining quite hard. A nice English summer's day. I hadn't brought an umbrella. By the time I got home my hair was drenched, flattened against my cheeks. When I let myself into the flat I was in a state that bordered on delirium. Mrs Binks was working with a borrowed Hoover, cleaning the lounge carpet. As she saw me, she flicked off the motor and stared at me – cigarette dangling from her lower lip.

'Crikey wot's come over *you?*' she began.

I surprised Maudie Binks by flinging myself into her arms and dancing with her all round the room. I dragged her down on to the settee, breathless and hysterical.

'He said he loved me. He said he loved me, Mrs Binks. *He said he loved me.*'

She drew away from me and tapped her forehead.

'Look, love, tyke it easy, I said you was queer when you come 'ome yesterday. Quite dotty … that's wot you are!'

'I am! I know I am!' I cried. 'But I'm so happy I want to die.'

Mrs Binks gained her feet and attacked the Hoover again.

'Well, go on and die, love, I've got me work to do and no time for dancing.'

I rushed into my bedroom. I flung myself face downwards on my bed and recalled every word that Esmond Torrington had just said to me. It was those last words that kept dominating the others.

'I do love you,' he had said.

He couldn't mean it, of course; not as I wanted him to. He was just using that phrase in a friendly or brotherly way. He hadn't said he was *in* love with me. It was only that he was rather touched by my silly sentimental poem. (Oh, how amazing the way things work out … fantastic that he should have found that poem and that I should have left it behind … I who am usually so tidy.)

But suddenly a kind of psychic recognition came to me and I knew that he *did* love me.

He would never have quoted that poem or made that declaration if he hadn't meant it. It became gloriously wonderfully apparent to me.

How was I going to wait to see him again? When would he come? When would I really know what he felt about me? I wished that I hadn't posted that long dreary letter to Robin just now, and hastily scribbled another air mail letter. I gave the address in Eaton Square and told him that I was going back into Mr Torrington's services.

I tore out then to a little hairdresser's shop that I used to patronise. I had my hair shampooed and set. I took a bus to the West End and went to a girl called Rita who gave marvellous facials. I knew about her through a friend of mine who was a model and used to have her face made up by Rita. I let her cleanse and beautify my skin. I left her looking quite glamorous. I got through the rest of the day *somehow*. Oh, and I forgot to mention that before I did these things, I sent an extravagant wire to Con and Kate – one each – so that they shouldn't be jealous.

'*Longing to see you tomorrow*,' I said.

In that way I thought my beloved Esmond would realise that I certainly meant to meet that plane from Nice.

I met it.

I hardly noticed young Jules De Vitte or Thérèse who carried a Continental-looking basket stuffed with parcels and was grinning all over her brown peasant's face. I only saw the children. Kate, adorable, in a little blue linen dress and jacket, and a hat with daisies on it. Con in a pair of grey flannel shorts, white shirt, and blue blazer, looking very English today. (I could imagine this attire had been approved by their father.) They flung themselves at me and gave me great smacking childish kisses that smudged my lipstick; but what did I care?

'Miss Bray, it was smashing on the Comet. It has four engines and a jet propeller!' shouted Conrad.

'It has a jet 'peller, Miss Bway,' echoed Kate.

I almost wept with joy, wondering how I could ever have thought it possible to desert them.

Thérèse put in:

'*C'était splendide!... Incoyable...*' She pointed to the Comet – the first aeroplane in which she had ever flown. '*Mon Dieu!*'

'I am pleased to see you, Mees Bray,' said De Vitte.

Being with them all, listening to them, brought me a breath of France and the feeling that all was right with my world again.

'Daddy told me to give you this,' said Conrad suddenly drawing a note out of his pocket. I took it from him, blushing, and put it in my bag. I didn't read it during the drive home. I couldn't. Everybody was talking and I wanted to be quite alone and quiet when I read what Esmond had written to me.

We reached Eaton Square. The June sun was shining now. The big elegant house looked inviting. A grey-haired manservant let us in. There was an early dinner waiting for us. I had never been there before but could see that décor and furnishings bore the unmistakable Torrington taste. Wonderful carpets, beautiful wallpapers, carved rosewood staircase. Queen Anne walnut furniture; a collection of fine paintings *and* another portrait of Veronica Torrington. I saw that as soon as I entered, for it was hanging in the dining-room and the door was ajar, when we entered the house. I could not resist stopping to look at it. Veronica, in a yellow chiffon evening dress, provocative but a little sad.

You again, I thought. Poor beautiful Veronica! I can pity you now with all my heart. You were a victim of that fiend who so nearly put an end to me, too. I understand how you suffered.

The children hadn't seen their London home for some time, and rushed into their bedrooms to examine some of the books and games that had been left behind. Mrs Williams showed me into one of the handsome spare bedrooms with two windows overlooking the square. Green carpet, white paint, rose-patterned wallpaper and rose satin-studded headboard. Painted Italian furniture.

I closed the door. I was alone and quiet at last. I took Esmond's letter from my bag. If I had expected a long epistle I was disappointed. It was very short, but enough to ease some of the torment in my mind and heart and fill me with a hope that could no longer be denied.

My dear sweet Shelley,

I do understand why you cut and ran but please never do it again – never leave the children or me for God's sake– We can't do without you. And don't break your heart about that score because I shall conduct many more for you, alone. À bientôt,

Esmond.

I read these words about a dozen times, still not daring to believe what they implied. Yet here was indisputable fact. He *must* love me. He said he could not do without me and that he would conduct many scores in the future for *me alone*.

I ate my dinner in a kind of daze, trying to concentrate on Con and Kate and Jules De Vitte's polite conversation.

Then at eight o'clock, after the children were in bed, the expected call came through from Monte Carlo.

'Thanks for wiring the children,' were Esmond's first words. 'You relieved my mind. It's good to know that you are with them again now. You gave us a few very bad hours, Shelley.'

'Haven't you forgiven me yet?' I asked.

'Entirely,' was his reply, then: 'I've just packed up and left Arc-en-Ciel. I made some kind of pretext to get away and I'm actually speaking to you from that hotel on Ez Plage – Le Cap Estel. I'm staying until the day after tomorrow. I've spoken to both Monica and Austen. I didn't intend to see my sister, but she wanted to see me. The poor old chap's very muddled and does not know what it's all about, but she does. She put on that "too ill to speak" act this morning but soon gave it up. I think she's seen the light. She was pretty sorry for herself and begged for my forgiveness, but I told her I didn't want to see her again for a very long time, if ever. I think Austen is taking her to Aix-les-Bains. I've got to meet a chap in Paris, but I'll be in London with you before dinner the day after tomorrow.'

I had nothing to say. I felt too shy, too nervous. His voice came again.

'Are you still there, darling?'

'Darling' I thought stupidly.

'Shelley!'

'Yes, I'm here!' I exclaimed.

'Thank you for forgiving us all and coming back to us,' he said.

'It's so wonderful being with Con and Kate again,' I said huskily. 'Leaving them for forty-eight hours was too long.'

'And it was far too much for me, finding you gone,' he said.

'It's hard for me to realise you cared,' I said.

'Shelley,' he said, 'I've had time to think. Something very strange and wonderful has happened to me. Once I left Arc-en-Ciel and came to Le Cap Estel, I felt as though I'd left all the ugly unhappy ghosts behind me. They've faded. I also have had time to realise too what *you* have grown to mean to me during the year you spent with us. It is so glorious here – I want you by my side. Shelley, when I get to Eaton Square, I'm going to ask you to marry me. I'd like you to think it over and give me my answer when I see you.'

Can one be mentally struck by lightning? I'm prepared to believe it now, remembering what I felt when I heard that totally unexpected proposal. Magnificent blinding lightning. So brilliant, so unearthly that little Shelley Bray was completely annihilated. I heard my own voice, strange and distant, saying:

'You can't possibly want to marry me.'

'But I do,' he said. 'Conrad suggested it.'

348

'Oh, don't be fantastic,' I laughed unbelievingly.

'But he did. When I told him he was going to fly to London to join you, he said he wished that you could be his new mother so that you would never have to leave him. You know I've thought for a long time that that boy was intelligent, and since he has stopped telling tales and started to work so well, I can almost believe that he will be a credit to me at my old prep. school, also that he'll pass his Common Entrance for Eton, one day. That is, if you'll promise to go on giving him such good ground-work before he gets to school.'

'Oh, Esmond!' was all that I could say, my eyes tight shut. I had a childish fear that if I opened them all this glorious nonsense would cease to be.

'Thank goodness he and Kate have got good taste,' went on Esmond. 'You'll make a very charming and sensible mother for them, and a very very wonderful wife for me.'

'But I thought you were going to marry Sophie de la Notte!' I exclaimed, swallowing several times.

'Marry *Sophie?* Heavens, no! I wouldn't dream of it. She's delightful but not for me. I never really intended to marry again at all. You know quite well how things have been with me, Shelley. I've been living in a sort of vacuum, but now the ghost of poor Veronica is laid, I know exactly what I want out of life and who I want: I promise you, my darling, that if you marry me I won't make the same mistake with you that I made with Veronica. I'll never leave you. I'll stop these damn tours. I won't conduct any more.'

'You will!' I retorted indignantly. 'I absolutely refuse to marry you if you don't go on conducting. I don't consider you should belong only to a wife and children. You belong to the whole *world.*'

I heard his low laugh – it sounded extraordinarily contented.

'Oh, Shelley,' he said, 'truly you're marvellous! I can't wait for your answer till I get to London. Give it to me now. Do you love me enough to marry me ... difficult ... temperamental ... all that I am?'

For a second I could not answer. He sounded so very ordinary, yet I knew that here was one of the most famous men in the word of music, asking me, Shelley Bray, to accept the honoured position as his wife.

My love for him was so tremendous that it overwhelmed me. At that moment, I actually felt his arms around me, and his lips against mine. I trembled. I answered him:

'Yes, Esmond ... my darling adored Esmond, yes, of course, of *course* I will marry you!'

The publishers hope that this book has given you enjoyable reading. Large Print Books are especially designed to be as easy to see and hold as possible. If you wish a complete list of our books please ask at your local library or write directly to:

Dales Large Print Books
Magna House, Long Preston,
Skipton, North Yorkshire.
BD23 4ND

This Large Print Book, for people
who cannot read normal print,
is published under the auspices of

THE ULVERSCROFT FOUNDATION

... we hope you have enjoyed this book.
Please think for a moment about those
who have worse eyesight than you ...
and are unable to even read or enjoy
Large Print without great difficulty.

You can help them by sending a
donation, large or small, to:

**The Ulverscroft Foundation,
1, The Green, Bradgate Road,
Anstey, Leicestershire, LE7 7FU,
England.**
or request a copy of our brochure for
more details.

The Foundation will use all donations
to assist those people who are visually
impaired and need special attention
with medical research, diagnosis
and treatment.

Thank you very much for your help.